A Walk in the Rain

A Walk in the Rain

A journey of love and redemption

UDAI YADLA

PARTRIDGE
A Penguin Random House Company

To order additional copies of this book, contact
Partridge India
000 800 10062 62
orders.india@partridgepublishing.com

www.partridgepublishing.com/india

CONTENTS

ACKNOWLEDGEMENTS

Writing is my passion and getting published is my dream. Pursuing a passion and fulfilling the dream is not as simple as it sounds. It involved a lot of people to whom I owe my gratitude.

Firstly I would like to thank my family for their immense belief in me. I would like to specially thank the most important person in my life, my mother, who despite not knowing anything about publishing, trusted me so much and did her best to provide me the best working conditions. I'm grateful to my wife for her tolerance towards my extended hours at my computer. I can't imagine how difficult it would have been, had she not understood my dream. I must thank my cousin Teju for her patience in reading every draft of mine and providing her valuable feedback. Any big accomplishment can't be a possibility without the support of a friend. I take the opportunity to thank my dearest friend Sathya for his moral support and unshakable trust in me. I thank all my friends for their help in keeping me sane throughout the endeavor.

I finally thank Partridge Publishers for accepting to represent my work. They might feature at the end of acknowledgements; nevertheless they are the people who made my publishing dream, a reality.

PROLOGUE

"*Eons ago, god created the world. It was nothing but a huge ball of rock: stark and dull. He was not happy with his creation. He wanted to make the world colorful. Hence, he created the oceans, the mountains, and the tress with beautiful flowers. It was beautiful, but He was still not satisfied. He wanted to make it eventful and interesting. Hence He created the animals, fishes, insects and birds which made his creation interesting, but there was no order in the world. The world was just wild and uncivilized, which demanded his governance every time. He wanted someone to rule the world, so that he could relax and just watch. Hence he created the humans, cloning himself.*

"*Hah… My job is now complete." The God prided.*

The humans ruled the world well, but they seemed to be listless and detached from each other. He kept wondering what he had missed. There was no bond between the humans, there was no love. The world was a mean place, only with materialistic purpose. He wanted to infuse love in the humans. It was the biggest challenge for him. He could easily create a zillion creatures in a jiffy, but to infuse love in them was a herculean task. It was a task bigger than creating life itself. He finally thought of an idea. He planned to tie the beloved hearts with a special bond which could make the human life on earth very special. Now he needed a special material to bind the hearts together. He summoned the divine goldsmith and ordered him to make special threads of gold. He imbued the threads with his divine soul. He called it 'The Thread of Love'. He then created the Kingdom of Love. The spirits of people who have selfless love for somebody earn a place in His glorious kingdom and they can physically communicate with the person they love, through the thread of love. Deeper the love, stronger the thread."

"It's beyond your consciousness that your soul lingers with the person you love and hence your mood will affect the one you love. This is the reason why you sometimes sense your mood changing mysteriously with no reason."

"Nice fairy tale, Sandy Candy… I'm enthralled actually." he ridiculed playfully.

"Thoughts are not physical, how can they physically affect others?" he questioned.

"You can only feel, but not see air. Air is physical.

You can only see, but not feel light. Light is physical.

You can see and feel your thoughts. Then why can't thoughts be physical?" Sandy's logical observation was irrefutable.

"Perfectly logical…" He was amazed by her ability of logical reasoning even for a fictitious fairy tale.

"Tell me about it." Sandy asked with curiosity.

"It's priceless." he exclaimed, staring at the exquisite beauty around his wrist.

MAGIC OF RAIN

Surya woke up to the symphonic pattering of the incessant rain drops on his bedroom window panes. He dragged himself to the window in a hypnopompic daze and sat on a chair beside it. He pushed opened the window and stared outside to witness the magic of the tender rain. It, actually, was a magical sight.

The tiny specks of rain slapping the leaves of the trees and the leaves swaying to the tune of the rain droplets.

The fresh sprouts of fluorescent green leaves peeking out through the nodes of the branches.

Chirping of the sparrows sheltered in their nests.

The fragrant aroma of the rain permeating the cool breeze.

And the cool breeze seeping in through the window, forcing him into a fetal position, gently caressing him.

It was magical indeed. The ringing of his phone on the table near him attempted to disturb his dreamy experience, so he silenced it without even looking at it and continued to enjoy the blissful beauty of the pluvial charm. There was a mystic bond between the two. He sat at the window, silently staring at the rain as if he were deciphering a coded message. The ringing of his phone interrupted him again. He didn't ignore the call this time. He shrugged in exasperation as he picked the phone. His frustration vanished when he saw who was calling. He smiled as he looked at the calling number.

"Hey Sunny boy... What took you so long?" screamed a voice at the other end, as he attended the call.

He had a close circle of very few friends, who call him Sunny. He maintained a formal relationship with those not in his old friends circle. He had to move away from the window to take the call as the sound of the rain was a disturbance to the caller. He had a short call with his friend, desperate to go back to his private conversation with the rain.

When he returned, he observed that the pattering of the rain drops had ceased its long and continuous endeavor. Sunny dropped his phone on the table and looked at the clock.

'Damn it... The rain tricked me once again.' He was late for his office.

He rushed to the bathroom and finished his daily chores in record time. Skipping his breakfast, which had almost become a habit for him, he wore a pant and a shirt, carelessly picked from his modest wardrobe. He didn't even look at the mirror to check how he looked. He didn't care.

As he rushed out, snatching his bag from the shelf, he made an abrupt stop at the window. He stared at the droplets clinging on the window pane as he slowly walked up to the window. He then connected the droplets and wrote 'SANDY' on the pane; his lips curved into a smile on his bushy bearded face without his knowledge, which he noticed in the reflection on the window pane.

Sunny was just over five and half feet tall, with a strong slender physique, which he had attained by hard labor, since childhood. He had a stony-face, devoid of traces of emotions. Despite an unkempt look with an unruly beard and untamed long hair, he possessed a wild look in his eyes and masculine features which attracted girls the most. His unprofessional outlook didn't affect his job as a system programmer, as the job naturally seemed to have suited him, with his brain working out complex algorithms with mundane ease. He was hailed as the topmost programmer in his company, which he had joined nine years ago. All through the years, he never made any friends in the company. His colleagues often mocked him as 'the machine', as he was emotionally impregnable.

"No wonder he is the best programmer... He's just speaking his language." One of his colleague joked.

"He looks like a weirdo to me. Look at his unkempt look and the way he is dressed, full sleeved shirt always cuffed at the wrists and that weathered denim jacket irrespective of the weather." A girl jumped in at the opportunity to avenge him for his rude rejection of her love proposal.

"Something about him seems mysterious since the day he joined the company." commented the other colleague.

"Sure seems to be a mystery. I would give away my month's paycheck to anyone who could unravel the mystery." joked another colleague.

SUNNY'S PARENTAGE

Surya, who was still not rechristened as Sunny, had a forgettable childhood, with nothing to cherish. He never knew any relative apart from his father. Though he lived with his father, he could be called an orphan, as his father, who worked as a mechanic in a private firm at Saltfort industrial estate, was more of a pain than support to him. He took Surya with him, ostracizing his relatives from him, not with the love for him, but hatred for them. He wanted to punish them for their deceit, by keeping him away from them.

Surya's father was a simple man with a modest job. He fell in love with a beautiful girl, who happened to be Surya's mother. His marriage with her was not a complicated affair, as both the families were happy with the proposal. She loved him so much that he thought he had all he wanted in life. They made a lovely pair. Every day was an opportunity to express their love for each other. He was delighted with the news of arrival of a new member in the family. Life was a smooth sail, until the fateful day when a tornado rocked the boat. One fine day he returned from his work expecting his wife to welcome him with a beautiful smile at the entrance, which had become a regular exercise. He felt disappointed when that didn't happen for the first time. He walked in and looked around for her, to know the reason for breaking their custom. He was shocked to find her on the floor, unconscious. He immediately rushed her to the nearby hospital. She was in her thirty fifth week of pregnancy and in immense pain. She was immediately admitted in the Intensive Care Unit. After various tests, they finally diagnosed her case. He was summoned into the doctor's cabin.

"Don't you know that your wife is affected by Marfan's Syndrome?" asked the doctor.

"What?" He said, in utter confusion.

The doctor stared at him for a few seconds and then answered "Marfan's syndrome is a genetic disorder. It's caused by the deficiency of a protein which builds the connecting tiss…"

"Is she doing fine?" He interrupted her conversation as he was not interested in learning genetic science.

The doctor was silent for a few seconds and then she replied "No."

The word shook the world around him. When he came to know that he was deliberately kept in the dark about her medical condition, he erupted in fury. He then banished everyone from his life.

He feared the inevitable and it happened. His wife gave birth to a cute baby boy, but she wasn't lucky enough to have a glance at him. Doctors couldn't save her despite their relentless efforts. He carried the child and walked away to lead a solitary life. He also hated the boy, because he believed that he had caused the death of his wife and also because he reminded him of the painful betrayal. After persistent attempts, he offered a slight reprieve to his mother, as she was widowed a year ago.

SANDY BEFRIENDS SUNNY

Surya was a lonely, timid boy who never made any friends, as he suffered inferiority complex. He was afraid people would reject him. His only business with school was studies, and he did very well with it. He restricted himself to solitude… until another fresh academic year.

He was in the fifth grade.

He sat on the last bench as usual and observed the incoming faces, of which most were familiar, without acknowledging anyone. He turned away to look outside the window, discontinuing his boring observation.

"May I sit here?" A melodious voice spoke.

He turned around with inexplicable curiosity, to find a cute girl. It seemed as if it was the first time someone had spoken so courteously to him. He didn't respond, but just moved a bit, indicating her to sit down. He liked her at the first sight, but still faced away from her as she sat beside him.

"My name is Sandhya." she spoke in a cute voice.

Surya looked at her and again turned away from her without any response.

"I told you, he's not the kind you make friends with." said a girl from the front row, priding her judgment.

"Come on… Sit with me." She offered her a seat.

Sandhya ignored her remarks and also his indifference, as she had already made herself seat beside him. As she was getting settled, he stole glances at her.

She had a chubby face with bright black eyes and a round nose. Dark curly hair flowed down her shoulders, occasionally falling before her eyes, which she blew away playfully. Her skin was fair and flawless. He noticed her pink palms, delicate and smooth, unlike his. She was as tall as Surya, but slightly plump. She had neatly arranged rows of teeth, enclosed in her pink lips, which sparkled as she smiled. As he looked at her radiant smile, he had an uncanny feeling that he also had a smile on his face. He was not sure whether he smiled or he felt as if he smiled, as her mood seemed to be contagious. As she turned to his side, he immediately looked away.

It was the first day of the academic year. The class started with self-introductions. She came to know that his name was Surya. She was a new admission in the school, yet she made a lot of friends on the very first day. Her confidence was evident from the way she carried herself. He felt uneasy sitting beside her. He probably felt uncomfortable because she felt comfortable with him. He was afraid that once she began interacting with other guys, she would come to know about him and hate him.

When he entered the classroom the next day, he saw that Sandhya was surrounded by her classmates, each very glad to make a conversation with her. She was an instant charm. She was seated in the same place as the previous day, but he saw that her adjacent seat, which was his usual place, had a bag placed on it. He understood that it was reserved for someone and started to look for another seat, when she spoke,

"This seat is for you."

He couldn't believe his ears. He looked back straight into her adorable eyes.

"How can someone make friendship with a despicable person like me?" he wondered.

He sat down consciously and placed his bag on his desk. She just smiled at him and then continued with her chatting. He appreciated the way she carried herself with confidence. He lacked it.

As the class progressed, Sandhya was amazed by his brilliance and wondered why he had no friends.

The class ended and everyone started to pack their bags.

"Hey Surya… You did a great job today." He didn't expect the conversation.

"Th… Thank you." he stuttered.

"Nice knowing you." She said as she extended her hand towards him.

He shyly extended his hand and held it hesitantly. She gripped his hand and shook it briefly. Surya felt as if his shackles of self-restraint were broken by her delicate touch. Since then, Surya experienced a different world around him. He made friends with everyone in the class. He began to smile a lot. Surya and Sandhya became best friends in no time. Days passed and their friendship grew stronger every day.

"You have a beautiful smile… just like the sunshine." she said.

"I'm going to call you Sunny." she declared gleefully.

Everyone started calling him Sunny. He liked the name very much.

"Hey Sandhya… I'm going to call you Sandy hereafter." Sunny announced.

Sandhya was thrilled.

"What's the meaning of Sandy?" she asked playfully.

He thought for a few seconds.

"Nothing… Just goes with your name."

"Isn't it cute?" he asked, blinking innocently.

She laughed at his innocence.

"It's so… cute." She held his cheek and gently pinched him, as she stretched the word 'so'.

Sunny gave a beautiful smile.

As months passed, they became special friend to each other. A year rolled by so blissfully for them.

"It's a beautiful morning, Sunny bunny." she said one day.

Sunny gave her an enquiring look.

"I don't like to call you the way others do." she spoke with childish charm.

Sunny smiled as he nodded his head in disbelief.

"Ok… What does bunny mean?" he asked.

"Nothing… I love them. It's just cute, isn't it?" she asked.

"Then, I'll call you Sandy candy." he replied instantaneously.

"What does candy mean then?" Sandy asked.

"You are as sweet as a candy. Simple, Isn't it?" he replied.

"So sweet…" she liked it so much.

They had lunch together, they took breaks together, they walked home together. They spent so less time away from each other.

One day, Sunny happened to assist his teacher with shifting the assignment books to the staff room. When he returned, he found that all his books had a sketch of a sun beside his name.

"What's this Sandy candy?" Sunny asked.

"Well… It's your logo." She giggled.

"Logo!!!" he blushed, as he felt like a celebrity.

She was a mountain of confidence to him. She changed his life altogether.

Sandy shared all her likes and dislikes with Sunny.

"I like sunflowers. I love the way they turn in whichever direction the sun goes. I like peacocks. I love bunnies. They are cute, aren't they?" She nudged Sunny with her elbow, hinting why she nicknamed him bunny and then again continued with her list.

"My favorite dish is brinjal fry. I like mangoes. My favorite ice cream flavor is strawberry. I eat ice creams, a lot. I love chocolates too. I like pink. I love to drive my mother's car. Someday, I'll take you on a drive. I listen to melodious music when I'm upset. It soothes me. I like to dance. I like to sing… when I'm alone, of course." She giggled.

"What do I love the most? Any guesses?" she asked playfully.

Sunny didn't guess anything. He just admired her enthusiasm.

"I'm waiting…" she warned him.

"Oh… Could that be me?" he joked.

"I'm not talking about people I like. I'm talking about things I like." she explained impatiently.

"I can't think of anything." He shrugged in defeat.

"Rain... I think it's god's blessings showering in the form of rain droplets. I love to get drenched in the rain. I love to walk in the rain." She spoke with immense appreciation.

"What do you like?" she asked him.

Sunny's smile turned into a frown, as he only then realized that he didn't know what his likes were.

He blinked at Sandy for a few seconds and then replied "I don't know."

Sandy was surprised.

Sunny believed that he didn't have a choice to like or dislike. Whatever life gave him, he accepted.

"Think again." She insisted.

He thought hard and then replied "You are the only one I like."

She stared at him for a long time... and then gently kissed him on his cheek, which he didn't expect. She was emotional. As his life moved on, her likes became his likes and her dislikes, his.

SUNNY DAYS

S ummers were always special for the school kids. Everyone celebrated the last day of the academic year, because they would get a long vacation. Each had their own plans. Some went to their native places, some enjoyed a summer trip to hill stations, some got enrolled for swimming classes and some enjoyed summer camps. Sunny didn't have any of those privileges, which he never brooded about. He was only painfully expecting to hear Sandy's plan for any those.

"What's your plan for the summer?" Sandy asked him.

"Nothing." he bluntly said.

"Great…" she shouted cheerfully.

Sunny didn't understand.

"We can spend the summer together then." Sandy said excitedly.

Sunny couldn't have asked for a better vacation. He was ecstatic. He realized that the lack of privileges had turned out to be a blessing in disguise for him. He was prepared for a memorable vacation.

"What do we do today?" Sunny would ask.

"Let's play - pick out the lie, Sunny bunny." Sandy would say.

"Pick out the lie?" he wondered. She would suggest new games, which he had never heard of.

The game was that one participant had to narrate an incident from their own life and the other had to find out whether it was the truth or a lie.

Sandy easily picked out his lies. It was as if she read his mind. He failed most of the times. He genuinely lost to her, but he realized how much fun it was, losing to her. Her childishly enthusiastic giggles were priceless.

"Shall we play riddles?" Just before his interest for the game faded, she would propose a new one.

Before he got tired of the games, she would amuse him with some fascinating fairy tales, which her mother shared with her as bedtime stories. They visited the Portshore beach few times. It was a great joy for both of them, holding each other's hands and walking in the soothing breeze along the magnificent sea shore.

She invited him to her house every day. Her mother served him snacks. He occasionally had lunch at her house. Her mother was so kind to him. He wished he had a mother too.

"Won't you invite me to your house?" Sandy joked once, as he had never offered an invitation to her.

He gave her a deep regretful look and then said "No."

Sandy was shocked and wondered whether she heard him right and if so, whether he was joking.

"What?" she asked in confusion.

He then spoke about his personal life for the first time. Sandy could not hold back her tears. She then understood the reason for his reclusive nature before he became her friend.

"Not a big deal. I don't have father. You don't have mother. It's even." Sandy tried to console him.

"Not even… You get love, I don't." he told her painfully.

Sandy was sad for him. She observed his mood change.

"Shall we go for mango picking?" she asked him out of the blue.

Sunny returned to cheerful mood with her enthusiasm.

"Sure." he replied gaily.

"Let's go." She snatched his arm and ran towards the backyard, where there was a huge mango tree. Sunny looked for a long pole, trying the ones lying around.

She giggled and said "That's not the way you pick mangoes."

He wondered how else. Sandy swiftly walked to the tree and climbed it with ease.

"Come on." She called Sunny. He was scared.

He hesitantly walked to the tree. He tried to hold the tree trunk and climbed up a few feet. As he looked down, he jumped off in fear. He was strong enough to hold the trunk, but was afraid of heights.

Sandy laughed uncontrollably.

"You stay there. I'll throw you the mangoes." She said and climbed even higher and threw him some ripe mangoes. As she looked down, she was amused to see him rub his nose in fear. He had this strange mannerism; he rubbed his nose when he got anxious or tensed. He was awed by her fearlessness.

"What are you doing there Sandhya? How many times should I warn you not to climb the tree?" Her mother ordered her to get off the tree immediately.

Sandy swiftly climbed down the tree and immediately ran to her mother and gave her a hug. Her anger vanished in an instant and she kissed her daughter on her forehead.

"Wow... Is this why she is called mother?" He wondered at how her mood changed with a hug.

"Blessed are those who have mother." He envied her.

They had loads of fun with a variety of games all through the vacation; he couldn't imagine a better vacation than that one. Since then, he made it a rule to spend the holidays together and she gladly complied.

His classmates once wondered whether he could smile, but then again agreed that he had the cutest smile. Within four years of friendship, they became inseparable. They were seldom spotted without each other's company. They came to school as early as possible and left as late as possible. They spent together, as much time as possible.

HEARTBROKEN

One morning in the classroom, he kept waiting for Sandy, but to no avail. He knew that she was never late to school. He finally came to a conclusion that she wouldn't come to school that day.

"I will not talk to her, even if she apologizes." He swore in anxiety.

He eagerly waited for her the next day, with lots of questions for her. He was earlier than usual to school that day, as he had even skipped his breakfast. As minutes passed, he started to worry. The class started, but she was still not seen. He eagerly waited for the class to end for the day as he counted down minutes. As soon as the class ended, he dashed off the classroom as his classmates stared at him in wonder. He ran to Sandy's house as fast as his feet could take him, anxiously expecting her to be sick. He got the shock of his life when he found her house locked.

He waited for days with the hope that she would return one day, but his hope went up in smoke. He gradually perceived that she had left him forever. Sunny's fourteen year old heart had endured a lot of grief, but the departure of Sandy was unbearable for him. The shock pulled him back to emotional hibernation.

Sunny never stayed back for any chit chat with his colleagues. He would step out of the office the moment he was done with his job for the day. Nobody complained had complaints about that either.

As he dashed past his gossiping colleagues, he heard his phone alert him of an incoming message. He picked it and read the message.

"Meet you up this weekend Sunny boy."

It was a message from his friend Imran. There was never a time he did not smile when he remembered him or his friend circle.

IMRAN'S BACKGROUND

Mohammed Imran was brought up by his elder brother, Mohammed Irfan, as their father was jailed for life term on a murder charge, which had deprived him of father's nurturing as a toddler. His brother was fourteen years older to him, which was also the reason for his fatherly responsibility.

Irfan was short but well-built, with a strong body and broad shoulders. He had a strong jawline and clam facial features, which could look menacing when he was angry. He was mostly cool and fun loving, but dangerous when provoked. He loved Imran very much, guarding him like an angel over his shoulders.

Imran was a short guy with well-built body, almost a younger version of his brother. He had large eyes brimming with innocence. He could fool anyone at first glance. Once they knew his nature, his innocent looks enhanced his foxy image. He was an obnoxiously stubborn punk, who wouldn't heed anyone's words when he had decided on something. Being the wiliest character and quintessentially the most unforgiving of the gang, he wouldn't spare a breath of relief to whoever messed up with him. His gang had constant feuds with other gangs. Their rivalry with the Michael gang was no secret.

Imran Gang comprised of four close-knit friends each one an amusingly unique character.

INTRODUCTION TO
IMRAN GANG
STEVEN

Steven was six feet tall and a lanky chap with a good amount of brain. He was more of a mischievous boy with a lively nature which made him an odd fit in the notorious gang. His elder brother, Philip owned Sound Systems, a rental store, which offered sound systems for hire and also took up contracts for public announcements, business promotions and political propaganda. With the influence of Irfan, he constantly won all the local contracts. Philip had no complaints about life, except for his brother's mischief, which sometimes got onto his nerves, but he forgave everything, as he loved him very much.

"Hey angel… Hey… Hey" Steven shouted as he sprinted to join Zahira, who was walking out of her house with a group of her friends.

Zahira looked around and back to her house to see if anyone was watching them. She gave Steven a stinging stare and scurried past him, followed by her friends.

"Hey… I need to tell you something very important." he said as he rushed to join her.

She bowed down her head without paying heed to him and kept walking, as she felt that her attention might encourage him to follow her, but in vain.

"I need to tell you something really very important." he repeated.

Zahira stopped walking and stared back in frustration.

"If my father sees you chasing me, he will kill you." she warned.

"Oh really! Lucky me…" he exclaimed, confusing her.

"I would then join the list of immortal lovers who died for the sake of love." he joked, not taking her threat seriously.

She was so desperate to get rid of him that she didn't want to build the conversation.

"Tell me what you wanted to tell, and leave." she said in haste, as she knew that she would be in trouble if any of her family members saw her conversing with some stranger boy on the road. She didn't know whether she liked him or not, but of one thing she was sure - she was afraid.

"You look most beautiful today. You never know how many angels turned green of jealousy after they saw your beauty." he complimented her.

Zahira secretly enjoyed his admiration.

"Let's get moving Zak, we are getting late." One of her friend offered to help her.

Zahira ignored her.

"You said the same thing yesterday." she said to Steven, forgetting her plan to get rid of him soon.

"What I said yesterday was not a lie. You seem to be more and more beautiful everyday as my love for you grows day by day." he clarified.

She blushed.

"I'm not sure if I would say the same thing if I wasn't in love with you." He deliberately added to provoke her.

"What do you mean?" she asked impatiently.

"Well… People say that when someone is in love, the girl would naturally seem to be the most beautiful, irrespective of how much beauty she possesses." He saw her cheeks turning red as he continued.

"I didn't mean that you look beautiful to me only because I love you."

"Well… Maybe you are really beautiful."

"Wait a minute… How can I judge when I love you so much?" He confused her and enjoyed her perplexed expression.

"Then why don't you stop loving me and get lost." she spoke with a mock smile and started to walk again.

"Don't worry dear… I would never stop loving you." he told her as if she was worried that he would.

"Really…? How glad would I be if you stop chasing me?" she said, frustrated.

"Not a chance. Your shadow might stop following you in the dark, but I would find you even in darkness." he responded with playful seriousness.

"Oh… Is that so? Then you don't need to search for me in the darkness. Find me tomorrow and propose me." She challenged.

"Is that a bet?" Steven asked enthusiastically.

She stopped walking again and turned towards him, slightly nervous.

"Yes… That's a bet. Promise me, if you lose, you will not pursue me. Ever…" she responded with hope that she might be free of trouble as she was confident that she would surely win the bet.

"I promise that I would not pursue you if I lose… But what if I win?" he questioned.

"Wh… What???" She stuttered, knowing where he was heading.

"Will you accept my proposal if I win?" he asked her excitedly.

"Let's see." she told.

"That's not fair. You should make the stakes clear." He persisted.

"Well…" She hesitated, looking at her friends for help, but they were not in a position to help her.

She finally made up her mind.

"Alright… Bet…" she announced and whisked away from that place, as he danced away in joy, celebrating, as if he had already won the bet.

His confidence scared her friends.

"What have you led yourself into, Zak." Her friends expressed concern.

"Don't worry dolls. I know what I'm doing." she said confidently.

Steven stood at Zahira's house compound gates, recalling her words.

Find me tomorrow and propose me.

He wondered what she had in her mind. When she challenged him with such a significant bet, she would have had some solid plan. He patiently watched her house gate for long, as he wondered about her options.

"Would she stay in the house all day long, without coming out? In that case, I will find a way to slip into the house, before which I need to make sure of her presence. Let me wait for some more time." he thought.

Somehow he was convinced that he was wasting his time waiting.

"She would not make it so easy for me."

"Let me confirm before thinking of a plan."

"But how" As he was observing the situation, he saw the postman at the end of the lane.

He got an idea.

He ran towards the postman who was riding his bicycle towards Zahira's house. He stopped him few yards before her house.

"What's up man?" The postman asked.

Steven directed the postman away from Zahira's house.

"What's your problem? What do you want of me Steve?" the postman asked him.

"I want you to deliver a mail to someone." Steven said.

"Drop it in the postbox, man." the postman said.

"Thanks for the mind blowing idea." Steven ridiculed."Just do as I say." he said.

"Hope I'm not a victim of your mischief today…" the postman said.

'Not at all… Never been so serious in all my life." he said, preparing to narrate his role.

"Ok… Listen. I want you to deliver a registered post for Zahira, which I'll give you." he said. As he was about to continue, he was interrupted by the postman.

"Sounds more troublesome than your routine mischief…" the postman said with disagreement evident on his face.

"I count on you, big brother." he said.

"If something goes wrong… I might lose my job, probably more than that." he said as he started to move.

Steven held him tightly by his arm and stared at him for a few seconds contemplating what to do further.

"Ok…" Steven made up his mind."If something goes wrong… you can point your finger at me. You can say that I threatened to kill you, if you didn't do this… Fair enough?" he spoke.

The postman was baffled by his seriousness.

"What's the deal?" the postman asked.

"Tell you later…" Steven winked at him.

The postman sighed. "Alright… Never again" he said.

"Let's get moving…" Steven nudged him excitedly.

Steven observed the postman walk into the compound of Zahira's house rather uneasily. Steven hoped he would execute his task well. The postman disappeared from Steven's line of sight as he walked towards the doorbell. Steven waited patiently for him. As more time passed, he began to get anxious.

"Did he blow it up?" he thought. Yet he boldly waited at her gate, ready to face anything.

As he was getting more and more tensed with anticipation, he saw the postman walking out, wiping his perspiration, which did not seem to stop flowing. He walked so fast that he could have run instead.

"What's up?" Steven inquired worried that he could have slipped up.

He narrated what had happened at her house nervously.

"What have you got, Ramu?" Zahira's father asked as he opened the door.

"I… got a letter for Zahira." He mildly stuttered.

"Ok… She's not home. I'll take it…"

"No… No." he said as Zahira's father stared at him suspiciously.

"Reg… Registered post." He stressed, stuttering more evidently.

"So what? Do you need a paternity certificate?" He snatched the envelope off the postman's hand as he spoke with frustration.

"Thank you and you may leave now." he said rather rudely prompting his envelope held hand to the gate.

The postman stared at the envelope for a few second and scuttled towards the exit.

"You assured me that no one will take it… She's not home. Now his father took it. He will find out that the mail was not from the post office as it did not bear any postal seal… My job is gone." he lamented.

"Hey… Listen to me. Don't worry. It contains only a few business promotional pamphlets and nothing else." he said. "You go on with your job… I will deal this." he continued.

"I saw that he was frustrated with me… He may…" The postman was telling him as he interrupted saying "Trust me."

"Couldn't be a worse day." The postman cursed Steven as he raced away on his bicycle.

He now knew that Zahira was not at home, but that knowledge was not sufficient for him to win the bet. He knew almost all her friends and their addresses, but he couldn't break into everybody's house to verify. Winning the bet seemed impossible. He had to find a way.

"I will surely find a way." he assured himself.

"Attention please… This is a personal message." boomed the speakers from an auto rickshaw.

"The announcement might sound strange. I plead you all to ignore this message as it is only intended for a beautiful girl named Zahira." continued the voice.

"Hey Zak… I know you can hear me. So, listen to what my heart has to say." He paused for a few seconds, building curiosity on the streets.

"No place in the world can conceal you from me. No force in the world can stop my love for you. My love will find you by your heartbeat." The speakers beamed, carrying the message in every street.

Zahira, who was busy chitchatting with her friends, was struck by the announcement. Her friends stared at her, perplexed with the message. She ran to the corridor to witness it.

The whole town was amused by the message. Some even appreciated his guts and bold mischief, but Zahira's family was utterly embarrassed and annoyed.

"Attention please... This is a personal message." The voice trailed off into the adjoining streets.

It wasn't long before he was arrested by the cops, concerning the complaint filed by Zahira's father.

He was liked by everyone in the town, including the cops, because of his lively nature and boyish charm that emanated innocence. All the goodwill was not able to save him from an arrest. He however escaped the traditional brutal treatment of the police.

"So... You have invented a new flavor of mischief, kid." the policeman joked at Steven.

"Not this time sir. It's serious love." Steven said.

"I would have loved to see you serious sometime, but forget about it this time, son." the policeman advised.

"Choose some other affair to be serious about... You know, the girl's parents are very serious about the case." He was genuinely worried about the kid.

"You might have trouble getting out of the case." As he spoke out the words, a cute girl in her late teens entered the station.

The girl glanced at Steven as she walked past him towards the policeman's desk.

"If you are glad that I stay in prison, I would gladly do."

"Look... I've got a better idea. Why don't you make me a prisoner of your love for the rest of my life?" Steven commented with his mischief fully intact.

"You mean to say that my love is a bigger punishment than imprisonment, huh?" She pouted her lips in mocked disappointment as she turned towards him.

Steven stood frozen with his jaw dropped as her words struck his ear drums.

"I hope this is not a dream." he was stunned.

"I don't care if it is a dream… Just don't wake me up." he thought as he winked excitedly at her.

She walked towards him and held his hand.

"You know what…? You won the bet." she announced with a wide smile, to his delight.

KRISHNA

"Guide sir... Guide... Do you need a guide, sir?" Krishna offered the tourists.

The place was not a renowned tourist spot. It was a ruined ancient fort with no special attraction, except the fact that it was ancient. People scarcely visited the place, and when they did, it was just to fill the extra time in their schedule or because of dishonest tourist guides, who exaggerated the facts to the tourists. However, it was not a fertile ground for the guides. Still there was quite a competition among the jobless locals, who knew everything about the ancient ruin - there was nothing much to know though. They also had competition from outsiders, sometimes. Krish, as he was called by his mates, was not a local and was not thorough with the history of the fort, but he was an expert bluffer. He had a slender body with height just a couple of inches short of six feet. He had cute brown eyes and an innocuous face.

"Guide sir... I work cheap, but you can get all you want to know about the fort." He offered, as most of the tourists, who were not interested in the history of the fort, ignored him. He didn't care, as he needed only one tourist for his survival for the day. He swept his sight across the fort for prospects. He found a couple, obviously newly married, clicking pictures of everything they came across. He gave a triumphant smile as he knew he had found what he had been looking for.

"You make a lovely couple, sir." Krish casually complimented them, as he walked past them.

They were surprised by such a remark from a stranger, but were flattered by the compliment.

"Oh… Thank you." the man said shyly.

Krish smiled in return and kept moving without asking them if they wanted his services, as it would steal away the sincerity of his remark. "Want a guide sir?" he asked a disinterested group of old men, still within sight of the couple.

"Excuse me." He heard the voice of the man, whom he had just complimented.

"Bull's eye." He thought, as he turned towards the voice.

"How can I help you, sir?" Krish asked the man as he walked towards them.

"Can you guide us, please?" the man asked him humbly.

"Sure sir. I would be pleased to." he replied.

"This is an ancient fort as old as 600 years." Krish spoke with the meager knowledge he gathered as he had overheard the other guides say.

He continued bluffing, hoping that the couple did not know anything about the fort. To his delight, they were not interested in the facts about the fort. They were only keen on taking photographs. Since they were alone on the trip, they took photos of each other, though the lady did not seem to be as enthusiastic as the man.

"Shall I take a photograph of you lovely couple?" Krish offered.

The couple was pleased as they themselves were about to ask him. Krish turned to be an enthusiastic photographer, much to their delight. He kept clicking photos of them endlessly. As they came to the watchtower of the fort, the couple was mesmerized by a sight of a ruined palace.

"Would you like to have a few photographs taken with this background, sir." He asked the man gesturing towards the palace.

"Why not…?" He gave the camera to Krish.

He clicked a few pictures of them in casual poses. The man was so crazy about taking pictures that he felt lucky to have his service. He started to take full liberty of him and posed with various backgrounds. Krish started to reflect their enthusiasm and he started to suggest a few ideas. As they moved to the palace's private art gallery filled with corroded wall paintings, they came across a romantic painting of a handsome prince on his knees proposing to a beautiful princess.

"Wow… Beautiful painting!!!" the lady exclaimed.

Krish gave them an idea of pose. "Why don't you two pose as if you are appreciating the painting? It'll make a very natural still." he suggested.

"Sure. That seems like a great idea." the tourist said and started to pose with his spouse.

"The bags on your shoulders don't seem pretty. It seems like an obstacle." he advised.

"You are right." the tourist said as he removed the baggage off his shoulders and stood to pose.

He clicked a few pictures, but felt something was artificial.

"Sir... It looks as if you are posing for photograph. Let us take some casual stills." he suggested.

"Fabulous..." The tourist appreciated his idea.

"You pose as if you are expressing your appreciation of the painting to your wife." he offered.

The lady felt embarrassed to perform such silly antics in front of a stranger and refused to comply.

"Do it for my sake darling." the tourist pleaded, to which she agreed unwillingly.

The couple posed in the most casual way they could. He turned back immediately, as he was curious about the photo.

"Please sir, stay in your position. I'm looking for the best angle to cover you both without obstructing the painting." he said as he struggled to get the best angle.

The tourist returned to the position, proud of Krish's commitment.

The man put one hand over his spouse's shoulder and extended the other hand towards the painting, as if expressing his appreciation for the painting. They stayed in the position for a few seconds, expecting him to get his angle right. They heard giggling and some funny comments.

"Hey... Have a look here. Isn't it strange that they have erected statues in the middle of the art gallery? I wonder if they are antiques too." a tourist quipped.

As the tourist couple did not get any comment from the guide for some time, they turned back.

"He's gone!" he exclaimed in utter shock.

They saw a few tourists passing by, giving a weird look to them, but the guide was nowhere to be seen and neither was their camera, nor their baggage.

"Want to have a look at the statue? Go, find a mirror, dumbo." She fired at him.

ALVIN

Alvin stood over six feet tall with a chiseled body, developed by a high protein diet and extensive exercise. He had fearsome eyes and high cheekbones. Complimenting his dark fearsome look, his cheeks were adorned by a vertical scar which he had obtained from a bike accident. Despite his intimidating outlook, his abject credulity made him the most vulnerable of the gang. No one could beat him with muscle power, but often manipulated by wits. He was nothing but a gullible giant. Their rivals always targeted him to bully his gang, but still he was the most lovable person of the gang. He always bragged about his muscle power, but it couldn't save him from embarrassment most of the time. Sometimes, it was the reason for his embarrassment. Just like the time he was cunningly tricked into a trap.

Al, as he was dearly called by his friends, walked into a chicken store through the vigil sight of Michael Gang's member, Jinnah.

"Get me some fresh tender chicken." Al ordered the shopkeeper.

"Enough of building muscles... Get him something that could develop some brain." mocked Jinnah.

That was enough to provoke Al.

"I'll break your skull and see how much brain you've got, son of a bitch." He shouted as he threw his bag at him and started to chase him. Even though he was no match for Jinnah in running, he didn't give up. Al chased him through the road adjoining the police station. By that time, Jinnah slipped out of his sight and that was when he noticed a group of young boys trying to push a jeep upwards a steep road. The vehicle seemed to have a starting problem, which needed some kinetic force to start it. Al noticed that the driver was hoping to use the force generated by the pushing, but that wouldn't be sufficient to start the vehicle.

"Push harder. Use more power." The driver encouraged the kids.

Al completely forgot about Jinnah as it was just the opportunity for him to boast his power.

"Hello boys... I reckon you need the help of some real muscles." Al said as he advanced towards the jeep, nudging the boys out of his way, indicating that he alone was enough for the job.

Al leaned, resting his palms against the rear door, faced down and jogged against the vehicle, pushing it up the steep road at a considerable speed. The driver tried to start the vehicle once with the speed generated by the push. The process of starting created a lot of noise, but failed to start the car. Al started to panic as it was a matter of prestige for him. He gathered all his power and sprinted against the vehicle, gazing at his accelerating footsteps, calculating his speed. As he kept moving for some time, he realized that no attempts were made to start the vehicle. Just then he felt an iron grip on his shoulder, bringing him to a stop. He looked up to find a cop with a stern look on his face.

"Where are you taking this vehicle, Rambo?" he asked ridiculously.

Al looked around perplexed. He neither found the boys nor the driver at the wheel. He then understood that he had been tricked.

"Bring him in." the cop shouted at the constable.

As he was taken into the police station, he looked around to find out who had played the trick with him. That was when he saw Michael and Jinnah hooting at him.

All it took for Michael to trick him was hiring a man and a few boys for a few minutes and a little bit of planning. He spotted an unmarked police jeep and decided to use it as an accessory in his game. He set one of his men to steer Al into the scene and the other to observe the movement of the cops and alert the team in case of any unexpected entry from them. They enacted the drama promptly at Al's entry, as Michael knew about his boasting tendency. The attempt to start the engine was carefully abstained till the entry of Al as it was supposed to attract the cops, soon after which the driver was prompted to inconspicuously jump off the vehicle.

Though he was let off without any charge, as the cops trusted his plea of innocence, it was a shameful defeat to his gang.

"Don't worry mate. We'll get them soon." Imran promised Al, who was so embarrassed to face him.

IMRAN

Michael Gang was having fun with booze already beyond the threshold.

"Seems to be a bad day today boss." The bartender told his boss as he saw Imran Gang enter the bar.

"How nice would it be if one of the gangs is wiped off!" the bartender wished.

"Well… For now, let's hope that the bar is not wiped off." the bar owner said with a sigh.

"Hey Ravi… You wanted chicken roast. You can order it, now that the stock has arrived. You know what? It's dressed too. Hah hah hah…" Michael shouted as he winked at Ravi prompting towards Imran Gang.

Al grabbed a plastic chair to smash at them, when Imran calmed him down.

"Strange… Really strange…" Al thought, as it was Imran who would mostly be the reason for any brawl they get into. He dropped the chair and followed him in shock as it was very unlike of him.

"There goes your chicken…" Jinnah gestured to Michael.

"Didn't have to wait for too long." the bartender told the owner sarcastically.

"Now, move your ass and offer them something." he ordered the bartender.

Imran led the gang to a corner of the bar. His gang stared at him in surprise.

"Let us hit them with brains, instead of fists." Imran suggested to his gang, who were even more confused.

"Let me do the planning. You just trust me and watch the show." He assured Al, as he understood the reason for his desperation.

"Call Krish…" Imran instructed Steven.

Steven dialed Krish's number without any argument.

"He'll be here in five minutes." Steven told Imran as he disconnected the call.

"Good." He kept watching Michael gang patiently, like a predator waiting its prey to approach its hunting range.

Imran saw Krish approaching them. His kept his eyes focused on Michael's mobile which was carelessly left on his table.

As soon as Krish reached their table, Imran retrieved his mobile and removed his sim card and handed it over to Krish. The whole gang observed his activities in confusion.

When Imran explained his plan to Krish, the gang realized that Imran was not the one to take bullying easily.

Imran decided to take advantage of his phone being identical to Michael's. His plan was to switch the phones and perform his trick with Michael's phone and then again switch them back. What trick he was up to, no one knew.

Krish felt that his task was very easy, as Michael's gang was already in stupor.

He kept watching the table for some time, waiting for some set up. He got to his feet when he saw someone walking into the bar. He waited for a few seconds, doing some calculations, and then he started walking in his direction when he was confident that they would cross path at Michael's table. He walked cautiously making sure that their paths converged at his target spot. As they approached Michael's table, he tripped the guy, toppling him on to the table, scattering the contents on it. Krish's sight was sharp enough to spot Michael's mobile phone. He first dropped the one in his hand and then bent down to pick up Michael's phone as he was conscious about the gang's focus on the guy who had tripped on to their table.

Imran, who was observing the whole trick, was very impressed. Krish walked inconspicuously back to Imran's table when the innocent guy was struggling to get out of the hook of the gang clouded by intoxication.

"Payback time…" Imran winked at Al as he walked out with the phone in his hand, patting Krish's shoulder in appreciation. His gang just stared at him as he walked out of the bar. He walked back to their table after a few minutes and handed over the phone to Krish.

"Let him have his phone back." he said as he winked at Krish.

No one understood what was going on, but Krish dutifully followed Imran's instruction. But he was not lucky this time as Michael had his phone in his shirt pocket. Imran saw his challenge, but he desperately wanted the phone back with Michael… and quickly.

"Do something… I want his phone back with him in 3 minutes." Imran ordered him.

Krish thought vigorously as he didn't want to let Imran down. As he was thinking of a plan to switch the phone, he noticed Michael walk towards the restroom.

"Thank you god... For helping me..." He prayed, as he followed him.

Imran curiously observed him, guessing his plan. Krish knew that he had to be careful, as merely getting in sight of Michael might cause a lot of trouble for him. As soon Michael walked into the restroom, he observed his position and switched off the lights. He then immediately dashed on him and skillfully retrieved the phone from Michael's pocket and dropped the other one onto the floor. Then he purposefully crashed onto some other guy, dropping him to the floor and rushed out of the restroom. He had the sight of a nocturnal animal, which helped him see better in the dark.

"Who the fuck was that?" Michael screamed.

Immediately the bar staff rushed to the restroom and switched on the lights.

"Sorry sir... The switches don't work properly. They get switched off sometimes." They apologized to Michael as they saw him infuriated. He picked his phone up, which lay on the floor and slipped it into his shirt pocket.

"Fuck with your switches... Who the fuck crashed on me?" He shouted as he looked around to find one guy who had just gotten up and was cleaning his elbows.

Michael understood that he was the one who had crashed on him and slapped him hard. The man who just received the slap opened his mouth in shock as he saw him rush out of the restroom furiously.

"You are the one who crashed onto me and you slap me in return." He screamed to himself, as he didn't have the guts to raise his voice against him.

Krish walked inconspicuously towards their table and quietly sat beside Imran, visibly flushed.

"What the fuck were you up to?" Imran grunted.

Krish retrieved the phone from his pocket and stuffed it in Imran's hands.

"You did it, son of a bitch!" Imran punched Krish's chest.

Krish was glad to have pleased Imran.

"Hey kid... Get me a bottle of rum." Imran ordered with a look of accomplishment.

No one knew what he had accomplished. They knew that they had to wait till he revealed what it was. As the kid placed the bottle of rum on their table, they heard police sirens approaching them. They were confused.

"Should we escape the sceneor stay?" Al asked Imran.

"We should definitely stay." he replied, as he didn't want the gang to miss the show.

The police jeep screeched at the entrance of the bar and a couple of policemen walked up to the bar.

"What trouble would come up on us today?" the bar owner wondered, as he walked to the entrance to receive them.

"Can I be of some help to you inspector?" the owner asked dutifully.

"Of course you can." the inspector said as he rushed into the bar with his team.

"Switch off the music." he commanded, which was obeyed by the bar staff.

"Call the number, now." the inspector instructed the constable, who called the number which was registered at the control room. A prompt sound emerged from Michael's shirt pocket. The inspector seized the phone from his pocket and checked the incoming number.

"Get the bastard." the inspector ordered the constable, who snatched him by his collar.

Imran watched with a sense of accomplishment as Michael was dragged out of the bar. Now Imran turned to look back at his gang.

"Curious guys?" Imran opened the conversation.

He only got a nod in unison, as a reply.

"Ok…" he said as he narrated his trick.

The gang was terrified with his guts of having conspired something like that, because the gang knew that manipulating the police was a very dangerous thing to do. But, he never cared about risk.

"The police would rip him apart for all the abusive language he used on them."

"Err… I used on them." he corrected his sentence and winked at the petrified gang.

"This one's for you Al. Scores level…" Imran had avenged Michael for Al.

GIRL IN A MENTAL STORM

The soothing breeze turned into a cold, rather spooky wind that shook even the strongest rooted trees. The wind was gaining momentum, growing wilder by the minute, scattering the dust and dry leaves around. The girls on the terrace, who were enjoying the soothing wind, felt threatened by the powerful slaps of the brutal wind. They started to scoot away from the open terrace. There stood one girl who seemed to be unshaken by the savage wind, though absolutely shaken within.

"Look at that bitch who is unmoved by the windstorm." commented a prostitute who passed by her.

"Probably one of the kind who enjoys wild things…" Winked another who was racing ahead of her.

The wind grew menacingly barbaric and soon started ripping the branches off the trees, but the young woman stood unruffled, holding the railings on the parapet wall.

Pooja, who was also rushing towards safety, sensed something unusual about her. She had come across many strange types of girls, but she seemed to be a mystery ever since her arrival a few weeks ago. She ignored her and rushed to shelter.

Pooja was an embodiment of native beauty, with dusky skin and perfectly proportioned body features. Dark long hair enhanced her native look, her charming bright brown eyes never failed to attract males. She was the most sought-after prostitute in the joint.

As Pooja settled in her room, she resumed thinking about the girl on the terrace. She could sense something familiar about her. Her thoughts were interrupted by the loud slam of the window which was jammed for many days. She understood that the wind was climbing to the peak of atrocity. She walked up the stairs and found her in same position. She hadn't moved even an inch.

"What the fuck are you doing here?" Pooja shouted at the pitch of her voice to beat the noise of the wind.

The girl did not budge. Pooja shouted again and was tempted to leave her where she was, but didn't. She walked up to her and drew her along with her, roughly snatching her by her arm. She led her to her room by force.

Pooja stared at her gloomy black eyes. She was a petite girl, five and half feet tall. She had fair skin, blotched by a scar below her right eye. She looked cute because of her innocent looks. Despite the scar, she was the most beautiful girl she had ever come across.

"What the fuck do you think you were doing up there?" Pooja shot at her.

The girl didn't seem to care.

"Look… I don't expect courtesy from you because I seem to be concerned about you."

"Just talk or fuck off from here, bitch. I just don't care." Pooja shouted.

The girl blankly stared at her for a few seconds in shock.

"People like you can't understand my feelings." she said and started to walk off.

Pooja swiftly raced ahead of her and blocked her way.

"What the fuck did you say just now?"

"People like me? What did you mean??? What the fuck did you mean?" Pooja screamed.

"People who treat their body like a pile of meat, ready for sale." she said bitterly.

"Who are you then? Did you come here for community service?" Pooja ridiculed her.

She didn't have words to speak.

"I... I was... I was forced into it." She stuttered.

"I... I was... I was forced into it." Pooja mocked her."What made you think that this was my career goal, or for that matter, for any girl here?" Her tone became serious.

Pooja somehow felt embarrassed exposing her pain that had been suppressed in her heart for ages.

"Did you ever come across a situation where you had to act ecstasy in extreme pain? Did you ever happen to live two contrasting lives at the same time? Did you ever feel that you have nothing to do with your life, you do not own it? Did you ever want to end your life, but were forced to live and you had to die every day?" Pooja screamed and stormed out of the place, ashamed of having gotten emotional.

Pooja had a pitiful past behind her façade of arrogant confidence.

POOJA'S MISERABLE
CHILDHOOD

Pooja had forced herself into prostitution out of despair as she had nothing left to feed herself and her family. The only thing she could trade with the mean world was her body. She didn't repent nor curse anybody. She was a brave girl who faced challenges boldly without grievance or fear. She earned the reputation of the most cooperative prostitute in the brothel, though she hated each second of it.

She was born in Paavanagudi, a small village not far from the Manchore city. She had a loving father and an angel for a mother. It was a small yet beautiful family. She was a princess for their parents. Her mother would never get bored of telling her unending series of happy ending tales. Her father would thrill her often with some surprise gifts. Her school was on the way to the factory where her father worked. He would carry his little girl on his shoulders till her school gleefully and her mother would pick her from school. She was not strong enough to carry her, still compensated by telling her some interesting stories to keep her entertained all through the way. They took it as a privilege to groom her every day. Their happiness was curbed by a disastrous accident at the factory, where her father was victimized by a forklift truck, which crushed his legs as they collided at a blind corner. On hearing the shocking news, her mother suffered a paralysis stroke. It was cataclysmic for little Pooja, who was barely thirteen years then.

Her father's hospital expenses were borne by his employer, who also offered him a meager compensation, which was not sufficient to support them for a long time, nor could they start a business.

Pooja took the responsibility on her delicate shoulders. Although her parents hated their daughter toiling at such a tender age, could not think of a better option. She worked as a housekeeper for an old couple who seldom had visitors, hence very less work. Pooja was glad that the lady, who had employed her, loved her very much. The old man used to give her gifts on all special occasions. She did not regret starting to work at such an early age. She was glad that she was placed in the perfect place. She worked for them for nearly three years. She turned from cute kid to beautiful lass. It's not only her physical appearance, but the intensions of the old man changed too. He used to occasionally pinch her, kiss her on her cheek and hug her, but she was too innocent to understand his cruel intensions. She didn't notice that he did all these naughty gestures only in the absence of the old lady. Once, he decided to break the pretenses of innocence and became bold to take it to the next level. He picked an occasion when the old lady was out for quite a long time and approached her when she was arranging the bed sheets. He gathered all his guts and hugged her tight from behind, grabbing her breasts. Even Pooja sensed that the hug was different from regular one. She shrugged off violently and stared at him in anger.

"What are you doing?" she screamed at him.

He got nervous, as he hadn't expected such a violent response from her. He realized that if he didn't get the situation under control, it would be an unpleasant experience for him.

"Look… If you cooperate with me, you could lead your life smoothly with all the support from me. Else, I can charge you with theft of some jewels and frame a criminal case against you." he threatened her. She was terrified by his threat. Luckily for Pooja, she heard footsteps at the doorway.

"Think about it." He said as he hastily walked away.

"The doctor rescheduled all his appointments as he had an emergency. It was all pain in vain." Lady Maria muttered as she walked in.

"If your work is done, you may go home Pooja." She told her.

She thankfully walked out of the house, hazy. She was not able to believe what had happened a few minutes ago.

"Filthy old man." She cursed.

She hated going back to that house for work, but also dreaded the old man's warning.

"Look… If you cooperate with me, you could lead your life smoothly with all the support from me. Else, I can charge you of theft of some jewels and frame a criminal case against you." she recalled his words.

"I would burn myself rather than succumbing to him." she thought.

But she also remembered her disabled parents.

"I can't let my parents suffer at any cost. I would do anything for them."

She kept thinking the whole night and she made up her mind the next morning. She walked to their house rather early. The old man peeped through the window with anticipation and lust.

"Robert!" The old lady shouted at the pitch of her voice so loudly, that it could have blown the roof away.

The old man started shivering, though confused. He walked downstairs hesitantly. He saw Pooja in tears, standing beside the lady. He could take a guess of what could have happened, but he wasn't sure.

"What's the matter, Maria?" He tried to hide the tremble in his voice.

"Aren't you ashamed of yourself, misbehaving with a girl of your grand-daughter's age?" she thundered.

"What? She is lying." He feigned shock.

"Stop bluffing me. Behave well and earn some respect you dirty old man." she fired back.

He started staring at her.

"Stop staring at her. If you cause her any harm, you will face dire consequences." She warned him with finality.

He walked away quietly, but kept staring at her with the corner of his eye.

"You don't worry baby. You go to work." she consoled her.

Pooja stood there hesitating for a long time.

"What's the matter Pooja?" she inquired.

"I could never face him again madam. It would always be embarrassing to face him again. I might not be able to work here anymore." She started weeping loudly.

"Be brave, my child. I can understand your feeling. Also I understand that you are the only source of income to your family. How would you support yourself and your ailing parents then?" she asked.

She had momentarily forgotten about that in her emotional outburst. She suddenly started to worry.

"Don't worry, child. I will arrange a better job for you. Just come back to me in the meantime for any help. You are like my granddaughter." she spoke, infusing confidence in her.

She was glad to hear her soothing words.

"Thank you madam" she said as she walked out of the house.

As she walked out of the house, she found that the old man was still staring at her with vengeance. She hated his sight that she walked faster to her home.

"You are early today, my angel. What made me so lucky?" her father asked with a smile.

"Madam told that there is no work today. Hence today is my lucky day too. I can spend the whole day with my papa and mama." she winked with a smile and hugged him.

His smile transformed into grief.

"Had I been capable enough, you would have been in school now. My heart aches to see you as a maid." he grimaced.

"With my papa's love, I'm always a princess. I want nothing more than your love." she replied with a kiss on his forehead.

"That, you can have more than you can weigh." he winked with a straining smile.

She moved to her mother who was enjoying the conversation between the father and daughter.

"So, what's my mama going to say about that?" She sat beside her mother.

"You are our princess darling." Her mother said.

"I know mama. I know." She hugged her mother.

"We must have saved the luck of all our previous births to have had you as our daughter. You are truly an angel." she said proudly.

"What more does the angel have than my darling princess?" her mother asked him.

"Wings, probably…. Could be nothing more" her father offered.

"Now, stop it both of you. Did you have your medicines?" she asked like a dutiful mother.

"Yes mother." her father mockingly replied, but with admiration.

She had fun the whole day with her parents. She knew that she had a big trouble, which she did not want to expose to them and spoil their joy.

"I'll face it all by myself." she told herself.

She trusted the old lady Maria. She was a very kind woman and she had also promised to help her. She counted on it very much. She forgot all her troubles and spent an ecstatic day with her parents.

The next day, when she woke up, she did not know what to do. She was in a dilemma. If she didn't go to work for the second day continuously, she would have to explain why she wouldn't go to work. She didn't think about it. She did not want to embarrass her parents with the cause. She thought for a long time and finally made up her mind to go to the lady's house, though she hated to encounter the dirty old man. She finished her daily chores and gave medicine to her parents. Just as Pooja was ready to leave, she heard a knock on the door. She wondered who that could be at the wee hour, as they usually had a very few visitors. She was surprised when she opened the door. It was the old lady Maria.

"It's a pleasant surprise to see you here madam. Please come in." Pooja invited her into her humble house.

"Hope I have not caused any disturbance." she asked with a benevolent smile.

"Not at all madam. I was actually about to come to meet you." Pooja responded.

"That's why I made it to you as early as possible." the gentle old lady told her.

Pooja understood that she didn't want to embarrass her as she had had a bitter encounter with her old husband.

"I have a contact in Manchore who could offer you a job of an apprentice tailor in a cottage textile industry. You would be trained and recruited there." She explained the details of the employment.

Manchore was a fast growing industrial city which contributed to the majority of the cotton production in the country and also gradually advancing into the IT sector.

"I think this is the best I can do for you, child." she told Pooja.

"This is great help madam. I enjoyed working for you, if it was not for…" Pooja trailed off as the old lady interrupted.

"I know dear. You no longer need to worry about that. I hope you could get all the good luck in your future." she wished her.

"Would you like to meet my parents, madam?" Pooja asked her.

"Some other time, child." the old lady replied.

As soon as the old lady left, Pooja ran to her parents to convey the good news. When she did, she got an unexpected reaction. They turned sad. She did not realize in the excitement of a new and better job, that she would have to leave her parents.

"We would not be apart for a long time. I would be living in the hostel with my coworkers in the beginning. Then I would take you with me after few months." she assured them. Little did she know that that wouldn't happen.

THE ORDEAL CONTINUES

She was excited about her new job. She had nice colleagues. Things went smoothly for a few days, until trouble started in the form of a male colleague, Raja. He came to know about her position and was tempted to take advantage of her helplessness. He would deliberately touch her whenever he got a chance. Pooja understood his intentions and despised him. He started making some advances and suggestive gestures. She ignored him.

"He is a slimy bastard." Pooja's colleagues would curse him.

They were used to the life they were living, but Pooja was not. She would be careful not to give him a chance of taking advantage of her. However, he would sneak in and brush her breasts or dash her whenever he would find a mild chance. She would feel as if a centipede was creeping over her whenever he touched her. She would spring off his reach immediately. His advances attracted the attention of other male coworkers. They also tried to take their share of ribald fun with her. Pooja was tired of running from them, but she had no other choice. Moreover, she lived in a spoilt neighborhood where prostitution was the main racket. He would sometimes follow her with lewd gestures till the ladies hostel where she stayed with her coworkers. She was approached by a few sex hungry dogs who presumed her to be a prostitute. She would walk away ignoring them, as she would feel that reprimanding them was not a wise thing. Few of her coworkers would accept the offer. She wondered how they could do such a thing.

"When you can't go against the tide, go with it. That's survival." One of her coworkers told her.

She hated the work. She hated the people. She hated the place. She hated everything around her. Life became totally different after she moved away from her parents. She felt lonely and vulnerable. She would go to meet her parents once in a month and would live all her life for the month in the few days she was with them. She wanted to stay back with them, but she had no other means of supporting them. After realizing her horrible state, she completely dropped the idea of bringing her parents to live with her. She resolved herself to take the situation all by herself. She became braver. Whenever her male colleagues would try to take advantage of her, she would ward them off with confidence. She was so determined, but her determination couldn't protect her. Once, when she was the last one to leave, she encountered Raja, who didn't want to miss the opportunity. He exceeded the limits and pounced on her. She slapped him hard and tried to escape, but he held her with an iron grip. She screamed and prayed for help.

"What's happening?" her boss thundered.

She thought her prayers were answered when Raja scrammed off as soon as he heard his boss. She felt saved.

"What do you think you are doing?" the boss shouted at Pooja.

"He was trying to…" Pooja tried to explain the situation when he intercepted her "Meet me in my cabin." And he kept walking away towards his cabin.

She feared her boss would hold her responsible for the act. As she entered the cabin, he stared at her for some time. He started to notice her sexual beauty.

"I could have you fired for your dirty acts." He played his routine game, which he had used with few of the girls working in his company.

"I did not do anything wrong." she tried to clarify.

"Shut up and just listen." He continued.

"I could let you continue here, if you would be nice to me." he said as he wound his hand around her waist. She warded his hand off in an impulse, which enraged him. He slapped her hard across her face, knocking her down and then held her to the ground. She tried to scream, but he sealed her mouth with his hand and mercilessly raped her. Her pitiful whimpers adversely increased the arousal of the beast. She wept hard as he wiped his sweat off his forehead.

"If you try to make a fuss about this, you would be charged on all possible felony. The cops are good friends of mine. So behave and cooperate. I believe you are clever enough to understand what I said." he warned as he walked away.

She was not able to sleep that night. She shed tears that night more than she ever had in all her life. She wanted to kill all the men in the world. She hated going to work the next day, but she could not let her parents suffer. She thought about trying for a job elsewhere, but she did not know where to go with her weak educational qualification. She knew that her boss would rarely visit the company, but she was terrified to witness the venue of the barbaric act. Her days at work seemed to be creeping slowly like a snail. Not a day went without the attempts of her smutty coworkers. She prayed for salvation every day before sleep and before work. She hated the news that her boss was going to visit the company that day.

"Meet me in my cabin." he told as he passed her.

Her women coworkers gave a meaningful whistle, which she hated. She understood that it was not a onetime affair. She was right. It kept continuing and she was helpless. She wanted to get rid of it as soon as possible. Visualizing herself in a jungle, she saw only hungry beasts around her, everywhere. Even while she walked home, not a single day was she left alone by the sex hungry jackals.

She had the usual sleepless night, dreading the prospect of yet another humiliating day.

She prayed that her fate should change, but next day at work was no different for her. Her hope was futile, which she finally abandoned.

"Hey girl... Would you like to have a paid company tonight?" someone shouted, as she was sulking with the bitter thoughts, on her way back to her hostel.

"When you don't get what you like, like what you get." Pooja remembered her roommate's secret of happiness. Her conscience suggested her to thrash the words.

She turned around and stared in the direction of the voice for some time and then... gave a nervous smile.

Her life changed since then.

POOJA'S NEW FRIEND, SALONI

The girl regretted her rude words when she came to know of Pooja's story through her brothel mates. She willingly made friends with Pooja after she got to know about her pitiful past.

"I'm sorry for what I said the other day." she apologized.

Pooja smiled in response as she instantly liked her.

"What's your name?" Pooja asked her.

"My name is Sa… Saloni." she told her hesitantly.

"Nice to know you… Honestly." Saloni continued.

"What's your age?" Pooja asked, although she felt that it was an awkward question.

Saloni stared at her for a couple of seconds and replied "Thirty one."

Pooja wasn't sure what she had heard was right, as she didn't look so. She could easily pass as an undergraduate college girl.

Saloni instantly struck a chord with Pooja and they became best friends in no time. She wondered how people could smile when they were subjected to such a pitiful state.

"I used to be a princess to my parents. Fate has turned me into a bitch to these filthy dogs." Pooja used to curse her fate, but remained strong to deal with it. Saloni appreciated her for her brave approach to life.

Saloni's fate was somewhat similar to Pooja's.

SALONI AND HER
RECKLESS UNCLE HARI

Saloni lived with her mother and uncle Hari in Manchore city. It had been more than ten years since they had shifted from their home town. Saloni was not happy about it, but she never expressed her concern. After she left her home town and more importantly her friends, she was unable to recover from the loss. She never made any new friends after that. Her mother understood her, but was not in a position to go back, as her brother Hari was supposed to be the only moral support they had. The purpose hadn't fulfilled though, as Hari proved to be an irresponsible, reckless gambler and a drunkard. He was more of a liability than a support. The house she owned was sold a few years back upon the insistence of Hari, that the money would serve for Saloni's marriage.

"Where's the money?" Saloni's mother asked Hari. She knew that their house was sold for a huge price, but they were still leading a mediocre life.

"Don't worry about the money, sister. I have safely deposited it for my niece's marriage." he told her, though he never showed the money to her.

She didn't trust his words, so she warned herself not to waste any more time as she had the risk of losing the money. She couldn't wait any longer to get Saloni married as she lost trust on her health and even more on her brother.

"I can take care of myself mom. You don't worry about me." She would always say whenever she faced marriage proposals.

Saloni's mother was even more worried with her stubborn stand, but she never compelled her on anything. She felt very uncomfortable sharing the roof with her unruly brother.

Later, when he exhausted the money, he even sold the car. Since then, Saloni missed the soothing, lonely evening drives, but didn't say a word.

Day by day, he became more and more troublesome.

"Hey… Look at Hari, man. He never seems to run out of money." His club mates used to flatter him in the beginning. Then he gradually exhausted all his funds and ran on debt.

Almost a year passed blissfully and then trouble started brewing for Hari.

"No more debt Hari. You have two weeks to clear your debt, before I slit your throat." The club owner, Rashid warned him.

Hari was terrified, because he knew that it was not a bluff. He couldn't even think of a way to get the money. He even contemplated the idea of escaping the city, but he could never be far from their grip, as he knew that he would be in the gang's vigilance the moment he owed them something. There was no other source of money for him. He then considered the idea of stealing, but he knew his weakness. He had heavy feet and also did not have the patience a thief should have. He would be caught at his first step.

Days passed without a ray of hope for Hari, as he wasted all the time in futile thoughts, hoping for some divine intervention, as he could not think of any other way of earning the money he owed. He was lost in thought for so long that he didn't notice that the deadline had already approached. He panicked all of a sudden, as if the moment was unexpected. He was consciously evading the thoughts for temporarily relief. Before he could seriously think of the solution, time had elapsed. As he was unable to arrange the money to remit, he naively chose to abscond. But he couldn't obscure the sight of the gang. He was caught red-handed in a bus while he was attempting to flee the town. He was taken to the gang's den. Hari was scared to death as he knew that the people he was dealing were ruthless criminals.

"You had your chance, but you threw it off. I assume you know the consequences of eluding me?" Rashid spoke in a menacing tone.

"I swear I didn't…" As Hari started to explain, he was rudely interfered by Rashid.

"Stop fucking with me." He warned him.

"Well… You know… Today was supposed to be your last day breathing." He paused, expressing his displeasure to continue. Hari didn't understand what he meant.

"Yes. I fucking hate to tell this, but you've got a chance to live a little longer. Chance…" he told reiterating the word 'chance'.

"Well… Here's your chance." he said, prompting towards Victor who had just entered the room. Rashid left the room allowing Victor to take control of the dealing.

SALONI'S WITNESS
SENDS HARI TO JAIL

Victor, for a long time, had been the security in-charge for Azkar Ali, who controlled all the illegal activities in the city like drug peddling, illegal gambling, contract killing, duplicate liquor and prostitution. Victor was not only his security in-charge, but also his most reliable lieutenant and second in line of power, which made him the boss for their organization after Azkar Ali's death recently during a police encounter.

Hari was awed by his monstrous figure, as he had never seen him before. He was almost seven foot tall with a well-built body. He had a flat square face with ominous deep eyes and a strong jaw. He could have easily scared a wrestler with his mere appearance.

He pulled a chair and sat before Hari, looking into his eyes.

"I hear you tried to dodge the man." He started calmly.

"It's bad. Really bad…You borrow money; you pay it… on time. If you break the rule, you ought to die. If you live, we are breaking the rule. It's not good. We can't break the rules? Can we?" Victor thought for a few seconds, faking dilemma.

Hari swept the perspiration off his forehead and silently hoped for Victor to come up with some good news.

"Alright..." Victor made a decision, much to the anxiety of Hari.

"We're already in deep shit, David. We've got to do better." Victor told his consigliere, as he knew that they were on the verge of complete demolition. Azkar Ali was shot dead in a police encounter the previous week. The encounter team had plans to wipe out the gang. The gang's survival depended on eliminating the officer who led the team, which was supposed to be assigned to Hari with wrong identity.

"He is not an experienced mercenary. What help can he offer us? He is the greatest fool I have ever known." Victor expressed his doubt over using him.

"That's exactly why we are using him." David shot back.

That day Hari boozed at the expense of Victor.

He was happy that he didn't have to die, but was terrified about the proposal.

As Hari walked back home, Victor's words resonated in his mind.

"Lending you the money and again wasting my resources on killing you is not a profitable business. It's no fucking fun... which is why I thought of splitting the debtors into two teams. One will kill and the other will die. If you want to live, you kill, or else you will be killed. It saves our time and resources.

Yes... It's a game. Game you have invited yourself into. Your lives are the stakes here. You have two days to kill or you will be killed by the one you are supposed to kill." Victor casually gulped down his drink. He thought for a moment.

"Yes... and in case both fail, I'll have you both killed." He shrugged as if he had no other option.

"I let you decide your fate. Along with your life, you may also earn yourself a job. Isn't that fair enough? I reckon you owe me big time." Victor winked at Hari patting him on his shoulder as he got up to leave.

"Kill or die?" Victor proposed to him an ultimate option. Hari would naturally choose the first option on any given day, but he had never considered it professionally.

He didn't sleep that night.

He was forced into a checkmate. He didn't think about whether or not to agree to the proposal as he didn't have that option. He only thought what it would turn him into. Whatever... He was in.

Moreover, the person he had to kill was not a big shot. He was just another debtor like him. He was just expected to do what was expected to happen to him.

"What would happen if I get killed?"

"Nothing..." He answered to himself. He knew that no one would worry if he was killed. And the killer would be forgotten if he could hide away for some time. So he applied the same thought to his target.

One of Victor's hoodlums pointed out the target to Hari from a distance.

"You're on your own now. You have two days. Remember... We have you tailed." he warned.

Hari didn't care to do a further background check on his target, as he thrived on the information provided to him. He knew his usual hangout points, dining places and the recreation park. Victor's men made sure that he didn't get to know more than what they expected him to know.

The only thing on Hari's mind was, *"Do whatever it takes to survive."*

"You could get him in the park during mornings, as he would be alone and least expecting an attack." the man gave a free advice to Hari.

Hari was prepared for the game. There was nothing great about his plan. It was simple – Confront and kill.

He chose knife as his weapon. It was a Nepali *kukri* knife which he won from a ludomaniac Gurkha during one of his rare gambling successes. He had it secured in a leather scabbard neatly tucked sideways inside his pant. He had used the knife few times, but never to kill someone. He decided the time and venue of the attack.

He impatiently waited for his target to show up, betting on his early morning jog and workout in the park. He never had the patience of a sniper. Thankfully, he didn't have the need to, as he saw his target approaching from the entrance of the park. His heart beat hiked suddenly as he nervously waited for the inevitable. He didn't know what would happen, but whatever happened, it was either going to change his life or end his life. He didn't like either, but he was sure that he chose the better of the choices. He was so keenly focused on his target that he suddenly feared some eye witnesses around. As he scanned around to make sure he was not watched, he feared he had let the target get away. His nervousness killed his hope for reprieve. He was already sure that he would fail. As he hid himself well inside the sideway bush, his desperation for survival forced him into action as the man was just a few feet away and a few seconds away from his reach. To his surprise, his grip on the knife grew tighter and his urge for survival threw him out of the bush as soon as the man walked on the path at his reach. As he pounced on the man, he didn't waste time and insanely drove the kukri into his chest until he was sure that he couldn't have failed, unknowingly getting himself drenched with the victim's blood in the act. He immediately fled the spot without even looking around if anyone had witnessed his act, with the fear of looking them in the eye. He darted himself to his home through the empty roads of the early morning, with his blood stained shirt on. With the shirt on, he felt as if he was confessing the crime.

He sprinted home and sped past the inquisitive Saloni into his room, shutting the door behind him. He straightaway walked to the backyard to bury his weapon deep down the ground. He then walked back to his bathroom, stripping off in hurry and jumped into the bathtub for a long hot bath. He then wiped every inch of his naked body hard, fearing he might spare some stains. He fell flat on his bed with a sense of accomplishment. He then remembered the blood stained shirt which he had ripped off before jumping into the tub. He immediately took the shirt to the backyard and set it on fire.

"Never knew that killing a person is such a simple thing." he wondered.

The initial fear transformed into excitement. He had thoroughly enjoyed the act. He jumped onto his bed and instantly drifted into slumber. He was then rudely woken up by heavy knocks on his door.

"How dare you disturb my sleep?" Hari thought furiously as he slammed open the door.

He froze to death when he found the cops at the door waiting for him.

He scanned around the room to find Saloni and her mother angrily staring at him.

"Is there something wrong, sir?" Hari asked composing himself with great difficulty.

"Yes sir. I'm sure there is." The cop mocked his fake innocence, violently snatching by his arm, pulling him out of his room.

"What's the charge?" he asked.

"Killing a police officer…" the policeman shot back, as he handcuffed him.

"Search the house." he ordered his subordinates.

"What? Police officer?" he asked in disbelief.

"Didn't you know that the one you killed was a police officer?" The cop questioned Hari, who realized his blunder.

"No… I mean… I don't know about any killing." Hari fumbled.

"We'll find it out." the cop said with finality.

"Sir, I see smoke coming out of the backyard." one of his subordinates shouted.

The police officer rushed to the spot, leaving two constables to keep hold of Hari.

By the time they reached the backyard, they could find nothing but ash. The officer strewed the ash across the floor to find buttons of the shirt partially charred by the fire. He gathered them for evidence.

"Well… You have a lot to explain." He said as he walked him out of the house.

"Thanks for your tip, Ma'am. We heavily depend on your witness. Would you testify?" the cop asked Saloni.

Hari stared at Saloni in shock.

"Sure sir." she said.

His expression of shock turned into look of vengeance.

"Guess you have a problem with your eyesight. Don't worry. We'll fix it." the policeman said as he fiercely knocked his knuckles on his spine, pushing him towards the door.

Hari was mad because of multiple reasons.

He was deliberately forced to the mercy of the gang and then was cunningly offered with a Hobson's choice. When he took the choice, which was eventually his only choice, he was deliberately provided with false background of his target. When he fretted over betrayal and manipulation of being used as a tool for murder and the backstabbing of Saloni turned him furious. It was a like an endless assault on him. The world had suddenly turned hostile to him.

Hari was represented by a lawyer offered by Victor, who had stakes in it. Hari accepted the offer without any resistance, as he still did not know his role in the drama. Moreover he didn't have the guts to deny his offer. Now, out of helplessness, he trusted that the lawyer could get him out of the mess. He trusted and followed him as instructed. He still suspected another foul play, but it was his only way out. With all the evidences and circumstances, he was sure to get maximum sentence.

"I'll take them all with me if they can't get me out." he resolved.

Despite the strong evidences, the case turned weak, owing to the skillful manipulation of the defense lawyer. He didn't have a convincing motive for the murder which helped his cause. A case of assault was interpolated to falsify the murder charge. In an unexpected turn of events, Hari was accused of an assault exactly at the same time of murder, which also concurred with the story of his bloodstained shirt. The defense lawyer conveniently diverted the murder case and helped Hari get away with case of assault with a sentence of 5 years jail term.

HARI SHREDS SALONI'S SERENE LIFE

Saloni led a calm life with her mother in Sundarawadi, a beautiful town far away from the reach of her evil uncle. It was a peaceful land strewn with green hills and a small pond. The scarcely populated town offered modest life to its residents, but more peace, with its serene atmosphere. She undertook a mediocre job as a salesclerk in a shopping mall, earning a meager salary. It still didn't make any difference to their lifestyle as they led a similar life as before due to the consequence of her mother's blind trust on her cunning brother. Saloni didn't care about losing all the wealth, but was somehow pleased that she no more needed to suffocate in the uncomfortable coexistence with Hari. Her mother still worried about her daughter's future. Nevertheless, she was also glad that they somehow got rid of Hari. Apart from her mother's anguish about her daughter's marriage, they led a happy and respectable life. They slowly forgot the painful phase of life with Hari. Saloni's beauty attracted many young suitors in the town. Couple of the most eligible bachelors of the town even approached Saloni's mother with proposal for her daughter's hand. She was delighted with the prospects, but her happiness was short lived as Saloni denied all the proposals outright. Her mother gently expressed Saloni's denials to the suitors, but she was not happy about it.

"How long are you going to elude your marriage, my child? When you are going to get married someday, why can't it be now?" her mother asked politely.

"I need some time, Mom." Saloni said, ending the conversation.

As days passed by, their position improved as a result of Saloni's diligence and honesty at work. More than five years had passed since they had moved into the town. They wondered how the town had turned out to be their hometown with all friendly people around. They led a peaceful life.

The peace in their life, however, seemed to be a passing cloud.

Saloni usually returned home every day before dusk. That particular day, she had to stay longer at work as it was a busy business day.

Saloni hurriedly wrapped up things and sped home, unwilling to let her mother get bored of solitude.

As she was walking towards her home, she observed that her mom was not at the gate as she expected her to be anxiously waiting for her as she was late from work.

"Maybe, she's not well." she thought as she rushed into her house.

As she entered the house, she was deeply distressed when she found her mother leaning on a couch in the corner of the room holding her head in discomfort.

"What happened mother? Aren't you feeling well?" She rushed close to her and was shocked to find her pale with fear. Her mother didn't seem to be pleased with her arrival as she stared behind Saloni.

Saloni was perplexed with her mother's expression. Her heart skipped a beat when she turned back to find the reason for her fear.

"Surprise… Surprise… Your loving uncle has come to pay you a little visit." Hari said.

He was sitting on a chair holding an iron rod in his hand.

Saloni regained her composure and put up a brave face. She was furious with him.

"Why did you come here?" Saloni asked fearlessly.

Hari knew that she was a brave girl.

"Very rude… You know? I have spent more than six months to locate you, and you give me such a cold treatment. Not good manners, darling." he said as he stood up and walked slowly towards Saloni. She moved a couple of steps backwards, careful in maintaining a distance to be out of his reach. Hari just moved forward without attempting to reach Saloni. When she observed that he walked past her, she instantly knew where he was walking. He moved towards her mother and casually sat beside her, wrapping his hands around her.

"Take your sinful hands off her…" Saloni screamed.

Hari mocked fear as he withdrew his hand in a reflex.

"I have suffered years of pain in prison because of you, but adversely, you seem to be angry about me. Isn't it unfair?" Hari said with an expression of a person subjected to gross injustice.

"Ok then... Go ahead and kill us." Saloni replied without concern.

Hari pretended to weigh the options.

"Well... It's again injustice. You have not killed me. You have subjected me to a perpetual pain. I might be happy to return the same favor." he said as if it was the most righteous thing.

"How do I do that?" he said animatedly.

As Saloni noticed that Hari was not watching her, she inconspicuously slipped towards the telephone and dialed the police helpline immediately.

As soon as Hari noticed her at the telephone, he knew it was trouble. He swiftly stomped over to Saloni, grabbed her from behind and scooped off her feet, crashing the telephone on the ground. She randomly kicked her hands and legs at him. Pissed off with her frantic repulsion, he hit her with the butt of the rod, on her face, wounding her just below the right eye. In the momentary tussle, he accidentally grabbed her breast.

"Ah... Ha... I had been a fool to have not realized that I was living with an angel of beauty all these years." Hari said as he tightened his grip on her breast.

"Get your hands off me, you dirty scoundrel." Saloni screamed trying to ward off his grip, but his grip was too strong for her. When she thought it was too tough for her, she swung her elbow at his face. He escaped the blow just in time.

Saloni's mother, who had been sitting dazed on the couch, sprang on her foot and pounced on Hari, driving her nails into his neck like a wounded predator, making him drop Saloni.

Hari could feel his flesh being ripped off by her. He yanked her away from him and swung his rod at her face, hitting her on her forehead. She fell down on the floor. He lustfully turned towards Saloni and slowly advanced towards her. As she noticed her mother fall on the ground bleeding profusely, she ran towards her for help, but Hari held her by her waist, scooping her away from her mother and dropped her on to the ground. As she tried to get on her foot, he swiftly moved towards her and stamped her ankle, not letting her rise. Saloni stared at him with an emotion mixed with pain and fury. She finally gave preference to save her mother.

"Please let me help my mother. I will never utter a word about you, I swear." she pleaded.

"You should have thought about this before you sent me to rot in the hole." he said.

"Now I shall clear the debts." he said as he knelt down, pinning her arms over her head.

He stared into her loathing eyes for a few seconds, enjoying her pain and then planted his coarse lips onto her beautiful shivering lips. She struggled to get off his grip, mostly anxious about her mother than herself, but he didn't care about the whimpering lady who was his sister. He was so totally lost in lust and vengeance that he tore Saloni's shirt and gobbled up her breasts like an animalistic sex maniac, as he ripped off her remaining clothes.

"For heaven's sake, spare her. She is your niece. Please… Please…. Please…" Saloni's mother blurted out feebly in a semiconscious state, which he didn't care to heed.

As they did not live in a town with tightly packed houses, she neither did have the hope of her neighbors hearing their screams. Hari knew that. He brutally raped his niece right in front of her bleeding mother. He lifted himself off Saloni's ravaged body and stared into her tear filled eyes with an evil grin.

"You can't get away with this, you bloody creep. Be prepared to go back to jail." Saloni spoke with threatening fury, tears flowing down her eyes.

Hari however had unshakeable trust in her love for her mother.

"I'm ready to go back to jail, if you are ready to lose your mother." He cruelly blackmailed her.

She furled her semi naked body on the floor and wept hard for not being able to fight him back and save her mother and herself. He immediately took his mobile phone from his pocket and dialed for the ambulance, mostly to safeguard his trump card to escape from any retaliation from Saloni. He knew that he had to kill Saloni in case her mother died, which he didn't want to do.

"I have called the ambulance to save your mother. See how kind I am." He faked generosity.

Saloni knew his purpose, but she did not care about anything other than saving her mother's life. She gathered her remaining scattered clothes as quick as she could, slipping herself into them and hurried to her mother who was in pain from his brutal assault. She wished she could kill him instantly. Hari plopped down on the couch and relaxed as if he was an invited guest.

After a while, they heard the sound of the ambulance siren. Saloni tried to fix her dress to safeguard her modesty. Hari chuckled as she struggled with her torn shirt. He witnessed murderous rage in her eyes.

Saloni visited her mother who was admitted in the hospital for treatment of a traumatic brain injury.

"God, help my mother and give me a chance to kill the scoundrel who caused all the troubles." She prayed, as she was returning from her hospital visit.

With a preoccupied mind, she opened the door to find Hari sitting cozily on the couch.

"How dare you come back here?" Saloni shouted in burning fury.

"Don't assume your ordeal has come to an end." He had planned more suffering for her.

"You know… I'm a righteous man. I know that your mother has done nothing wrong to deserve all the punishment. Hence I will pay her medication bills. I will take care of her. My debt is with you which I'm going to repay in full. You do as I say, or you'll be responsible for your mother's death." he threatened Saloni.

"Good evening Victor. Got a gift for you…" Hari shouted gleefully as he lustfully stared at Saloni.

POOJA'S FLIRTING GAME

Pooja felt sorry for Saloni when she came to know about her past, which was no less tragic than hers. She mentally adopted her as her sister and vowed to be her strength.

"It's a jungle out there. There are always hungry predators on the prowl. If you are helpless, they will hound you. Remember one thing, baby. When you are out in the jungle, be the beast, not the prey. Be strong." Pooja told Saloni.

Saloni appreciated her in every aspect except one.

Hey Eva… This is my new number baby.

- Sheila

Pooja messaged to a number which she'd just got through a brothel mate.

She giggled as she saw the message delivered.

It was a teenage boy who was intrigued by the message from a girl. He was inexperienced with girls, but his curiosity got the better of him.

Hi...

He messaged back.

Pooja, with her experience, could read his pulse by his message. She understood his inexperience and his desperation.

"Easy" She smiled.

Sheila: Actually not sure about your number. Glad I got you.

She messaged back.

She understood his predicament, but she always enjoyed it.

He was indeed in a confused situation. He wanted to continue the conversation with her, but he couldn't guise himself forever. He was afraid his confession would cease the conversation. Nevertheless, he made his decision.

This is not Eva. My name is Alok.

He responded.

Pooja figured out his interest. She also understood that she had to lead him, as he seemed to be timid guy. *"It's always easy with this kind of boys."* She thought.

Sheila: Oh... Wrong number. Sorry to have troubled you.

Alok: No trouble at all. Nice knowing you.

"Naïve" Pooja thought.

Sheila: Nice to know you too.

Sheila: Wondering if you knew Lisa. I got your number from her. – She bluffed.

Alok: Let me think... I may have known someone by that name – He was desperate to hang on.

Pooja smiled to herself.

Alok: May I know about you?

Sheila: You can't know me through phone messages.

Alok: Can we meet then?

"Piece of cake" Pooja casually remarked as she threw her phone on the couch.

"Won't I ever get a real challenge?" She bragged playfully, as she winked at Saloni.

Saloni noticed her act all along and wondered what she was up to as she didn't know her traits in the beginning.

"Why do you do this?" Saloni asked her hesitantly.

"Do what?" Pooja did not understand her.

"Why do you lure innocent people into this, when you have sufficient income here?" Saloni asked her hesitantly.

"I mean… It's all the same money right?" She tried to clarify.

"Well… Actually, I don't earn money from these people." Pooja took a pause as she spoke, because she was never used to clarifying to anyone about anything. She sensed a strange bond between them.

"You know… I do this to quench my thirst for freedom." She found it difficult to explain.

Pooja's inmates did it for extra money, but not Pooja.

Saloni was interested to know more.

"I did not quite get that." Saloni further probed.

"Well… you know… Here we are thrown to men, whoever chooses us. There, we could live the life, we dreamt of. We could throw tantrums. We could have the guy wait for hours, but he still would kneel down before you and say 'It's a beautiful day.'" she explained.

"What about cheating on him in the end? What about breaking his heart? Remember… Guilty conscious hurts you more than anything baby." Saloni spoke with concern.

"They won't be cheated or heartbroken, baby. You are speaking to an expert." Pooja assured.

Saloni, however, was not convinced.

THE ULTIMATE
CHALLENGE

Pooja became obsessed with the luring game, as it gave her the opportunity to pretend that she led a life of her will.

"He is such a waste of time, you know. He does not seem to be interested in girls at all… I suspect if he is impotent." One of her mates commented about a guy.

"No man is impotent when you know how to deal with him." Pooja commented.

"Deal with him darling…" They challenged her.

"Deal…" she agreed.

"What did you say his name was?"

"SAM" They said in unison, as if they were curiously expecting it to happen.

Pooja weighed her options to deal with him.

Is he a shy punk who is afraid to take initiative? Couldn't be… as he was dealt by shameless girls who would readily open up for sex.

Was he brought up in a conservative way that his morals obstruct him from engaging into carnal affairs? There is a turning point in everyone's life.

Is he reluctant to spend money on girls? I don't need it.

Is he afraid of commitment? So am I.

There are two types of men:

The first - who are desperate for sex and would jump at an opportunity.

The second - who are desperate for sex, but need an excuse to embrace it.

After comprehensive analysis, she came to a conclusion that she was going to deal with the second category.

She could have easily neglected him and looked for a more willing participant, but her obsession with the prospect of a true challenge to gauge her ability compelled her to accept it.

She was an expert in dealing with men, but she was dealing with a rare kind.

"I need to know him before I deal with him." she decided.

She didn't want to expose her details, before she was ready for the game. Hence she borrowed Saloni's phone.

Hey Ritu… How're you doing, baby?

- Julie

Pooja used different pseudo names every time. She confidently waited for response after sending the message.

"What's going on Pooja?" Saloni asked puzzled.

Pooja looked at Saloni and gave a meaningful smile.

"Hunting…" she replied, though she knew that Saloni wouldn't like it. Moreover she was using her phone.

Saloni responded with a hopeless sigh.

"Why don't you give up?" Saloni asked Pooja.

"Well, you know..." Pooja started answering, when Saloni interrupted her.

"Maybe I should give up on you." Saloni said disgustedly and got up to walk out, when Pooja, laughing aloud, held her by her arm and pulled her back to where she sat.

"Stop laughing. It's not funny anymore." Saloni shouted.

Pooja gradually calmed down as she stared at Saloni for a few seconds.

"What do you want me to do now?" Pooja asked her.

"Go to hell... I don't care what you do." Saloni said dismissively.

Pooja was silent for a minute.

"I'll quit after this." Pooja told crisply.

"What?" Saloni was unable to believe it. Pooja was serious this time. Saloni knew that when Pooja talked seriously, she really meant it.

"Yes. You heard it right. I'll quit after this." Pooja repeated.

Saloni suddenly felt guilty that she was intruding into Pooja's affairs and thought she had no right to object to her fancies.

"Hey... I'm sorry darling. I didn't mean to persuade you. I was just pissed off." Saloni told.

"I know you are, Sal... I know. But I meant what I said." Pooja said.

"You don't have to do that. I mean... Why do you do that?" Saloni asked completely calm now.

"After my parents, nobody ever really cared about me as a person, until you came into my life. You loved me like a younger sister I never had. You get angry when I make mistakes. You get anxious when I'm not around for a long time. You are the one person with whom I would share my happiness and sadness." Pooja said as she wrapped her arm around Saloni's shoulders with pride.

"I know I have bothered you many times, but never knew you were so pissed off with my affairs." Pooja confessed.

"Don't get emotional baby. I was just worried you would get hurt." Saloni spoke in a fervent tone. She was emotional actually.

"I know baby… I know." Pooja said.

"I can't quit now, as I have accepted the challenge and I don't want to lose to those bitches. But surely after this…" Pooja reminded her of the deal. "Aren't you glad that I would quit?"

Saloni surely was. "Of course. Very glad." she smiled.

Pooja punched Saloni's cheeks gently and hugged her. She then realized that it had been quite some time since she'd sent the message. She knew that the response might come after many hours, as people might not notice the messages immediately and sometimes, men at work respond at the end of day.

"Today is Sunday. Probability for delayed response is less." Pooja thought. She normally would have waited till she got a response, as she believed that desperation would always be a disadvantage. Since the mobile number did not belong to her, she had the option to gauge his responses.

What's up? No response. Don't say Peter is screwing you. Share a piece of cake with me too. ;-)

Pooja knew that she wouldn't have to wait for too long after this message. And she was right. She gave a triumphant smile when she heard the beep of the message alert in less than a minute. Saloni shook her head sideways in a hopeless gesture.

Pooja's expression changed from excitement to confusion and then to frustration when she read the message.

> *Flee fornication. Every sin that a man doeth is without the body; but he that committeth fornication sinneth against his own body.*
>
> *- Corinthians 6:18*

Pooja then understood that she was dealing with the third type of man, which she believed never existed.

"What happened?" Saloni asked.

Pooja threw the phone to Saloni.

"You have made the wrong pick this time baby. Drop it." Saloni suggested after she read the message. Pooja promptly nodded in approval.

"Think we got the wrong guy, girls. Better we drop him." announced Pooja to her mates.

"Had a nice sermon, child?" mocked one of them.

"Hope you have learnt that you aren't as good as you think you are." the girls ridiculed her.

"So, you knew it? Bitches…" Pooja hated losing to them.

"Seems like the champion has lost for the first time…" The girls mocked a pitiful expression.

"Stop blowing your trumpets punks. Game is still on. So, hold your celebrations." Pooja warned the girls.

The girls thought it was foolish of her, trying to hit on him. Nevertheless they wanted her to try and fail. They were also jealous of her privileges, due to her proximity with Victor.

"Don't let your ego mislead you baby… Let it go." Saloni advised.

"One last time Sal… Don't try to talk me out of this." Pooja curtly responded. Her ego was badly hurt.

Saloni knew when to stop trying with Pooja. She just shrugged off in defeat.

Pooja understood that she was in for a difficult challenge, but believed that it was not impossible. She thought about all the possible ways she could deal him with.

"Here you go" She made a decision.

She decided to wait for a couple of days to start her plan, as she knew that she would have the disadvantage of the impression created on the guy by the earlier encounter. She then sent a message which read:

> *The son of god was born in a manger and*
> *suffered crucifixion. He shed his blood for our*
> *sake. Let's spread love on his name. Share your*
> *love to the ones who suffer from drought of it*
> *and earn the love of the Lord.*
>
> *- Chris*

Pooja turned into Chris. She waited eagerly to check the outcome of her plan. She had ample alternate plans, but she heavily counted on this one.

She was discouraged by the lack of response. She anxiously waited for more than six hours without any good news.

Just as she was pondering over her alternate plan, she was alerted by an incoming message.

"You are a man with a golden heart, Chris. God bless you."

Chris was delighted with the response as she didn't have to go for plan B.

Chris: Hi... I don't know your name. But since you appreciate it, you should be good too.

Sam: You don't know even my name. Then how did I receive the message from you?

Chris expected this obvious question.

Chris: I sent messages to random numbers. I just want to spread the message. Most people ignore such messages. You are nice to have valued it.

Sam: I'm actually inspired. By the way, my name is Sam.

The conversation between Sam and Chris continued. Once she got the hold, she magnetized him into the groove of her artful eloquence. She however was extra careful in dealing with him as she didn't want to need a second chance with him.

Initially, when she had the prospect of a true challenge, she was thrilled, but not anymore. She felt very uncomfortable and wanted to end it soon. The friendly conversation continued for a few days when Sam invited Chris to make her next move.

Sam: Now that we had been friends for quite some time... Can we meet up?

Chris knew that it was time for her next move.

Chris: Sam... I have a confession to make.

Sam: Yes?

Chris: I'm a girl.

No response from Sam.

Chris: Still want to meet?

Sam: Yes.

Chris could not read the expression of his last response, but she was confident that she could deal with it. They met up at a modest café, revealing their identities. It was a strange meeting for both of them. They exchanged formal pleasantries and took their seats in the scarcely occupied café. Sam had chatted well with her, until he knew that she was a girl, and then suddenly turned shy. Pooja as Chris probably felt nervous for the first time in her life while dealing with a man. She composed herself and decided to lead the conversation as usual.

"I owe you an apology. I kept you in the dark." Chris started the conversation.

"It was only my assumption. You didn't lie to me. You don't need to apologize?" Sam responded with a smile.

"I don't want to exculpate myself since I have an excuse. I knew you believed that I was a man and I let you believe a lie, which is equivalent to a lie." she said.

"Only a person with a noble heart could be so righteous. You are an angel." Sam expressed his wholehearted admiration. He immediately felt that his words seemed to be flirtatious.

"I mean you are a nice girl." Sam mitigated his comments. Chris needed no explanation, as she knew that it was a genuine appreciation.

"I know what you meant. And thank you for thinking so." she replied.

"By the way… I didn't know your name yet." Sam, who seemed to be more relaxed now, asked her.

"Strange that you are going to know the name after you made a friend, right." Chris winked playfully.

"My name is Christy. Friends call me Chris." she said.

"Then you haven't lied at all." Sam pointed out.

"You seem to be hell bent on proving me innocent." Chris laughed aloud.

"You are such a wonderful friend. I'm lucky." Her comment made him blush.

"Since we are friends, I would explain to you why I give the impression of a boy when I send messages." she told."Promise me you won't laugh." She asked him to swear.

"I swear." Sam said laughing.

"See… You are laughing." Chris complained, sounding childish.

"Ok… Ok… Now tell me." Sam asked eagerly.

"Well… How do I put it?" She thought for a while and then continued."I do it…because boys naturally tend to pester for friendship. I finally end up knowing that their intensions were not pure." she reasoned thoughtfully.

"Boys… Yeah, boys like me?" Sam asked, as he was slightly guilty himself for persuading to meet a stranger girl.

"You know, you don't fall in that category. You are the most truthful and honest person I have ever met." she complimented him.

Sam instantly liked her. From then on, they met frequently. She could not go on her normal pace with Sam, as she was forced to go slow.

"Tomorrow is my birthday." Sam informed Chris.

"Wow… Then I'll be part of a grand celebration tomorrow. And I'll get you a special gift." She said as she was so glad to have got an occasion. She wanted to wrap it up soon. She had dealt with many men. Still, she'd never proposed to anyone till date, but had skillfully made them do. That was a record. She knew that her record would no longer sustain.

She dressed in a pure white long gown flowing down like clouds and walked like an angel to meet him. She prepared herself to declare that *she* was his gift although she hated to say that. She was surprised to find that she was the only invitee.

She walked graciously towards him not letting the surprised look off her face.

"Surprised that you are the only invitee?" Sam asked her.

She just nodded her head in affirmation.

"I never celebrated my birthday since the death of my foster parents more than a decade ago."

"Well… In fact I don't know when I was born." He winked at her.

She was confused now. She didn't say anything as she waited for him to continue.

"I only know the day when I was found at the doorsteps of an orphanage. That is what I consider as my birthday."

Pooja then came to know everything about his childhood.

It was an autumn evening when an adorable infant was abandoned at the doorsteps of the *Sacred Mary Home for Love,* run by the benevolent, Sister Teresa. She picked up the cute baby who had tiny eyes and a wide smile. She wondered how one could forgo such a lovable child. She disapproved people orphaning innocent children, but again believed that they did it out of helplessness. She always believed that everyone on the earth is naturally good and circumstances force them to do what's not good. She looked at the child, fascinated by his gentle features. She named him Sam.

Sam grew up into a cheerful and mischievous adolescent. He always broke the rules set by the Home. There was not a single one from the staff who did not have complaints about him, but Sister Teresa always forgave him. She loved him like her own child. Sam never fretted that he was an orphan. Sister Teresa never let anyone feel so, which was why she didn't call the place as an orphanage. She named it "Home for Love". She had abundance of love that she could bestow sufficient to everyone in the home. Sam had a good bunch of friends, but every now and then, he would lose a few friends. Childless couples picked their heir and adopted them. On one such visit, Sam was chosen by an elderly couple, who were past fifty.

"Today is your lucky day, Sam. You have got yourself a lovely family." Sister Teresa told Sam as she gave him a compassionate hug.

She then witnessed that Sam had his eyes filled with tears. She knew that it was common of kids, because she gave everyone so much love. But Sam seemed more independent than anyone else, which was why his tears were unexpected.

"Don't you like me here?" Sam asked Sister Teresa in a trembling voice.

"There could be no joy greater than having you here, my child." she confirmed.

"Then why do you want me to go?" Sam asked innocently.

Sister Teresa ran the home on meager funds. She picked helpless children, groomed them with love and waited to get them a loving family. She could not afford to go any further with inadequate funds she received from the limited number of donors.

"Son… Listen to me. Everything happens with a purpose. You are born in this world with a purpose. You are chosen by purpose."

"You have lot to achieve in your life. The home may not be able to provide you with all the facilities. This opportunity to you is the gift of God. Do not deny God's gift." Sister Teresa convinced him.

Sam half-heartedly walked towards the door.

"Son…" Sister Teresa called him as she walked up to him and knelt down to hug him.

"Before you leave, I would like to tell you something, son." she started.

"The biggest sin in the world is not being able to love someone. Do not judge anybody by what they are, because life may have played unfair with them. You be fair. The one who loves would be the closest to God. Do not choose whom to love and whom to not. Love everybody. Remember… Love is the language of God."

Sam always remembered those words.

He seemed to bear a curse of eternal orphan-hood as his foster parents died in a car accident just when he had passed teenage, leaving behind sufficient wealth for his survival.

As she heard his story, she felt an emotional touch for the first time.

"Then why do you do it now?" she asked him.

"Because I didn't want to disappoint you…" he said.

She stared at him for a few seconds.

"Well… Good that you are celebrating your birthday now at least, because it is the day when you express your gratitude for the greatest gift from god – your life." she said and before she could continue, she was interrupted by him.

"If I had to celebrate the day when I got the greatest gift from god, it would be the day I met you." he spoke with immense sincerity.

He stunned her with his words.

"Yes… You are the greatest gift of god to me." he said, hesitating to complete what he had in his heart.

"I never thought I would say this to anyone… But, I love you, Chris." She was surprised by the proposal.

"Damn… The bitch did it." Her mates cursed as they couldn't believe it.

Pooja, however, was not proud of her achievement. She had won the bet, but felt like a loser.

IMRAN'S VISIT

Manchore, 26th July

Imran visited Sunny on the eve of his birthday without any announcement.

"Hey Sunny boy..." Imran shouted as Sunny opened the door for him.

"I have planned a surprise birthday gift for you." he hinted to Sunny, unable to hold his excitement.

"You have already surprised me with your visit, buddy." Sunny welcomed him with a warm hug.

"Quit your tricks dude... You can't deny my gift." he insisted.

"Well... I can't, can I?" Sunny winked at him with a beautiful smile."At least tell me what my gift is." Sunny pleaded.

"You can't know it until you get it. That's what you call a surprise, ain't it?" Imran teased him.

Sunny smiled at him and nodded in defeat.

"I'll get you something to drink." Sunny said as he walked to the refrigerator and threw him a coke.

Imran caught it promptly and gulped it in a hurry as he was thirsty after the tiresome travel.

"Care for an egg sandwich?" Sunny asked as he walked to the kitchen.

"Make that a double. I'm damn hungry." Imran told.

Sunny smiled as he walked to the kitchen, knowing that he wouldn't do with one.

As Imran finished his drink, he casually walked to the trash can and dropped it in.

As he looked around, he noticed an open diary with something written on it and a pen lying beside it. He walked closer and found that it was a poem.

The vast sky gaily smile in blue, which the dark blanket calmly shrouds
And the ever mighty sun humbly hidden behind the ubiquitous clouds,
Gush of cool breeze defeat the scorching heat of the veiled fire ball.
The lutarious aroma spread in the air, portend imminent rainfall.

When the rumbling thunders warn, the world scrams to safe abode.
On the contrary, crazy you would jump and shout in blissful mode!
When the gray looming clouds threaten to tear open its aqueous balloon,
You walk like the winter breeze, eager to embrace the celestial boon.

*When the sky begins to sprinkle, scaring to soak me down to
the bone,*
*I rush to shelter in fear, wondering if it would transform into
a cyclone.*
*Gracious as the magnificent rain itself, you offer your hand, I
hold fain.*
*And invite me in the cutest voice – Shall we have a walk in
the rain?*

"Here you are." Sunny walked in with his sandwiches.

Imran gobbled them up in no time as if his survival
depended on it. Sunny watched him in amusement.

"You saved my life Sunny." Imran said rubbing his flat
belly, as if he was starving.

"That makes it twice then." Sunny joked as Imran
would often remind him of his once life-saving feat.

"Yeah, twice..." he replied laughing loudly."Don't worry,
I'll return the favor today." he joked.

"Really? Let's see." Sunny replied in the same flavor.

"Would you do something for me?" Imran asked Sunny
after a thoughtful silence.

"Anything for you, buddy. Tell me." Sunny assured him.

"Why don't you forget Sandy?" Imran asked him,
prompting towards the poem he had written, presumably
sometime before he came.

"Something else, buddy. Anything at all..." He politely
declined his appeal.

"Whatever makes her so special to you, I think you have
done nothing wrong to deserve all the pain you self-inflict."
Imran spoke with concern.

"Don't worry, I'll fix it today. You just listen to me." he said.

"Alright, my friend... I'll listen to whatever you say. Ok?" Sunny agreed.

Imran gave him the broadest smile."That's like a good boy. I have some work to do now. I'll be back in a few hours." he said as he walked out.

Though Imran had already revealed that he had a special gift for him, he didn't reveal the details.

Sunny stood proudly, watching Imran leave, shaking his head in disbelief.

He wondered about the mysterious ways fate deals with life that turned the person he had hated the most into his greatest friend.

SUNNY'S PAST
WITH IMRAN

"What a beautiful day!" Imran blissfully announced, inhaling his cigarette smoke.

"Why don't you enjoy the beautiful day all by yourself?" Steven replied ridiculously as he lit his cigarette.

"Come on pal. Why is your head so hot?" Imran said patting him on his shoulders.

"The sun is making every part of me hot." he said, wiping the sweat off his forehead. Since it was exam season, students came to school late as their exam started at 10 am. The duo got settled at their regular place, which was a compound wall of an unoccupied house on the way to school.

"You need to be patient to achieve something." Imran said, knocking him gently on his chest with his elbow.

"What do I achieve by charring my ass in the sun?" he shot back with mock anger.

"Come on bastard… I want to show you the girl I love." Imran said.

"You have already shown me last week." Steven reminded him.

"This is a different girl dude. I fell in love with her yesterday." Imran said in a mockingly shy tone.

"Shameless bastard…" Steven playfully threw the cigarette he was smoking at him which hit his shoulder and fell in his shirt pocket. Imran jumped to his feet with the fear that it might damage the shirt. It did. Imran was quick to remove the cigarette, but not before it made a hole in his pocket. Steven could not control his laughter and as he laughed uncontrollably, jumping off the wall.

Imran stared at him for a long moment and suddenly burst into laughter without any warning. Steven was baffled as he sensed that he had the boomerang getting back to him.

"That's a beautiful shirt, you are wearing." Imran said pointing at Steven's shirt as he removed his, right there in the open and threw it at Steven, which fell at his feet.

Steven held his forehead as he sighed with defeat.

"I should have committed the worst of sins to have been born as your friend, bastard." Steven said as he removed his own shirt and threw it at him. He then dusted the dirt off Imran's shirt and wore it which was a little short for him.

"Perfect. Your shirt fits me better than mine." Imran said as he tucked the shirt into his trousers, as it was a bit large for him.

"Now, tell me… Where is your angel for the week?" Steven asked Imran.

"Be patient, my friend." Imran told Steven.

"Is it… My friend." Steven mocked him. "It's already past ten. You don't make a fool of yourself. Forget about the girl… Not a single bird is flying into the school." Steven explained him.

Imran suddenly realized what Steven had said. He looked around in horror, hoping to see someone walk into the school. The gang used to make a person a fun object for the day, whoever was found ludicrous. Imran knew that if something funny happened, he would become the entertainment for the day to his gang. He seldom became the fun object. He didn't want to become one, that day. He saw a boy riding a bicycle in their direction. It was Sunny.

"Hey punk… Come here." Imran shouted.

As Sunny hesitantly rode towards them, he realized that it was not his day as he knew that Imran generally derived a lot of pleasure bullying him.

"Why does no one come to school today?" Imran fired at Sunny.

"Today is a school holiday." he replied, getting off his bicycle, trying to be as humble as possible.

Steven suddenly burst into laughter, which surprised Sunny as he hadn't expected it. He couldn't seem to stop his laughter, which irritated Imran, who, in extreme anger, kicked the cycle which flew off Sunny's grip and fell at a distance. Steven, still laughing and coughing by uncontrollable laughter, walked to Imran.

"Come on pal. Why is your head so hot?" Steven ridiculously repeated Imran's lines.

Imran couldn't control his anger.

"Go and tell the girl, that I wanted to meet her, now." Imran ordered Sunny.

"I don't know whom you love." he tremulously responded.

"Don't you know the girl I love?" Imran swung his hand to slap him when Steven pulled him away.

"You get out of here." he told Sunny and resumed his laughter.

"What's so funny?" Imran asked Steven

"Even I don't know the girl. You don't even know the name yourself. How would he know it, bastard? Moreover, you fall in love with 5 girls in a week. Who would keep track of it? You lose your mind when you are angry, dude." Steven patted on his shoulder.

Steven walked a few steps to a payphone and took a sudden halt.

"I was worried that you would spoil my day, but as a matter of fact, you made my day." He resumed his uncontrollable laughter.

When Steven dialed a number from the payphone, Imran knew what was coming.

"Do you know what happened today?" Steven started narrating the whole incident to his gang, trying to suppress his laughter with great difficulty.

"Let's meet for a drink… Ok… Be there in ten minutes." Steven hung up and turned to Imran with a wicked smile.

Sunny was upset with the bad beginning of the day. Imran was the person he hated the most. He hadn't expected to encounter him on a holiday and spoil his whole day. Though he didn't resist Imran, he utterly hated what he was doing to him. He rode his bicycle to his favorite leisure spot. The old cycle he was riding had been almost dismantled by Imran's kick. He just rolled it along where the wheels automatically led him, as they knew where to take him when he felt sad and lonely. He approached a place surrounded by a barbed fence coiled with creepers, which was where he found peace whenever he felt lonely. The place itself was lonely and rather spooky, but Sunny found solace in that lonely, unattended place. He found strange resemblance between him and the place, which did not seem to be owned by anybody, with its fence overgrown with creepers and weeds. The land was fully grown with unwanted milkweed and strewn with dry leaves from the great banyan tree stretching its branches throughout the land, blocking the sun rays from all directions. There was an uncovered well in the centre of the shabby piece of land, with broken weathered concrete rings around it. The unpleasant mood of the place was an advantage for Sunny, as no one would like to visit the place, hence providing him with loneliness. That was the only thing that he wanted when he was in bad mood - loneliness

Steven, along with Imran, walked to their regular bar. They crossed the crowded counter, signaling the service boy to come to their table. The bar was crowded despite being afternoon time. They found their gang already there eagerly waiting for the rare fun. Yes... Imran was a rare fun. He was so careful about not being ridiculed. Krish and Al were banging the table welcoming Imran and Steven.

"Welcome boys..." Al greeted with open arms, imitating a welcome gesture to a grand event.

"Get me a bottle of rum, and two plates of chicken roast." Al shouted his order to the service boy.

"Sure big brother." The service boy replied with a big smile, who liked Al very much. Al might be hated by anyone who had a first look at him, but liked by most who knew him.

The gang started having fun at the expense of Imran. They were famous for their extreme tolerance among themselves and also their commitment for each other, which made them a formidable gang.

They started having their second bottle of rum and ordered for more chicken.

"So, you haven't seen his girl?" Krish asked.

"No… But I wish I had." Steven replied

"Never trouble yourselves. He'll show you some other girl tomorrow." Al joked.

"Next time… Make sure that the school is open before wasting your day." he ridiculed.

The whole gang broke into laughter. They did not observe that Michael's gang was seated a few tables away from them.

"How long do we need to wait for the chicken roast?" shouted Krish.

"Don't worry dude. I will get it for you." Al said as he staggered to the side dish counter.

Michael silently observed Al walk to the counter, waiting for an excuse to start a fight.

"Where is the chicken roast?" Al shouted at the counter.

He saw the service boy carry two plates of chicken roast which he snatched from him and told him "Thanks."

The service boy was terrified as it was supposed to be Michael's order. Michael gladly stood up in his way to stop him. Al was so fully drunk that he had to squint his eyes to make out who was blocking his way. He then identified him after a focused gaze.

"Just move out of my way. Don't make it a bad day for you." Al blabbered, shoving him out of his way with his shoulder, carrying the plates with both his hands.

Michael took an empty beer bottle from the nearby table and crashed in on his head in a split second.

Al, who was already in drunken stupor, did not have enough time to react. He could only sense something crash on his head and warm blood oozing from his head. He fell down unconscious the next instant.

Imran, who was facing the direction where the incident took place, was stunned at the sight. He banged the table, scattering the items all over the table. Steven thought he was frustrated by their mockery, but realized he was wrong. He followed Imran's eyesight and saw the scene in horror. Imran threw a plastic chair towards Michael, running in his direction and pounced, with his leg stretched towards him. Michael didn't expect him coming. Imran's kick landed right on Michael's chest, which tumbled him down the floor and sent him crashing on the nearby table, scattering the dishes and the bottles on it. Imran rolled along and regained his position on foot. In the meantime, Steven ran to help Al. He removed his shirt and wound it around his head to stop the bleeding.

"Get an auto immediately." he shouted at the service boy, who ran out to get one.

By the time Michael stood up, Imran got an empty bottle and crashed it right on his head above the ear. Now Michael started bleeding. Krish blocked the rest of Michael's gang from approaching Imran, while Steven rushed Alto the hospital. Imran approached Michael, who found a glass filled with liquor and splashed it right at his face. He closed his eyes on time, avoiding the burn of alcohol. Michael aimed the glass clumsily at Imran, who easily ducked away. Michael took the opportunity and fled the spot as fast as he could, but Imran did not fall short as he chased him at shot range. Michael took a beaten road, which was not used much by people. He snatched a cloth drying on a rope in front of a house and tied it around his head to stop the flow of blood. Imran chased him in blind rage.

Since Sunny was a regular visitor to the place, he had made a place for himself at a corner, where he usually sat. He forgot the bitter incident of the morning as soon as he started thinking about Sandy. Her thoughts always offered him reprieve from pain and carried him to the virtual world of joy. It had been two years since she'd left him all alone, but not her thoughts. He felt punished by her haunting thoughts in the beginning, but later found peace with it. He stretched out his legs placing one above the other, leaning against a tree with his hands resting behind his head and closed his eyes, relishing the loneliness. He forgot everything about his grief. He just leaned back, following his heart to the lovely land of dreams where Sandy waited for him.

"This is what I wanted: A place where no one would disturb me." He thought, relishing the silent atmosphere.

THUD! He heard a loud noise just a few feet left of him. He hated the disturbance and wondered who could have caused it. He saw a man fall across the fence, with a cloth tied around his bleeding head and his shirt drenched with blood. He stood frozen in shock at the sight of the blood soaked man. He was in for another unexpected shock when he saw Imran dive across the fence, knocking the man down and punching him hard across his face. Sunny visualized Imran as a beast pouncing on a hapless victim. He seemed to be the most barbaric person he ever came across in his life. He cuddled himself in the corner to stay away from the scene as it seemed to him that he was the most ill-fated person in the world to have encountered the beast twice in a day: Deadlier the second time.

Michael kicked Imran in the chest and rolled away from him. As Imran fell back, Michael had time to run away from him. As he tried to run away from him, Imran sprang on him, sweeping him off his foot and both of them then rolled towards the unprotected well. Michael sensed that he might fall unconscious anytime. He needed to get away from him as soon as possible, as he knew that he would be dead, the moment he fell unconscious. Michael gathered all his power and punched Imran on his face, attempting to run away. Imran was not the one who gave up easily. He grabbed Michael's shirt and tried to get up. When he was about to get on his feet, Michael yanked his shirt off, making Imran lose his grip as he wobbled backwards and leant on the ruined concrete ring. Michael randomly threw a kick at Imran as he staggered aimlessly away from him. The weathered concrete wall was not able to support the weight of Imran, and it crumbled, letting him fall in. Imran could only get the grip of the weathered concrete ring, which was about to crack anytime.

"Help… Help me." Imran started shouting. Sunny wanted to let him die for all the sufferings he has inflicted to him. He started walking away with the relief that he would be redeemed of the trouble from him thereafter.

"Help me... Anyone there?" Imran shouted again, in a rather commanding voice. Sunny was surprised that, even on the verge of death, he would not lose his arrogance. He wanted to get away from the spot as soon as possible, but the prospect of a death he could prevent did not let him move away. He walked cautiously towards the well, still speculative about what he was about to do. He looked around to see if he could find a rope or a strong branch to offer him, but luck was not in his favor. He walked inch by inch to have a look at him by hesitantly peeking into the well.

He was ready to take two big risks. To save him, he needed to take a risk and saving him itself was a risk. He didn't care about that. The weathered cement ring which Imran was holding, broke off from one hand's grip. He was holding himself up with his other hand.

"Help me... Is anyone there?" Imran shouted.

Sunny made up his mind and prostrated on the floor, stretching his legs wide apart as he moved towards the well, crawling by folding his leg forward towards the well, one leg at a time. He was growing more nervous as he proceeded towards the well. He shut his eyes for a couple of seconds and strictly made up his mind to enact the rescue. He moved forward and stretched his hand towards Imran. Imran didn't know who was helping him. He just projected his loose hand to him. Sunny held his hand and tried to pull him out. As Imran tried to pull himself out, he pulled Sunny towards him in the effort. Sunny was terrified as he moved closer towards the well. He spread his legs wider to find whatever he could to get a grip of. He gripped some herbs spread across the ground, which helped him a bit. Imran pulled himself up to rest his elbow on the open area where the cement ring was totally wiped off by his fall. The support which was held by the other hand suddenly crumbled off, which disturbed his hold of Sunny's hand. Now Sunny was shaking with fear, yet he didn't let his grip loose. He closed his eyes to avoid the visual treat of the horrific scene. He spread his legs as far as he could and tried to pull Imran with all his power. Imran also took the advantage of his elbow resting on the ground and transferred most of his weight on it and stretched his other hand to Sunny which he held tightly. Sunny was a bit relieved of his strain and Imran transferred more weight on his other elbow. Sunny looked into the fearless eyes of Imran, as he gradually rose up. Imran didn't seem to be terrified about the prospect of his death, but was in a hurry to come out of the well for some other reason. He stared at Sunny for a long moment with his sullen eyes. He rested his other elbow also on the ground. Now Sunny held him by his underarms and pulled him gradually out of the grim hole. Imran supported both his hands on the ground and tried to get his legs on a grip in the inner circumference of the well. Sunny tried to pull him out with maximum force, cautious at the same time, to not fall forward. As Imran set his foot on a fissure inside the well, he sprang out of the well and fell on him and rolled away. Sunny couldn't believe what had just happened, not even as a dream. He knew that, what he did was right. But whether it was for him, he was not sure. Both of them got up breathing hard.

"Are you fine?" Sunny asked without his knowledge.

Imran closed his eyes pressing his fingers against his eyelids and turned towards Sunny, opening his eerie eyes, which terrified him. Sunny knew the very instant that, what he did was not right for him. Imran immediately knocked him hard off his way and ran in the direction he'd come from.

"What a crude personality." Sunny thought bitterly.

John, who was irresponsible and unruly, was often punished and advised to learn discipline from Sunny. John's hatred for Sunny grew day by day with his growing popularity at school. He wanted to vent his grudge on him somehow. He had all his focus on him, and was looking for a chance. He knew that Sunny would be a vulnerable target out of school and he was looking for the most convenient chance. Finally he got his opportunity during the annual exams. Sunny actually never had any clue about the vengeance of John waiting to erupt at the best suited time. Hence he never worried about him. He wrote his exam with complete satisfaction while John was eagerly waiting for him. Sunny walked out of the hall as he completed his exam. John followed him out of the school campus. Sunny observed him follow him, but it never occurred to him that he was craving to thump his vengeance out on him. As John followed him looking for the most convenient place to confront him, he saw Imran sitting with his gang at their usual place. John was delighted as he thought it couldn't be a better chance, as he knew that Imran didn't need a reason to torment Sunny... he just needed to sight him. He increased his pace to block him within the sight of Imran and he succeeded in doing so. Sunny did not understand why he'd followed him then, but now he understood.

"What do you want?" he asked John.

"You cause all the trouble and try to get off easily, don't you?" he shouted at Sunny, purposely to draw Imran's attention and he succeeded.

Imran looked in the direction of the sound and spotted Sunny. Their eyes met. Sunny hated him at the sight.

"Yet another bad day." he thought, cursing his fate as he saw Imran staring at him.

After John was convinced that Imran was watching them he started abusing Sunny with all the false accusations. Sunny didn't care to justify as he understood his intensions and he considered it a trait of weakness. He hated Imran more than John. Imran broke off from the gang and started walking towards them.

"Look there… his punching bag has arrived." Steven told his gang prompting to Sunny with a sigh of resignation.

As Sunny was blankly facing John's accusation with his sight partly focused on Imran through the corner of his eye. John didn't have Imran in his field of vision, but he trusted that he would have some sadistic fun with Sunny to his delight. As he was cherishing the scene in his mind, he held Sunny by his collar and raised his fist to punch him. Sunny was staring at his fist descending on him and also with the corner of his eye, he saw Imran rushing towards them. He was prepared for the double assault. To his surprise, Imran held John's fist midway in the air and punched him on his lower jaw, knocking him off his foot.

"Stay away from the thought of troubling him. Else I will rip your skin off." Imran warned in an ominous tone that terrified John, who scrammed off the spot.

The unexpected turn of event surprised not only John, but also Sunny and Imran's gang.

"What could have changed the devil?" Steven exclaimed to his gang.

The mood of the whole atmosphere was reversed as Sunny stared at him in confusion. Imran shifted his gaze towards Sunny, but this time, he saw a glint of friendliness in his eyes.

BIRTHDAY SURPRISE

"*It's not the person who is good or bad, it's the side we rub of him.*" Sunny thought as he recalled the memories of his friendship with Imran and wondered how the other side of him was a stark contrast.

The ringing of the doorbell pulled him back to the present. He guessed who it was, as he rarely had visitors.

"Sunny boy… Get prepared to rock." Imran shouted in his usual enthusiastic tone.

Sunny sometimes wondered how he was still a child at heart despite having crossed forty years which made him 10 years older to him.

10:00 PM

Sunny drove as per Imran's instructions.

"Don't you think I have the right to know where I'm being taken?" Sunny asked curiously.

"Right." Imran told.

"Boy, I'm so glad. Now, tell me." Sunny did not hide his relief.

"I meant, drive to your right." Imran mocked him.

"You are a bloody scoundrel." Sunny said smiling at his adamancy, as he dutifully drove according to his instructions.

"Tonight's going to be a life changing night for you." Imran told.

"When did you turn into a fortune teller?" Sunny ridiculed him.

"My prophecy shall never fail." Imran replied with a naughty wink.

"Turn to your left and that's where you'll find your surprise." he announced.

Sunny didn't know what to expect. Even though he had lived in the city for nearly a decade, he didn't know most of the places. He turned left as instructed to find it himself, as he was too reluctant to guess. He was surprised. Rather shocked. Now, he knew where he was.

"Bastard… I should have guessed it already." Sunny shouted in a displeased tone, looking at the huge two storey building with scantily dressed girls strewed all over the corridor. Though he had never been to the place before, it wasn't a difficult guess.

"Look my friend. Life is a mix of good and bad, joy and pain. It all happens to you in the flow of life. Don't obstruct it with self-restraint. Stop living in pain. Let it flow. You will find that life is beautiful." Imran spoke in a bit of rush as if he would forget the lines.

"My life is already beautiful." Sunny thought of saying, but he knew that Imran wouldn't agree with him.

"Where did you steal the lines, rascal?" he said, gently knocking him on his chest.

"I don't remember, but it surely cost me lot of time." Imran giggled.

"Now, will you get off the car, please?" Imran had no intension of wasting any more time.

Sunny got out of the car and walked behind Imran like a reluctant child going for his first day at school.

"Ok Sunny boy… Here you go." Imran said as he led him towards a room in the first floor through the corridor crowded by prostitutes.

Sunny walked through the crowd of giggling girls, averting their gaze.

"Here you are, at the door to heaven." he said stopping at a room located at the centre of the corridor.

As Sunny stood motionless at the door, Imran pushed him in.

"Celibacy is not a pride. Give it up, now." Imran said as he winked at Sunny, showing his thumbs up.

"Forget Sandy and allow the flow of life." he said and walked towards the other door nearby.

"Forget Sandy…? Is that possible?" Sunny asked himself.

Sunny finished his chores, gobbled up his breakfast, picked his bag and sprinted to school.

"Oh god… I must hurry." Sunny thought, even though he was not late. Sunny and Sandy had a custom of arriving to school well before the classes started. They set their own time. They chatted and played together until the classes began.

That was the most joyous period of their school schedule. She was an intelligent companion who always pushed him hard. He liked the discussions with her. She most often defeated him on any argument and he loved losing to her.

It was such a joy for him, seeing her smile. Her rosy lips and sparkling teeth accentuated her beautiful smile.

Despite his efforts, he was late as usual. He saw her sitting in the last row, staring angrily at him as he walked into the classroom. She prompted her sight to the wall clock, indicating that he was late. Actually, he was very late that day.

"Yes I'm late." he agreed.

"What's your reason today?" she asked.

"I ran out of ideas." he said, unable to invent one for the day.

"I am fed up of your tardiness" she turned her face away from him.

"Sorry…" he apologized as he placed his bag on the desk and got himself seated beside her.

"You know, it took the whole night for me to complete my Math assignments. How did you do with yours?" he asked her.

"I was not able to complete my assignments" She frowned as she tried to pull his leg for coming late.

"Oh no…" He was terrified.

The first session was Mathematics. The Math teacher was so strict that all the students shivered at the very mention of her name. Her punishments were so severe.

"How much is pending?" he asked anxiously.

"Actually, I haven't started at all." she replied, turning her face away from him trying to suppress her laughter.

"How can you be so careless? Why don't you try to finish it now?" He panicked.

Sandy enjoyed his nervous stutters. She was proud of him.

"Hey pal. Early as usual…?" Nilesh asked Sunny as he entered the classroom. He turned to find more classmates appearing at the entrance.

"You seemed to have broken your custom of coming late." Ashika, who just followed him into the classroom, ridiculed him.

"Don't you remember? First session of the day will be taken by Sheeba Ma'am?" he replied. Sunny got lost in the terrifying thought of Sheeba ma'am opening the class for the day.

The whole class room was bustling with various discussions.

"Hey Gopal, did you see the match between India and South Africa?" Peter asked.

"No buddy. I could never think of anything other than the assignments. We had a huge lot yesterday." he responded.

"Can't you do it now? I can help you finish it…" he asked Sandy after long silence.

She gave him a brief stare. She began to say something, when they heard the terrifying slap of words from behind.

"Why can't you maintain silence when you are in the classroom?" Sheeba ma'am screamed from the entrance.

"Now come on. Get back to your seats and maintain silence."

He sat beside her, but did not dare to speak up. She was blushing. He thought that she was terrified. He didn't notice that she was trying to suppress her laughter.

Let me enjoy his anxiety for some more time and then surprise him when I submit my assignments." Sandy had a naughty thought.

The class started to come in full attendance. The teacher asked them to stay out until everybody came.

Now there were four students standing outside. The teacher looked at the clock. It was exactly 8.30 am which was the scheduled start time.

She stood up and gave an angry stare at them. They began to feel their spines chilling up.

They knew that they haven't done anything wrong, but still it was Sheeba ma'am they were facing.

She stared at them. After few agonizing seconds of stare, she spoke. "Why don't you try to be a few minutes early to school? That does not hurt, does it?"

"Sorry ma'am." the whole bunch of pupils sang in unison.

"Now come in and take your seats" she whipped.

"Ok students. Now, all of you rise for your morning prayer." she said.

Class prayer was done, not his. He kept chanting god's name, but did not know what to pray.

"Should I pray that there should be a sudden strike and the schools declare a holiday for the day with immediate effect? Or should I pray that the teacher get an urgent call from her home for an emergency and she should leave immediately."

First thing, he wished he would faint so that he would not have to see Sandy being punished by this brutal teacher. Thoughts were running at lightning pace within him. He prayed that the teacher should forget about the assignment. He knew she wouldn't.

"Students, let's get the roll call done." she said.

"Anand"

"Yes ma'am."

"Ashika"

"Yes ma'am."

"Can the assignment be completed by the time the roll call is completed?" he thought.

"It might have taken the whole night for me, as I had to work out each task. Now since it is just a carbon copy, it might take lesser time." He ran senseless thoughts in his mind.

"Lavanya"

"Yes ma'am"

"Mustaq"

"Yes ma'am"

He had been getting endless thoughts in fear. None might work out.

"Sandhya"

"Yes ma'am"

"Surya"

"Surya." The teacher called him as he was lost in thoughts.

"Surya…" Now she shouted his name. Sandy nudged him with her elbow when he woke up in horror.

"Are you day dreaming…? If you want to dream, go home. This is not the place." she scolded.

Sandy felt bad for him.

"Sorry ma'am, this won't be repeated again." He fumbled as he stood up.

"Sit down." she growled.

He felt his heart slip down to his stomach.

"The roll call is done. Here comes the most terrifying part of the day." Sunny thought.

"Now let's recap what we had discussed yesterday."

He was relieved a bit as it might procrastinate the horrific scene, which was scaring him from quite some time.

"Before we start the session, let me have each one of you submit your home assignments"

His relief did not last even as long as he thought about it.

"Now, before that… Do we have anybody who has not completed the assignments?" she asked.

Sunny felt weak on his legs as he stood up with his eyes shut tight.

He did something which shocked everybody, including himself, as he stood up, because the class had never seen him in the list of exceptions.

"Why did I get up? I have completed my assignments." he thought. He didn't want Sandy to be lone exception. He wanted to share the punishment with her.

He gave a grieving look at her. She was stunned as she saw him stand up. She wasn't able to understand what was happening. Her mind was not permitting her to think of anything except the impending punishment for Sunny. She was so worried for him. She looked around and found that he was the only one who stood up. It troubled her even more. Now she rose up slowly. She wondered whether she was sane to stand up despite having completed the assignment, but she knew that she couldn't let him alone in pain. Sunny saw her with sad eyes, as he was more worried about her than himself. They were the best two students of the class and now they were the only two who had not completed the assignments. The teacher felt so bad. She didn't want them to set a bad example to the class.

"Sandhya… Do you two have any acceptable reasons for not being able to complete the assignment?" she asked turning towards Sandy.

"Po… po… power failure ma'am." she stuttered.

"What about you?" she asked Sunny.

"I forgot ma'am." he said hastily as his mind had closed all its thinking doors.

The teacher boiled with anger. "All lame excuses from you people! I can't believe it."

She looked at the shelf to find the cane missing.

"John." she called out.

"Fetch a cane from the next class room."

"Yes ma'am." he said obediently.

He hurried away immediately as he was so eager to please her to earn some goodwill from her.

She liked the two very much. She counted on them every time. She used to pride on them. Now she was angry that they had let her down. She gave them a brief stinging stare and turned away.

"You two get out of the class and kneel down." she shouted.

They sadly walked out without looking at each other and fell on their knees.

"The last thing I would do as a sacrifice to anyone is to take a punishment from her." he thought.

"But anything for Sandy…" he thought again

They gazed at each other. He smiled at her with all his efforts which ended up with nothing more than a wince.

She also looked at him and tried to smile, but she failed too.

They had never been punished in the school so far, since they were perfect in studies and discipline.

Even though the teacher knew that, she had to punish them, as she didn't want to exhibit partiality.

John, who was jealous of the two, was so internally very happy because he was about to see what he had been yearning to see for a long time. A double delight too, as both Sunny and Sandy were going to be punished. He hurried back like a dutiful student and handed over the cane to the teacher. She took the cane and advanced towards the duo.

"I thought you were the best students of my class," she spoke in displeasure. "But you two let me down. I know that you are disciplined and sincere."

"I cannot excuse you with that credit. Everybody has the same set of rules. You are no exception."

She took the cane and swung it like a tuning fork. The sight of the cane terrified him worse than a nightmare. She marched towards him with the weapon in her hand.

"Stretch your hand." she ordered as Sunny outstretched his hand exposing his palm.

The teacher raised the cane so high in such a way that she was about to slay a dragon.

"Brutal lady." Sandy thought.

Sandy couldn't bear the sight of Sunny being punished as she preferred herself being punished instead.

While Sandy despised the teacher because she was punishing Sunny, she forgot that she was next in the line.

"Don't worry; you will get your turn." she thought to herself sarcastically.

She was physically not as strong as Sunny to bear the pain of caning, but the sight of her best friend being punished was more painful to her.

The cane landed on his outstretched palm with a terrifying slap of sound.

"She is the person I hate the most." Sandy thought.

Sunny took the caning with all his strength, to avoid exposing his pain. Now the teacher turned towards Sandy after finishing with Sunny.

She was so lost in the world of pain, of seeing her friend being punished, that she came back to reality only when she heard footsteps towards her. She had her eyes fully open, but the sight of the teacher approaching suddenly came into her view as she came out of her trance, which made her heart skip a beat.

Sandy slightly moved backwards involuntarily at the sight of the approaching assassin.

"This will pass." she thought.

"Stretch your hand." the teacher shouted.

Sandy hesitantly stretched her hand out as if in breaking frames of a slow motion picture. Sunny looked past the teacher at her tender palms. The teacher raised the cane in her typically tyrant way and smashed her beautiful palm. Sandy let out a loud scream followed by weeping.

"Brutal lady." he cursed her.

There couldn't be a worse sight for Sunny. The caning left blood red impressions on her delicate palms. The tear filled eyes of Sandy felt like a dagger in his heart. Nothing could hurt him more than a tear rolling out of her eye.

"I wish I could wrap myself around her, shield her from anybody hurting her." he thought, unable to bear the immense pain.

"You two kneel down at the entrance till the end of the session." The teacher said.

They both knelt down turning away from each other, hiding their pain from each other. Sandy, who was not familiar to pain, tried hard to suppress her weeping, but could not avoid feeble whimpers. Her knees were paining like hell, but she hid it from him by turning away. The entrance of the classroom where they knelt was rough because of the sand scattered. It felt like hundred bees were stinging her. Though he couldn't see her expressions, he felt her pain. That was the most brutal way anybody could punish him. She was trying too hard to tolerate the pain, but she was on the verge of collapsing. She tried to get some support from the classroom wall as she leaned her shoulder on it.

"Stay erect." shouted the teacher.

Sandy suddenly came back to her senses. She tried to stay erect, but it was too much for her that she fainted where she had knelt. Sunny froze in pain as he saw her faint. There was a sudden murmur in the classroom.

"Silence." barked the teacher.

"Somebody, bring water for her." she ordered.

A couple of boys and girls rushed to help her. Sunny immediately stood up to fetch water. "Not you... You kneel down." she shouted.

He instantly gave an angry stare at her which surprised her. She stood with her jaw dropped, utterly shocked as she did not expect it from him. He seemed like a wounded animal snarling at her. Meanwhile Mustaq, who was standing beside him, squeezed his shoulder, hinting him to stay calm and hurried to get water. Sunny fell on his knees and threw his head down letting the tears flow down. He clenched his fist tight and punched on the floor. He felt like getting up and slapping the lady. Meanwhile, Mustaq splashed water on Sandy's face to bring her back to consciousness. She squinted her eyes with a wince. The girls supported her to her desk.

The two menacing hours of class came to an end with the closure bell ringing, spreading an air of relief to the whole class, but not to him. He was burning with rage. He wanted to punish the brutal lady in some way.

The teacher's eyes met his as she walked out when she saw terrifying anger in his eyes. She stared at him for a moment and then walked away without a word. He immediately stood up and rushed towards Sandy. He couldn't dare to look into the eyes of the girl he liked the most. The pain in her eyes seemed to rip his heart out of his rib cage. He sat beside her and thought of consoling her, but he was at loss of words. It was the interval session and the class started to disperse out for break as soon as the teacher left.

"We will take her out for some refreshment, Sunny." the girls told him.

He nodded, as they took Sandy out, who gave him a straining smile as she walked out with the girls. He knew that she was trying to ease him despite her pain. It was a 15 minutes break.

"I can manage it myself." Sandy told them as soon as they came out of the class room, as she wished to be alone. She walked weakly to the washroom to wash her face. As she was washing her face, she revisited the events of the unfortunate morning.

"You know, it took the whole night for me to complete my Math assignments. How did you do with yours?" she recalled him saying.

She felt too dazed at the prospect of the teacher's punishment for Sunny that she instantly forgot everything.

The facts were right in front of her, but she was not able to reason it.

She finally came to the conclusion that he had completed his assignment. Immediately, she dashed to the classroom as she wanted to talk to Sunny without wasting a second. As she walked in to the classroom, she found that Sunny wasn't there. The classroom was empty. She quickly walked to his desk and retrieved his bag, shuffling all the books in it and found the one she had been looking for. She took the book out quickly and opened it to find that the assignments were completely done.

Her head started spinning. *"What made him take the punishment then?"* she wondered.

It was only then she remembered herself lying to him that she had not completed the assignments.

She then understood that he took all the punishment because he didn't want her to be alone in pain. Tears started rolling down her swollen cheeks.

"I had been such a fool. He suffered all the pain because of me, yet he never had slightest complaint about that. What have I done to earn such a friend, who would want to accompany me even in pain?" she thought with a mixture of pride and pain.

She closed the book and lay her head down on it, kissing it. She wanted to hug him instead of the book. She had never felt so emotional.

"Hope you are feeling better now, Sunny?" Mustaq spoke to Sunny as they walked into the classroom.

"Better." he stiffly responded.

Sandy sat erect as soon as she heard his voice. She wiped her tears, though it was clearly evident that she had cried a lot.

Sunny saw Sandy sitting in his place. He hesitantly walked towards her, not daring to have a word with her.

«Do you have an explanation for this?" Sandy asked, raising the completed assignments in her hand.

"Oh! Where did you find that?" he acted surprised.

"Well, I thought that I had forgotten it at home." he sighed and turned away from her, arranging his bag.

"I would rather be punished for not completing my assignments than be punished for absent-mindedness. It looks so ugly, you know" he said, surprised at how conveniently he could lie.

"Well done." he thought.

Sandy stared at his eyes for a few moments.

"Stop lying. Your eyes strain from your lie. I can read it."

"Great effort, but not good enough." she spoke in trembling voice.

"Well…" he tried to explain.

"I know why you lied" she interrupted.

A thin sheet of tears formed in her eyes. She beamed at his friendship.

"I had been such an idiot not to have known." she spoke with pride as she stared straight into his eyes. As she spread open his palm and saw the bruise, she felt more the pain than him. She blamed herself for his suffering.

"You are hurt because of me" She wept with a sense of guilt.

"If you really don't want to hurt me, do me a favor." he said.

"I'll do anything for you. Tell me what I should do?" she asked

"Don't hurt yourselves." He said as nothing could hurt him more than her tears.

She was tempted to hug him tight and bury her face on his chest. She smiled through her tears. His sacrifice was making her feel guiltier for her lie.

"You know what...?" She hesitated to continue." I too lied... Sorry" she said after a lot of hesitation, fearing that he might hate her for it.

"What...! I was not able to make out you lied" he was shocked, but winked immediately, to let her know that he was amused.

"If you have completed the assignments, then why did you take the punishment?" he asked her.

"How can I let you suffer in pain alone?" Her response made him forget his pain.

"There is no pain when you are with me. Promise me Sandy, that we will always be together." Sunny waited for her response.

He expected her to respond in affirmative, but she didn't. Instead she looked into his eyes without blinking, letting the tears roll from her eyes. He looked straight back into her painful eyes and did not understand the meaning of her pain. She hugged him without a clue and pressed her eyes over his shoulder. Sunny felt an inexplicable stirring in his heart as he tightly wrapped his hands around her.

She didn't answer his question.

TRAGIC TWIST

10:30 PM

"Yes... She didn't answer."

"*Perhaps she knew that she wouldn't always be with me. But that didn't change the fact that I was her best friend, and she mine... always.*"

"*No... It is not possible to forget her. I love her more than anything in the world.*"

"Are you going to dream the whole night or get into the act?" He heard a harsh voice of a girl disturb his beautiful memory.

"*I hate her more than anything in the world.*" he thought as he hated the girl even before he looked at her.

The room was dimly lit. He glanced in the direction of the voice, where he saw a girl sitting on the bed, leaning against the wall.

She was a petite girl. She had high cheekbones and grim eyes complemented by a scar below her right eye. She was just as tall as him. She wore a sleeveless shirt revealing a portion of her cleavage and a loose fitting track pant. She was Saloni. He hated her instantaneously. Her fair skin had a black patch on her left upper arm, which he vaguely noticed in the dim light.

He noticed her surprised expression when he walked away from her to the window and sat on a chair, staring outside without minding her.

She waited for some time to get him settled. She sensed something wrong when he didn't seem to make a move, even after an half an hour.

"Are you going to waste your time staring out through the window?" she asked him.

"I haven't come here for what you think." he said without even looking at her.

"What else do you want?" she asked impolitely.

"Mind your business." he fired back.

"This, actually, is my business." she responded back.

He didn't need any more reasons to hate her.

"If you need me, just let me know." she murmured as she plugged the earphones resuming her favorite melodies.

"How are girls so casual about selling themselves for money?" he thought bitterly as he glanced at her.

The phone shivered in vibration as a message arrived.

Hope you are enjoying, Sunny boy.

He smiled to himself as he stared out of the window. It was a brightly moonlit night.

She stared at him for a few seconds in confusion. She didn't understand why he had paid so much just to sit in a corner without doing anything.

"Who cares as long as he does not hurt me?" she thought.

He was longing to get out of this room as he felt suffocated. He kept staring through the window and was constantly looking at the time in his mobile phone. She was still confused.

"What is he waiting for? There is something creepy about this man." she thought, as she had never come across such a customer in the few months of her experience.

"I need to pass at least 1 hour more before I leave." he had set himself a time target, as he didn't want to dishonor his friend's efforts to make him happy.

11:30 PM

He kept staring at the road outside the window. He had nothing to pass the time which made him feel so uneasy until he couldn't take it anymore. With great difficulty, he achieved his time target. As he rose from his seat, Saloni thought that he had prepared himself for the action and removed the headset. To her surprise he started walking outwards.

"Who cares?" she thought.

She was glad that he left, as she'd felt something scary about him, though she couldn't read the face that hid behind the beard. He stormed out of the room and almost collided onto a man is his late forties, who was couple of inches taller than him, but was heavier for his height. He had droopy eyes, large ears and barrel nose which gave him the appearance of an evil cartoon.

"Miss your mojo, mate? I have the right stuff for you." he said chuckling, which infuriated Sunny.

"Fuck off." he said as he pushed him aside and walked angrily down the stairs which converged down from each end. Unexpectedly his push destabilized the man and he fell heavily on the ground crashing against the balustrade columns.

As Sunny went down the last step of the stair case, he saw the man standing in front of him.

He sensed trouble.

"Sorry, I did not mean it." He apologized to him and started walking, though he didn't like the way he spoke to him. He just didn't want trouble.

The man quickly walked ahead of him and stopped him by blocking his chest with his fist.

"Who the fuck are you?" he screamed.

Saloni put on her knee-length semi-transparent pink chiffon coat with pleated sleeves, slipped on her sandals and rushed to the corridor when she heard the high pitched voice.

"Look, I'm sorry. I was a bit upset." he said.

"Don't worry. I have the cure for it." he said as he punched him on his chest.

Sunny was really getting impatient with his approach, but did not want trouble from people like him.

"Please let me go. I don't want any trouble." Sunny said.

"That is what you get when you misbehave with me." the man said.

"Ok. What do you want me to do?" Sunny asked.

The man held his collar and thought for a few seconds, staring straight into his eyes and shifting his sight from his head to toe.

"Kneel down and apologize. I'll let you go." he said, though he didn't intend to spare him so easily. He liked to dominate people who became his victim.

Saloni was watching all the action from the corridor. Sunny stared at the ground with raging anger. He didn't want to show his angry stare to him as it might aggravate the situation.

"Kneel down, son of a bitch." he shouted.

Imran heard the shouts and thought some drunken punk was having his routine fun by victimizing an innocent passerby.

"There is no way I would kneel down before him." Sunny thought

The man tried to push his shoulders down to kneel but sensed resistance, which enraged him.

He slapped Sunny, disturbing his patience. On a prompt reflex, he punched the man so hard on his chest that he was swept off the ground, and stepped back a few feet.

It scared a passerby, who scurried away from the spot as he hadn't expected the sudden burst of action.

For an instant, Sunny forgot all the crude facts about the thug.

"I will kill you, son of a bitch." the man shouted as he ran towards him.

"Look...I'm sorry. That was unintentional." Sunny shouted at the pitch of his voice, but the beast did not listen. He jumped on Sunny with his fist swinging at him, landing his punch right on his jaw.

This time Imran recognized Sunny's voice and hurried out of his bed, jumped into his pants and ran down the stairs, still wearing his shirt.

Now the guy held Sunny from behind and pushed him down forward and tried to reach his *kukri* from the leather scabbard tied around his waist. He succeeded in picking it and was about to dig it into him when Imran jumped from twelve stairs above, on to him and kicked right on his face. The *kukri* slipped out of the man's hand as he fell on his back. As Imran regained his ground, he continued delivering punches hard on his face.

"I can't take it alone." the man thought as he shouted for help.

Now Saloni started walking downwards as she sensed an ugly melee. This kind of trouble was common in this racket, but this time it seemed to have exceeded all the limits.

He got response from his gang. There came two people; one guy had iron rod and the other had a sickle. Imran was cool as ever, but Sunny was terrified, as he was never subjected to anything like that before. He knew that he had no other option than to fight. Now Imran stood before him, guarding him from them. He raised his hand on the person with the sickle and ducked down, deceiving him and punched the other guy. The punch was so hard that he rolled down on the floor, which gave him time to handle the guy with the sickle. When the man swung his sickle at his neck, he ducked down and punched him hard on the lower abdomen. Meanwhile, the guy with the iron rod was dangerously close to Imran that he did not have time to block him. Sunny jumped in and held the hand holding the rod and dragged him as he swung him along like a merry go round threw him away at a distance. As the man got up, dazed, Sunny punched him hard on the face. This gave Imran convenient time to overpower the guy with the sickle who crashed onto an electric post, which knocked him down. More people were coming in.

Saloni was anxiously watching all the action, as she expected it to turn into a nasty one. She was disgusted with the people's approach, especially the one who started it.

"Hari, that's enough. Have a drink and go to sleep." Saloni shouted scornfully as she walked down the stairs. Hari was in no mood to listen to her. He brought extra men to fight them.

The aggravating fracas disturbed the sexual fun within the brothel, gradually filling the corridor with spectators, some with fear, some with frustration and some with the excitement to watch some real time action.

Sunny and Imran were back to back, so that they had their vision in all the directions. Sunny, who was glancing at the people around him, saw her. He stared into her eyes for a brief moment and then shook her off his glance, focusing on the danger in front of him.

After the two were knocked down, came four other people. The duo jumped on them, dividing their rivals between them. Sunny was rolling with one guy on the ground, and succeeded in pinning him down the ground and punched him on the face. As the other guy was trying to crash him on his back with a big rock, he immediately rolled away, exposing the other guy, thereby knocking him out. Now it was easy for him as he had only one guy to deal with. He twisted the other guy's hand and was about to punch his neck, when Hari grabbed his *kukri* from the ground and ran to stab him. When Sunny knocked him on his neck and turned around to find Hari approach with his knife, he thought was dead.

Just then, in a flash, Imran held Hari's hand holding the *kukri*. Hari cunningly pulled it out of his grip in such a way that the blade cut through his palm, splashing his blood on Sunny's face. Imran kicked him away from Hari's reach, rolling him downwards along the sloping road. Hari swung the knife at him again, which he tried to block with his forearm. The blade tore the skin from his forearms. Sunny ran towards him for help. Just then, a guy crashed on him pushing him to the ground. He punched the guy on the face and kicked him away from himself and watched as Hari raised the *kukri* again to stab Imran, who was powerless, as his hands were tightly held behind him by a guy. Imran then kicked Hari on his chest and knocked the guy holding him from behind with his head thrown backwards. As he was free of the grip, he kicked him in the groin, as he was not able to use his hands effectively. Sunny was happy that Imran was able to cope with the guys. He turned to move towards Imran, when one of the guys held him by his legs and toppled him down. Sunny wrestled with him and twisted his arms and knocked him on the spine with his elbow, which made him cry out of pain.

Sunny then turned around to see the status of his friend, who was valiantly fighting only with his legs, kicking anyone confronting him. Now Hari regained his position and kept swinging the *kukri* at him. As Imran kept dodging at him, one of the guys swept him off his ground by tripping his legs. Sunny jumped to his feet and ran towards him, but it was too late as Hari drove the *kukri* through Imran's neck and blood splashed all over his face. Hari retrieved his weapon and immediately fled the spot, when he heard the police sirens at a distance. It was clearly evident that Imran was lifeless by the time Sunny reached him. Sunny knelt beside him and wept.

"You saved my life Sunny."

"That makes it twice then."

"Yeah, twice..."

"Don't worry, I'll return the favor today."

Sunny recalled his conversation with Imran from that evening and wondered whether the brutal fate foretold his death, resuming its sadistic game with him.

The police sirens scared the curious spectators, dispersing them in random directions.

Sunny swore to avenge his friend's murder, as he looked around for the murderer.

SUNNY'S ADVENTURES
WITH SALONI

11:50 PM

The police vehicles screamed into the scene, causing commotion among the panicking customers and also the prostitutes. Everyone started scrambling away from the spot, including Saloni. Sunny looked around for the killer, but he was gone. He ran around in search of him but he lost him. As he reached the parking space, he noticed that the cops had by then, reached the murder spot and had surrounded Imran's lifeless body, looking around for suspects or witnesses. Sunny thought he could not walk into the cops and lose the chance to avenge his friend's murder. Just as he turned away, he found Saloni running in his direction.

"She knows him by name. She should have known more about him." he thought.

He stood next to his car waiting for her with the front door open. As she ran to his reach, he grabbed her and tried to push her inside. She struggled to escape, but he overpowered her and pushed her into the car. Then he pushed himself into the driver seat across her and closed the door. He started the car immediately without the headlights on and silently escaped the proximity of the crime scene, getting on to the main road. When he drove unsteadily without any sense of direction, Saloni started to scream and kick him to let her out, which frustrated him.

"Shut up." he said as he slapped her hard across her face.

She instantly responded with a hard punch on his face and threw her hands and legs at him. Sunny started to worry that her struggle might attract unexpected trouble. He drove the car to the sideways at a safe distance and stopped it there. He then held her hands tightly above her head arresting her movement.

"What the hell do you want?" she screamed in irritating cacophony.

"Look, I am not going to hurt you. I just need a favor from you." he said trying to calm himself down, but without any success, as he held her by her throat against the door.

"Did you think that by forcing me into your car, you can control me like a doll?" she croaked through her strangled throat.

"I didn't mean to control you. I just need a help." he shouted, still unable to control his temper. He then gradually loosened his grip.

"What makes you think that I'll help you?" she fired back warding his hand off her throat.

"What would that be anyway?" she continued after regaining her breath.

"I need to get the whereabouts of the guy…what did you call him?" He thought and thought hard through his turbid mind resulted from the savage slaughter of his best friend.

"Hari…Yes Hari." He remembered

"I don't know anything about him." she carelessly responded and tried to open the door to get out of the car.

"I can't force her to help me. I need to find a way to persuade her." he thought

"Yes, she doesn't have any reason to help me, but she has a reason to defend him. He is her pimp, after all." he bitterly explained to himself.

"How do I win her support?"

"Look…I will pay you as much as you want. I want that bastard." he said, holding the door closed.

She abruptly stopped trying to get out of the car and turned towards him, interested.

"Bull's eye" he thought

"How much will you pay me?" she asked.

He was relieved that he had convinced her to help him.

"I will kill you bastard." he swore within himself.

"How much?" she repeated.

"Bloody bitches… They would do anything for money." he thought with hatred.

"How much do you want?" he asked.

"Three lakhs." she said

That was unexpected shock for him, though he did not want to bargain on his vengeance.

"But I do not have so much money now." he reminded himself.

He couldn't find him all by himself as he didn't know anything about him. Moreover, he should have fled somewhere. He needed all the help he could get.

"Guilt will kill me, if I don't kill him soon." he thought.

"I don't have that much money now." he said.

"Find him yourself." she said and turned to open the car door.

He punched hard against the door above her shoulder with his open palm, almost brushing her ear. She was frightened for a second, but concealed it immediately.

He stared into her cold eyes with so much hatred that he never hated anyone before.

"These are people who take advantage of helpless people. They are not fit to be human." he cursed within himself.

"Look… If money is all that matters to you, I will give you what you wanted. But I need some time." he said.

"Anyways… I don't expect a free favor from people like you." he grunted through his teeth. He was never that rude to anybody, but couldn't help it this time.

"Then give me some advance." she said ignoring his rudeness.

"Yes." he said scornfully. He hated her the most. He hated her for making business out of his helplessness. He hated her for not understanding his emotions.

Is there any other reason why he hated her?

He released his hand from the door and returned to his seat. Something was disturbing him very much. He didn't know what. His mind was dodging some mysterious thoughts without comprehending it. He shook all the thoughts and concentrated on the drive.

"What if she takes all the money and dumps me or leads me into a trap?" he thought for a fleeting moment.

"I have to take this chance. In fact this is my only chance." he convinced himself.

He held the steering wheel tightly with his eyes shut revisiting the horror that had occurred just a few minutes ago. Tears rolled out automatically as he wept with suppressed moans.

"I will not let him get away with this." he promised to Imran.

He wiped his tears and turned towards her.

"What a brutal lady?" he thought as she was staring out of the window, unmoved by his emotional outburst.

Hari knew that the police would have faxed his photo to all the check-posts to sieve for him. He needed a foolproof plan to get through the police vigilance. He knew that he didn't have time to think or devise such a plan. His instant thought was to get out of the place, as he would get caught, just if he stayed minutes longer. He chose a simple plan – to bushwhack through the police gates. He didn't have the patience or intelligence to draft a better plan. Just then he received a call. Hari knew that he would get that call.

"Hey, Victor… It's not my fau…" Hari started to justify, when Victor snapped him.

"Just cut the shit and get the hell out of there." Victor commanded.

"I'm just few hundred yards from the check post. I have already planned to run through the cops and…" Hari was not able to explain his plan completely.

"Son of a mongrel… You don't follow anything that comes out of your shit head. Just listen to me." Victor explained his plan and instructed him "Just stay where you are. Someone will pick you up."

"The cops are looking out for me everywhere. I would be inviting them to grab me, if I stay here a few minutes longer." Hari complained.

Victor gave a long breath, trying to tolerate his non sense.

"You... will... get out of there... in less than five minutes. Now... shut the fuck up and stay calm." Victor stressed on each word expressing his frustration and disconnected the call immediately as he didn't have any more patience.

"Son of a bitch." Hari growled at the dead phone.

Sunny heard the police car rush past his, which was parked on the sideways with the headlights turned off. It was a dark road without street lights, which hid his car from the cop's sight. Just as he was relieved, he saw the police car slow down. They seemed to have sighted something as they drove past them. Sunny froze in his position, afraid to turn back as his heart was beating so heavily. Saloni remained silent beside him. When he saw the car driven in reverse towards them, he held the steering wheel tight as he feared getting caught. He turned back slowly to find the car stop a few yards away from his car and saw someone get out of it. Saloni saw Sunny's face sprayed with blood and knew he would definitely be arrested red handed. As the cop approached them, Saloni turned on the engine hinting him to drive away. Sunny took the hint and sped away from the cop, who was actually going to ask them to help him get the car out of the pit where its wheel was buried. The cop immediately rushed back to his car, turned on the engine and struggled to get the wheel out of the pit. The wheel spattered the slush, thereby driving it deeper into the pit.

He then got out of the car and tried to lift the wheel out of the pit, but it was too heavy for him. He put all his efforts digging his foot in the ground, transferring all the power onto his hands. His hard work paid off as the car moved out of the pit. He jumped into his car and turned to their direction. The cop's struggle with the wheel had given Sunny some time. Sunny drove as fast as he could, nervously staggering on the road, bumping on the speed breakers, still without the headlights on. As he drove unsteadily in the meager moonlight, he didn't notice a man standing along the road, who was swept into the sideway bushes as he drove past him. Sunny then consciously turned on the headlights, but couldn't spare a thought about what happened to that man as he tried to focus on the road ahead as well as the road behind, keeping the chasing cop at a distance.

Escaping an accident by a narrow margin from the car without headlights, Hari cautiously emerged out of the bushes, making sure it was safe for him. He was getting impatient as he repeated the act with each passing vehicle. Just as he saw a vehicle approach him, he jumped into the bushes and peeked out. This time the vehicle didn't drive past him. It just stopped a few yards away from him and blew the horn thrice. Hari understood that it was the one sent to transport him. He knew the signal. He ran out of the bush towards the vehicle which was actually a haystack carrier tractor.

He immediately dialed Victor's number who received the call on his Bluetooth headset.

"Victor…" was all he said when Victor disconnected the call as he wasn't interested in talking to him. Hari knew that it was no use calling him again.

He was not happy with the tractor as transportation, but he didn't know worse.

The officer at the check post inspected the vehicle.

"Let it pass." He signaled the gate keeper.

The vehicle zoomed past the check post gate and stopped after a few miles. The driver jumped off the wheel and walked towards the rear. He removed a few piles of haystack down and saw Hari coughing, as he emerged out.

"Son of a bitch… How long did you expect me to survive without breathing?" Hari growled as he was still coughing.

"I have no pleasure in stealing your breath…" he replied and immediately stopped speaking any further when he saw Hari glaring at him.

"I won't have any more conversation with him." he swore as he walked back to the driving wheel.

Hari followed him and sat in the front seat beside him this time. He actually didn't even know where he was going to be taken. It was such a tiring ride that it shook his whole skeletal structure. He hated the ride more than anything.

Sunny noticed a police check post a few hundred yards ahead. He abruptly stopped the car and resigned in his seat with the engine turned off. Saloni quizzically looked at him without speaking out anything for a few seconds. She knew that a cop was on their trail and wouldn't be too far from reach.

"Get off the driving seat." Saloni shot at him.

He was puzzled at her sudden instructions.

Just as he was about to open his mouth, she said "There is no time for argument."

"Get out of the driving seat now." she repeated louder this time.

He felt offended by her authority.

"This is not the apt time for an ego clash." he thought as he got out of the seat and walked towards where she sat. She swiftly shifted her seat from within the car across the gear box and sat on the driver seat in a split second. He was surprised by her agility. She turned on the engine and shifted gears even before he had gotten into the seat. He hurried into his seat, fearing she might leave him. She turned backwards in a second and started driving towards the direction from where they had come. More dangerously towards the cop who was chasing them.

"Are you insane?" he shouted.

She didn't budge. She just kept shifting gears as she drove, until they heard the police sirens approaching them. He doubted that she was deliberately rushing him into his ill fate.

"Is she walking me into a trap? I am a fool to have fallen for her trick" he cursed himself.

He also wondered why he had let her take control of the situation. He shut his eyes, questioning himself what justice he had done for the sacrifice of his friend. He felt the car riding on a bumpy road. He still did not open his eyes with the fear of failing in his mission. He heard the sirens approach closer to a striking distance. He shut his eyes even tighter, as he was terrified of getting caught, before doing what he was supposed to do. He could hear the laughter of Hari getting louder and louder, who was mocking his inability to touch him. He shut his ears also. All he could feel was pitch darkness and graveyard silence. He thought that it was a good way of hiding from his conscience.

"No… I could escape anything but my conscience." The thought shook him like a leaf in a storm wind. He felt his body tremble by a violent force. He felt being swung around left and right on his seat. He did not know what was happening and also did not want to know as the reality was so scary.

"I'm going to get caught… I'm going to get caught." he thought with his eyes tightly shut. He swung around as if he was caught in a whirlwind. He felt a sudden calm which was more ominous than the violent agitation. He was soaked in perspiration, when he felt someone nudge him. It felt like a sledge hammer striking his heart at a full swing.

"This is the end of the road." he thought as he slowly opened his eyes, afraid to face the cop standing outside with handcuffs stretched towards him. He saw Saloni standing out at his window and saying something in muted way. As he took his hands away from his ears, he could hear the siren receding away gradually.

He got out of the car with a bottle of water and washed Imran's blood sprayed on his face. He sat in the driver's seat facing out with the doors open. The prospect of getting caught took his breath out.

"How long are you planning to stay here?" she asked sarcastically.

He returned an angry stare.

"You have the risk of getting caught if you stay here even for a minute longer. You decide." she said as she shrugged coolly as she got back to her seat.

He sat for a few moments to regain his composure. He took a deep breath and started the engine, firing away from the spot, conscious about not getting noticed by the cops.

He was thankful to the darkness that hid the car number, saving them from a police trail.

"Drive away from the main road." she instructed him. He looked at her, trying to resist his sense of gratitude for her timely action. He complied with her. He was also happy that she started cooperating with him.

"Give me the money, or get me out of this havoc." she fired at him out of the blue.

"How wrong was I? These tramps count money and nothing else." he thought, wondering how she proved him wrong in an instant.

He needed to find some place to work out his plan. Before that, he needed to get some money to get her to start cooperating with him.

12:05 AM

He drove about 3 miles away from the spot and started looking for an ATM. He withdrew 50,000 rupees as per his daily withdrawal limit.

She stared at him with a puzzled look as he offered her the money.

"I will pay rest of the money soon." he said as he gave her the money.

She grabbed the money with irresistible greed. He saw the luminous glow in her eyes as she held the money in her hands. It was then he realized that she was wearing a flimsy tops and loose pants without pockets. She removed her scarf tucked at her waist. He wondered what she was up to. She folded the currency into the scarf and tied it around her wrist.

"Strange ways of pocketing money..." he thought. *"Don't they mind anything other than money?"* He hated her for her desperation.

"Where do we find him?" he asked her.

"Drive to Hotel Sun Shine" she responded.

"Do we find him there?" he instantaneously asked her with curiosity.

"No… We stay there for the night and start searching for him tomorrow morning." she carelessly responded.

He was furious with her casualness.

"It's not a funny moment now. Your humor is offending me." he said, controlling his rage.

She looked at him for a fleeting moment.

"It is unsafe to keep driving on the roads at odd time when there is a serious crime scene in the city and you seemed to be very much involved. I believe if you are not ready to waste the night, then you should be ready to face an inquiry from the police. If your luck is bad, you might be charged with a murder case." she responded.

He knew about his luck.

"I should listen to her." He agreed.

"It's a nice hotel which is hassle free." she continued. "Now move fast before somebody gets interested in us."

"No wonder she knows all the hotels." he thought scornfully as he drove according to her directions. He hated being so negative about somebody, but he couldn't help it when it came to her.

"Why am I so unnatural with her? Why do I force myself to hate her...?"

"Nothing unnatural. Anybody would hate her." he argued within himself.

12:15 AM

He halted the car before an old fashioned hotel, according to Saloni's directions. The name board read "Hotel Sun Shine" with a dull orange light. The hotel didn't seem to attract the travelers much, as it was hidden from the highway. He had noticed the hotel for the first time, though he lived in the city for nearly a decade. There was no organized parking zone.

He parked the car in a vacant place and turned off the engine. He sat in the car and glanced at the Hotel façade which read 'SS'.

"We might be at risk if we intend to stay here for long." she spoke out.

He stared at her for a few moments and walked out with her. He slowed down to maintain some distance from her, as he didn't like walking with her. When she looked back over her shoulder, she understood his intensions. She turned back and walked confidently towards the reception.

"Dev... Do you have vacant rooms?" she asked and winked coquettishly leaning on the reception desk of her usual hotel.

Customers sometimes preferred hotels as they felt uncomfortable at the brothel house. They were permitted to take the girls to the prescribed locations at an additional charge.

Sunny was at a distance from her, but noticed her gesture. He despised her act, but Dev was flattered, as he knew that Saloni was the most conservative prostitute he had ever seen. It was so unusual of her to flirt.

"I hate saying no to you. Let me check." he said turning to his register.

Sunny walked up to her and stared at her uncomfortably.

"Act normal. I believe you don't like any inquiries of who you are and why you are here. With your expressions, people can make out something's wrong." she whispered to him

She nudged him with her elbow and curved her lips up with her thumb and index finger indicating him to smile.

He hated her touch. *"It's true. I didn't want any dampeners."* he thought as he feigned a smile.

It was a bad effort. Dev looked at him suspiciously.

"First time..." she quickly explained him in a husky whisper.

He laughed aloud "Come on bro, you'll like this."

"Quite late to be the first time though…" He chuckled as he whispered back to Saloni. Sunny heard him, but did not care. Saloni took the key and walked towards the room.

Dev filled the register himself, with some fake details as he was used to it for quite some time, but stared at them suspiciously.

She held his hand and led him to the stairs. He walked with her till the stairs and as soon as he climbed a few steps which got him out of the attendant's sight, he pulled his hand away from her. She didn't like his rudeness. They walked with hostility towards each other.

She walked past him and stopped at a room which bore the number 55.

She unlocked the door and swung it open. He followed her, hating to stay with her in the same room for the second time in the same night.

As they entered the room, she threw the keychain engraved with sun on the bedside table, which attracted Sunny's sight. He kept staring at the dangling sun of the keychain as he drifted into his past.

It was the last day of the academic year and the whole school was buzzing with excitement. It was a bright sunny day, yet was drizzling constantly. The sun and the rain conflicting each other was a pleasant sight. It was a warm day with cool, tiny specks of rain caressing the exposed skin of arms and faces.

"It is the most beautiful day of my life." he thought to himself as he saw Sandy walking towards him.

Every day he was with her, he felt the same way. The world is a stunningly beautiful place, but without sunshine, it would all be chaos. His life without her was the same. She was the sunshine of his life. Every beautiful thing in the world reminded him of her. He wanted to give her something which could remind her of him... all the time.

He would like to meet her everyday and spend every moment of his life with her. Yet he was ready to sacrifice the joy of her company for the whole vacation for a special reason.

"I will not be available for the whole summer vacation." Sunny said flatly, concealing the pain, as he did not know a better way to put them into words.

"What?" she asked in an utter shock, as they had promised to spend the vacations together.

That's all... He was stuck with loss of words. He had rehearsed all night, what to say to her, but still failed.

He was tempted to say that he was just kidding, but he did not.

"What for?" she repeated, a little louder this time.

"Well… My grandma has invited me to stay with her for the vacation." he said bleakly. Sunny knew only his paternal grandmother as a relative, as his father had disowned everyone of his relations except her.

"Are you going to stay with her for the whole two months?" she asked in an almost trembling voice, hoping to get a negative answer.

"Yes…" he answered laconically.

She stared at him for a few seconds and forced a smile.

"So… you are going to have a nice time, huh." she asked him, sounding rather sarcastic.

"I don't think so. I'm just going to please her." he replied, very satisfied as that was the most convincing line he had spoken so far.

"I wish to meet you the very next second you return." she told with a heavy heart which hurt him a lot.

"Waiting to meet you again..." he said with utmost sincerity.

"If at all, I could succeed in the self-imposed ostracism from my world." he wondered, as Sandy was the whole world to him.

"You should have packing to do. You go home. I have some stationary to purchase." She said.

They stood facing each other for a long time without speaking a word. She stared into his face for a few more seconds and then started walking away from him without a word, just waving her hand bidding adieu.

"I shouldn't have hurt her. Nevertheless, I'm hurt too." he thought painfully, but he had got to do what he got to do.

He kept watching her walk away from him till she disappeared at the turning of the road. He stood there even after she disappeared. He seemed to have frozen where he stood. The pleasant weather before few minutes turned into hell as he saw Sandy disappointed. What added more to his pain was that she seemed to be annoyed with him.

"It will pass." he thought. It was not as easy as he thought.

"What next." he thought again looking in the direction where Sandy walked, still unable to believe what had just happened.

He turned to walk home with a heavy heart. He didn't observe that she was hiding in the corner of the street, watching him stare at her path.

She was so glad that he was truly missing her a lot, but she dreaded missing him.

She kept staring at his path as he disappeared at the turning of the road and then started walking back to her home with sadness.

What Sunny hated the most was talking to his father. Though they lived together, they lived like total strangers. When he reached home, he saw his father drunk as usual. He was lying on the sofa in the hall. He wanted to tell his father that he would be going out for a couple of months. Not that he would object or even mind if he found out that he had lied. He just didn't care. Sunny wanted to inform him for a formality.

"I'm going out for a free summer coaching. I'll stay there for two months." he told his father who just nodded in response.

"Finally... I'm going to earn my first money." he told himself proudly as he recalled his employment scenario.

The proprietor at the lumber depot was absolutely against child labor. When Sunny had approached him for a job during his summer vacation, the proprietor had denied outright.

"First thing: we are against child labor, as I feel that it would affect their education. Second thing is: we don't have vacation jobs." he declared dismissively.

"I'm not a child and this job is not going to affect my education, as I'm working only during my vacation. And if you think the quality of work would not be up to mark, you can reduce my pay, if you find so." he responded immediately. Though his talk seemed matured for his age, it still didn't impress the proprietor.

"Go back to school kid. Concentrate on your studies and you can earn a lot more later." he said.

"If my education is only what you are concerned about, I can show you my report cards till now and also for the next year. This could only boost my self-confidence, but in no way could hurt my education." he said, realizing he might have been a bit rude with his high pitch voice without his knowledge, but he had only impressed him with his confidence. The proprietor immediately offered him the job, though it was not common of him.

He then requested one of his coworkers to allow him to stay with him for that duration.

Everything was perfectly set.

His job was to load and unload lumber from the trucks.

He was strong for his age and performed his task very well.

"Come on man. It's time for a tea break." his coworkers would say.

"I'll join you after I finish unloading this last truck." he would say.

He wouldn't take a break from an unfinished task. The proprietor was very much impressed with his commitment and honesty at work.

Sunny was very happy at the prospect of earning his first wage and even happier about spending it for a very special purpose. His work ended for the day at dusk every day. When he went to bed after his first day at work, he realized how contented he was about being self-dependent. He had never slept better. His job was the same every day, but he performed his job with renewed vigor. His boss had his focus on Sunny, as he wondered about his commitment and his adaptability at such a tender age. Though he had no complaints about the job, every day seemed like eternity to him as he missed Sandy more than ever. He had never imagined how long a single day could stretch. Every day seemed longer than previous day. He counted down days every day, but found that there were still many more to go.

It was the same case with Sandy. She missed Sunny so much. She would walk on the path, which she used to walk with him every day from school. She recalled their conversation and lived in her memories. She laughed to herself, recalling the laughs they'd shared together. She grieved, realizing the bitter truth of separation.

"I wish I could shut my eyes and live in the world of thoughts forever. The world where I would never have to part with him" She would think, whenever she missed him.

The brief separation further strengthened their bond.

By the end of the stipulated employment period, he felt he had already lived uncountable years. He realized how painful his life could be without Sandy. This had compelled him to resolve not to let this happen again for any reason, for any duration. It was not long before he would taste the fruit of his sacrifice. His proprietor called for him at the end of his last day at work.

"I appreciate your honesty and dedication at work. I reckon you would continue to be as good with your education. You could come back to me for any help which would be in my ability. I wish you good luck." he said handing him his wage for his hard work. Sunny received it as if he was presented with the most coveted trophy.

"Thank you so much for trusting me and giving me the opportunity." he said as he excitedly left the lumber depot, proudly turning back to have a glance….

He ran straight to the shop which he visited several times before that.

"Hope you have got it ready today." he said, extracting money out of his pocket as he saw the shop keeper nod in approval.

He walked home so fast that his heels ached. He was so excited that he didn't notice his father sitting in the hall. Neither did his father care. He walked straight to his bed and started dreaming about the next day.

Separation is the most painful test to measure the sustainability of love.

He understood that separation had extended the boundaries of their love beyond imagination, but he knew that he would never dare face it again.

It was inexpressible and immeasurable joy he experienced at the first glance of Sandy after the eons of separation he had experienced. He had never felt so much joy ever in his life. He felt as if he had lived his whole life, died and born again, at the first sight of Sandy.

"I feel like I was dead and was born again." Sandy said in ecstasy.

Sunny was stunned as he heard her speak his thoughts. He kept staring at her for sometime, forgetting everything else.

"I have a gift for you." he told her, unable to hold his excitement.

"What is that?" she asked him.

"Close your eyes." he said with uncontrollable excitement.

She was unable to bear the suspense. She shut her eyes immediately so that she could be relieved of the suspense sooner.

As she was eagerly expecting Sunny to tell her to open her eyes, she felt his hands slightly brush the sides of her neck. She felt a strange tingle at the touch, which made her blush. Then she felt his hands retract.

"May I open my eyes?" she asked with unbearable curiosity.

"You may." He was also as excited as her.

She didn't waste a second after that. She immediately opened her eyes to get a look at her gift. She was stunned at the sight of the gift hanging around her neck. It was a silver chain with a golden pendant in the shape of a glowing sun. Anything that Sunny gave would be a treasure for her, but the one she was gazing at was exquisite.

"This is breathtakingly beautiful." she said as she held his hand still looking at it. She sensed something odd in the grip of his hand. She stopped looking at the gift and pulled his hand towards her. Her heart ached when she spread open his palm. His palm was coarsened by the blisters caused by the grating lumber work. When she got to know the whole story and the reason for his painful disappearance for the whole summer vacation, she brimmed with pride and joy for being blessed with such a wonderful friend.

"This will remind you of me every time you look into the mirror." he told her.

"I remember you every other time too. I don't need any object to remind me of you." she responded.

"Will you keep this as a token of my friendship?" he pleaded.

"This will stay with me… till my end." she promised him in tears of joy, holding his callously beautiful hands.

12:20 AM

"Give me your phone. I need to make a call." Saloni spoke, pulling him out of his memories, yet again.

He stared at her with disgust, hating her request, rather demand.

She stared back for a few seconds and then turned to move away. He didn't want to ask why she wanted the phone and whom she wanted to call. He just threw the phone on the couch. She picked up the phone without looking at him. She moved to the corner of the room and dialed a number.

"Hey. It's me." Saloni said

"Where the fuck are you?" Pooja asked with a sigh of relief.

"Drop that. I need a little help." Saloni replied.

"Don't be so sure. You might need much more than that." Pooja replied sarcastically.

"What are you talking about?" Saloni exclaimed. Her shocked expression invited the attention of Sunny.

"The police inquired about the incident and who were involved in it. It was revealed that the person who instigated the bloody chaos was with you last night and you are missing too. Now, they are looking out for you. Perhaps they need some help from you too." she replied.

"That's wonderful news." Saloni ridiculed her luck.

"Ok... I'll take care of that. Now, tell me. Do you know where Hari is?" Pooja was shocked to hear this from her.

"If you aren't with him, then where are you and what the fuck are you doing?" she asked Saloni.

"I don't have time for that. Tell me if you know where he is?"

"I don't know where he is, but I have some vague information that he fled somewhere."

"Now tell me Sal, what's going on?"

"I'll tell you later. If I can't get out of this soon, you don't forget to visit my mother. Bye for now." Saloni told.

"Sure darling, but stay away from our regular places. The cops are on a hunt and hey..." There was silence for a few seconds.

"Careful." Pooja finally said, sensing something terribly wrong.

"Thanks for the tip." she said as she hung up the call.

Sunny looked at Saloni with curiosity. She walked a few steps towards him and threw him his phone back. Though he was so curious to know what she heard, he hated to ask her for it. He waited for her to speak out as she walked to the window in a deep thought.

"We are in trouble." she spoke out.

Sunny hated the word 'We', even though they were bound together by fate.

"What is the trouble that 'we' are in?" he stressed on 'we'.

Saloni promptly caught the sarcasm.

"I was identified as a witness for the crime and the police are on the lookout." she answered plainly not willing to contest with his sarcasm.

"Great!!! Do we have enough problems yet?" he ridiculed.

"Not yet. They might come here looking for us." she ridiculed back.

"Wonderful. And where does that 'we' come from? Why did I come to you in the first place and why did I get along with you? Despite all the problems I currently have, I have to keep expecting more because of you." he shouted at her.

"Shut up…" she responded.

"I'm not so pleased to use the word *'we'* either. All the havoc was caused because of you. I was identified as a witness for your crime. If the police are looking for me, it's to lead me to you. You get your friend killed because of your whims. You involve people into your crime and blame them for your faults." she growled in fury.

"Shut up, slut..." was all he said with a murderous slap which threw her few feet away from where she stood.

She lay there still trying to regain her composure. She knew that she had provoked him, but she herself had been provoked. This was not something which Saloni intended to forgive. She laid down still, seething in anger at his uncivilized behavior.

Sunny got furious with the accusation of Saloni. What aggravated his temper was that he believed it was true and blamed himself for everything that happened that night. When Saloni blamed him, his guilty conscience stabbed him, which provoked him to hit her. He was straining hard to calm down and think about the situation on hand. He knew that he couldn't afford to lose her help at any cost. Nevertheless he couldn't make up his mind for an apology.

Saloni wanted to slap him back and walk off, but she badly needed the money. She was willing to help him for the money he was about to pay her, whatever may happen. She promised herself never to forgive him. She slowly crawled to lean on the wall beside her. She leaned on the wall breathing hard, trying to digest the ill treatment. She could sense her ears ringing from the slap she had received. When she tried to subside the noise, she felt the volume rising. She couldn't understand that they were police sirens until a few seconds later. Both Sunny and Saloni felt the heat creeping up their nerves. She instantly got to her feet.

"I... am leaving this place. You... can stay here." she said furiously, walking swiftly towards the window, as she switched off the lights of the room.

He understood that it was a response to his sarcasm, as she stressed on 'I' and 'you'.

She walked past him, leaning out through the open window and looked around. He did not understand why she was looking out of the rear window when the cops were approaching the entrance of the hotel. He was shocked when it suddenly struck him what she was up to. She was planning to get down four floors through the rear of the hotel, with the help of chimney pipes and sun shades. The pipes ran beside the sunshade on each floor. She planned to use the pipes to get down each floor resting at the sunshade, as continuously sliding down would be impossible. He couldn't dare think of such a stunt. He was surprised at the ease with which she had thought of this idea. He was literally scared of her guts. He couldn't afford to be left behind by her as he needed her help. Moreover he was sure to be caught if the cops raided the hotel. As he was lost in the thoughts, he saw her disappear through the window. He swiftly moved to the window and looked out to find her valiantly sliding down the pipeline and stepping onto the nearby sunshade of the lower floor. As she stepped on to the sun shade, she looked up to find him staring down, rubbing his nose nervously. She stared at him for a few seconds and then looked for the pipeline to slide further down to the next floor below. As he closed his eyes to gather his concentration and guts to perform the insane stunt, he heard the sirens approach closer and then shut off. He still could not gather enough guts to throw his leg out through the window. He leaned out and looked down to find her sliding down to the first floor.

"Damn gutsy tramp." he thought.

He thought of running through the cops, but he knew that he could not take any chance as it could destroy his mission. He could not stay there any longer, as he was running the risk of getting caught.

Even the fear of getting caught could not inspire him to emulate her feat. He shut his eyes hard and thought why he needed to do the stunt. Images of the brutal night flashed in his mind, which was inspiration enough for him. He took a deep breath and made up his mind. He looked out and saw that Saloni had already climbed down and was standing there waiting for him. He wondered why she was still waiting for him.

"No one with self-dignity would deal with someone who treated them the way I did to her. Cheap souls never mind anything other than money." he thought disgustingly as he hated her more with every second he spent with her.

He threw his leg outside and held the pipeline, supporting his feet at the base of the window. He held the pipe tight, but his nervous grip seemed to deceive him. He just blindly held the pipe and threw his other leg out and slid down to the sunshade. He feared falling off, as he was not able to control the momentum, but luckily he fell steady on the sunshade. He could not stand straight with his shivering legs, as he looked down. He tightly gripped the pipeline as vertigo crept into his mind. He thought of finishing the whole downward journey at one stretch, as he didn't want to experience the terror in installments. He didn't let his mind go on with the debate as he just closed his eyes and jumped off the sunshade sliding down. He could not slide down continuously as the clamps at regular distance obstructed him. He had to shuffle his hands at the clamps. Climbing down at one go, was not as easy as he thought. He kept sliding without looking down, skipping one sunshade. He realized that it was a foolish thing not to use any support. He got off at the next one. He felt as if time was frozen and he was sliding down the pipes forever. He was so desperate to land, as there were two more milestones between him and land. He took off from the next sunshade and held the pipe which shook off the clamp, letting it loose. The pipe started to sway along as he started to slide down carefully, fearing that it would break off. As he looked down calculating the distance he had to slide down further, he noticed Saloni carefully watching him. He wondered what was running through her mind. As he was about to shift his sight back to the pipe, he saw her gaze shifting beyond him. He also noticed a change in her expression. He followed her gaze leading to the room from where they had jumped off, which was flickering with light which was just switched on. He sensed that the cops had finally made it to their room. He started to slide down faster than before and jumped off the pipe when he was fifteen feet from the ground. He fell down rolling along, stopping a few feet away from Saloni. She gave him an unpleasant stare. As he regained his balance and stood on his feet, she pulled him by his arm below the sunshade of the nearest room. He yanked off her grip as he hated her touch. She gave him an obnoxious look, as she peeked towards their room. She stood back stiff and subtle without making any noticeable movement and noise. Someone seemed to have peeked out of the room looking for suspects. He sensed the seriousness and waited for her lead. Saloni carefully bent down and removed her sandals. Sunny got a cue from her act and followed her. She concentrated on the dark road leading to the place where they had parked the car. She thought for a few seconds and made up her mind. She held the sandals in her hand and tip toed towards the place where the car was parked. Sunny followed her, just looking up occasionally to check if they were being watched. He saw someone look out of the window and panicked. He started to run hastily with a thud, which also compelled Saloni to run fast behind him.

They reached the car and jumped in. Everything that had happened to him since he had entered the brothel was happening for the first time in his life. He sat still for sometime, regaining his breath and cursing his fate. Saloni knew that it was not safe to stay there any longer, but she didn't want to engage with him in any conversation. She just kept looking back towards the hotel prompting him that they were at risk. He understood the signal and started the engine. He was glad that the hotel didn't have a parking space, as they would have been easily trapped in that case. His relief was not long lasting, as he heard the sirens again, just as he turned the engine on. He thought that running on a chase was not a good idea. He immediately turned off the engine, switched off the lights and ducked down in the car. The turning on and off of the engine seems to have attracted the cops. Saloni thought it was foolish, but did not utter a word. As the police vehicle approached, he cautiously peeked towards the path careful not to form a silhouette in the windscreen. As he saw the patrol car drive promptly towards them and slow down when it approached them, his heart started to beat like a sledgehammer. He understood his foolishness. As they slowly approached the car, he kept the grip on the key to turn on the engine and crash past them, if necessary. As the police car was about to stop near his, they saw another car recklessly speed across the cross road. The cops set their car on chase behind that car instead. The diversion saved him. The adrenaline rush he was experiencing that night was much more than he could handle. He wondered why Saloni didn't suggest an idea when they were in a very tight spot. It was then he understood that just by paying the money, he couldn't get her complete cooperation. He misread her association with him, despite such an ill treatment as acceptance. She expected to be treated well too. He also wondered how she got that self-respect, despite her profession.

12:45 AM

He drove away immediately as quietly as possible, still fearing that the cops might track them back. As he drove some distance from the hotel, he stopped at an unnoticeable place, unaware where to go further.

"I can get off here. You take your money back and find him by yourself. I have had enough trouble for my life" She couldn't afford to lose the chance to earn the money, yet she told him so, knowing that he needed her support. Sunny was in a tight spot, as he neither could afford to let her go nor plead her for help.

"I will pay you rest of the amount soon." he said hitting the wrong spot again, though he hinted her to stay with him.

She hated his rudeness, but she understood that she couldn't squeeze courtesy out of him. Clenching her teeth, she sat staring out the window, waiting for him to proceed. She knew that she only could guide him, but still, decided to give him a hard time. She stayed silent without a word.

"He has to ask for what he wants." she thought to herself.

TRACING THE KILLER

Sunny kept driving aimlessly without a sense of direction, still waiting for directions from Saloni. Both kept silent without a word for quite some time. Sunny stopped the car at a lonely place. He knew that she had to lead the way. He expected her to volunteer, but her silence explained him that he had to ask for it.

"Where to?" He broke the silence.

Saloni looked at him for a couple of moments and turned away from him, realizing that they were sailing on the mid sea without a compass. She thought for few seconds. He was not patient enough to wait till she spoke out.

"Do I have any directions to drive?" he asked ridiculously.

1:00 AM

"Where are you taking me?" Hari impatiently questioned the driver.

"Err... I don't know." he responded.

"What the fuck is that? You don't know where you are taking me?" Hari growled, scaring the driver.

"I… I was only supposed to transport you to another vehicle at the highway junction before the next toll gate, which is one hour from here." he answered calmly, expecting the conversation to end with that. And it did.

Hari didn't pose any more questions. He only kept pouring profanities at Victor for dealing so clumsily with him. It did not take long before reaching his next transport, which was a three wheeler milk van with a single seat.

"Yes man… I've got him. Yes… Yes." The van driver was speaking to someone as he saw Hari's vehicle stop behind his van.

"What the fuck is this?" Hari growled to himself as he hated his next transport even more.

"Who the fuck were you talking to?" he shouted at the driver as he disconnected the call.

The puzzled driver did not understand at once that it was him he was talking to.

"Talking to me?" he asked.

"Who else is fucking behind you?" he growled with uncontrollable fury.

"Well…" The driver didn't know how to react.

"It was the one who is supposed to receive you." he reluctantly revealed.

"Give me his number." he asked the driver, who was scared to deny.

Hari immediately called the number from his mobile as he didn't like to be blindly led by someone.

"Hello…" the person answered.

"Where the fuck am I getting transported to?" Hari asked sarcastically.

"You will know it in few hours." the person coolly told.

"I know that I'll know. I called you to know it now… Just now…" Hari screamed like mad.

"I'm sorry… I'm not permitted to talk. Please let the driver lead you here." the person said and disconnected the call, though he didn't know why he was instructed to be so deliberately rude with him.

1:00 AM

Saloni called a number from the dialed list.

"Is Victor around in the town?" Saloni asked Pooja without any preamble.

"I don't understand what the fuck you are up to." Pooja replied, worried.

"Is he there?" she persisted.

"Yes. What now?" Pooja asked.

"Use your charm on him this once for me and find out where he hid Hari." Saloni asked, which worried Pooja.

"I thought you are already in enough trouble. You seem to be looking for more, honey." Pooja spoke with genuine concern.

"Cut the crap darling. Please…" Saloni told with a hint of urgency.

Pooja sensed her urgency and interjected "Don't tell me you are in trouble now."

"Cops came hunting for us to the hotel. We just slipped out of their mouth." Saloni told.

"What…! You still seem to be starving for more adventure, baby. Now get the hell out of there, will you?" Pooja shouted.

"Don't know where to go, dear. The cops seem to be everywhere."

"Listen sweetheart. The person you are with seems to be dangerous. Be careful with him and do as I say." Pooja instructed on Saloni's further course.

Saloni stared at Sunny suspiciously for a few seconds and concentrated back on the call, which confused him.

"Ok…I'll do it." Saloni said as she disconnected the call.

"What now?" Sunny queried.

"Drive to your right." Saloni said handing over his phone back.

Sunny followed her directions through a beaten road. He wondered if she was walking him into a trap. He had no other option than to trust her. And he did. There were neither street lights nor any traffic. He had to rely on his car head lights to illuminate the path. It was a rough ride through an almost uninhabited land. He did not know where he was driving to as it was a pitch dark night.

"Would you throw some light on where I'm driving to?" Sunny asked sarcastically.

Saloni just gave an expressionless look for a few seconds and turned away from him.

1:05 AM

Pooja knew that Victor was a ruthless beast. Hari had not only caused a lot of damage to Victor's business, but severely marred his peace of mind with a reckless ruckus. Victor was boiling in rage because his business was put on hold. Worse was that he didn't know whether it was a temporary one. His business had always invited trouble from all quarters, especially the police for the disturbing impact it had on the neighborhood, as he did not involve only in prostitution, but also drugs, duplicate liquor and various other illegal activities. Victor always used to grudge that Hari was a liability to the business with his impulsive nature, but never expected such a fiasco.

Pooja feared she would have a nervous breakdown, when she imagined baiting Victor for information. She knew that Victor would love to get Hari killed, but she could not gather enough courage to meddle with his affairs. Though Pooja enjoyed maximum liberty, he didn't encourage her intrusion into his business.

"What the fuck are you getting me into?" Pooja cursed Saloni.

Pooja knew that she would do anything for Saloni.

She thought for a long time.

"I have to do it for Sal." Pooja resolved.

She then took her mobile phone and dialed a number. She didn't have to wait for long, as she heard the click of the call immediately.

"What the fuck is it with you?" Victor shot his words out reflecting his eruptive mood.

"I feel so relieved to hear your voice. The cops have been pestering me with threatening questions. I awfully miss you. Can we be company tonig…"

"Shut the fuck up and stop fucking with me." Victor grumbled as he slapped the call off. Pooja felt her heartbeat stop for a few seconds, after which she felt her heart hammer against her rib cage at express speed.

"Sorry darling, I did all I could do." Pooja thought as she was regaining her breath.

She felt the mild ringing of her phone like a thunder. The display showed the number she'd called a few seconds ago, which pushed her heart to her throat. She swallowed it back and picked the call.

"Wait for me in my apartment." That was all she heard before the call got disconnected.

She didn't know whether to be anxious or excited, but she had to do what she had to do. She knew she had to be careful handling him, as he was in a volcanic mood. Pooja immediately moved to Victor's apartment.

1:20 AM

She waited in Victor's bedroom for some time, which seemed like eternity. She had never been so afraid in her life. She suppressed her fear and concentrated on her task. She was drafting and redrafting her dialogues to squeeze out information from Victor. She however wondered how this information could be so vital for Saloni. She would know it soon. She only trusted that Saloni would not do anything foolish. As she was lost in her thoughts, she heard footsteps rattle the silence of the night. She shuffled and shifted on the bed, wishing she had some more time to prepare herself to face him, with her plan better drafted. She saw the door crash open and Victor barge into the room like a vicious, wounded animal.

"I'll rip your skin off, if you screw with this." Victor growled at one of his hoodlums and then disconnected the call through his Bluetooth headset and walked past Pooja. He didn't care to acknowledge her presence. He seemed to be quite drunk already. He threw the headset on the bedside table, tore his shirt off in fury and yanked his shoes off which flew across the room. He gave a brief angry glare towards her and plopped himself on the bed and took a deep breath.

"What the fuck are you waiting for? Make a drink for me." he commanded.

"Strong." he said and fell on the bed, staring at the ceiling.

Pooja walked towards the mini bar set up in the corner of the bedroom and poured a strong shot of whisky as he would always prefer. She heaved a sigh of relief as she was mixing his drink, as it was not as bad as she had expected, at least not yet. She carefully carried the drinks tray and walked to him.

"This would make you feel better." she said as she handed him the drink.

Victor snatched the drink from her hand, spilling some on the bed and rest into his throat. Pooja was so eagerly expecting him to finish it, so she could pour him another. She was so desperate to get him drunk, retrieve the information, set him to sleep and quit the place as soon as possible. As Victor finished his glass of drink, she carefully took the empty glass from him and made another drink, stronger than the previous one and handed it to him. She was struggling to make a start, as her plan had collapsed as soon as she saw him.

"Where the fuck is Saloni? Who is she fucking with now?" Victor asked as he gulped the next round of drink. Pooja was relieved that she didn't have to take the trouble of starting the conversation.

"She should have stuck along with Hari." She baited Victor.

"She's not with him. She didn't carry her fucking mobile with her. I don't want that bitch to be caught in anyone's sight, until the issues get settled." Victor grumbled.

Pooja was not happy to persist, but she was not lucky this time. She had to make another try.

"Sure. I would warn her, when she gets in touch with me. I was thinking that she fled the spot with Hari." She tried the bait again.

Victor did not care to respond. Pooja understood that she had to toil for the information. She decided that she had to be more persuasive and direct. She retrieved the empty glass from him and poured another drink, strongest this time.

"Hope Hari does not fall into the cops hands." Pooja handed the drink to him as she spoke, unsure whether she should have.

Victor turned violent, shouting "Son of a mongrel…" as he quaffed down the third shot also in a hurry and threw the empty glass at her face, which she caught in reflex, saving an injury. She gave a mute sigh of relief. She realized that it was getting tougher. She poured another drink and moved closer to him with all her courage gathered.

"Are you trying to get me drunk, bitch?" he shouted, which terrified Pooja.

"Thought this could sooth you down" She tried not to stammer as Victor snatched the drink off her hand and gulped the last one too.

She knew that Victor was not the one to fall for flattery. She somehow had to get the words out of his mouth. She waited for the drink to have its effect, but found no hope.

"The cops are hounding for Hari like wild dogs. He better be safe somewhere, for your sake darling."

Pooja made a futile attempt. She knew it the instant she spoke as Victor slapped her hard and fired back saying "Mind your fucking business. Now… get yourself fucking useful. Get undressed."

The slap was so hard that she was dazed for a few seconds. She was beginning to lose hope, as she got undressed. She joined him on the couch nude. She noticed that to her favor, Hari was getting into Victor's head, driving him crazy. Victor suddenly started to blabber which was a rare sight.

"Let the police noise come down, I will cut you into pieces while you are still alive, son of a mongrel." Victor screamed as he threw the glass, which shattered on the floor.

"Why don't you kill him now?" Pooja asked hesitantly, despite the slap she had received.

"I do not want him through this so quickly. His death should be a deadly warning to whoever fucks with my business." Victor barked.

"I believe the cops will take care of him." Pooja said as she kept kissing his chest and proceeding towards his groin, gradually undoing his trousers.

"Nobody can touch him until I'm ready to relish slicing him into pieces and feed him to the fish." Victor blabbered in an inebriated tone.

"Where is he right now?" Pooja asked cautiously and rightly faced the ire of Victor.

"Don't you dare intrude into my business, bitch." he screamed.

Pooja immediately took his organ in her mouth. Victor groaned at the sudden assault and gradually calmed down. He started to snore in a few minutes. She knew that she had been lucky that despite confronting him in such an explosive mood, she had escaped with just a slap, though it hurt her jaw like hell.

1:30 AM

"The son of a bitch is deliberately causing inconvenience to me." Hari mumbled to himself, as he climbed onto the carriage filled with milk cans and squatted in the corner, hiding behind the cans. He didn't know where he was going, as the milk cans blocked his view. Also the dark hour of the night made it difficult for him to figure out where he was being led. His only thought was to escape from the cops. He tried to keep awake so that he could be alert to situations, but his tired body gave up to the soporific breeze and he fell asleep instantly.

4:30 AM

Hari was unaware that he had travelled for around three hours as his sleep had enabled him to forget the discomfort of the milk van. He was harshly woken by the cans crashing on to him, caused by the sudden stop of the vehicle. He woke up to find that it was still dark. He blinked his eyes few times in the moonlight and saw to his horror that his ordeal hadn't ended. He jumped out of the van and stared at the charred structure in the background of the dark sky, with bright full moon and the gray clouds passing over it like smoke blown in gentle winds.

"Son of a bitch… He didn't seem to end his sadistic jokes on me." Hari cursed Victor.

The building had been devoid of human habitation for a really long time. It stood isolated, with not a brick of construction within its proximity. The building, which was once a movie theatre, was rumored to have been haunted by the souls of the dead, who had died in the incinerating fire, which had spared none in it. No one dared to approach it since then.

"Why do you dare get into that building? I would never do that." The driver spoke out of curiosity.

"What's wrong it?" Hari asked impatiently.

"It's believed that the building is haunted by hundreds of souls, which were victims of a fire accident a decade ago." the driver said.

Just as he was staring at the demonic building, he saw a boy approach them on a bicycle, smoking a cigarette. He seemed to be in his late teen. He was a lean boy of average height.

"There comes your guy. His name is Bhuvan. He'll take care of you." said the driver as he zoomed away in his van, waving at Bhuvan as he went past him.

"What the fuck…! A boy is going to take care of me?" he shouted to himself.

The boy heard it and instantly hated the guy. He parked the bicycle behind a wall and walked towards Hari.

"Can't you find a better place than this? Human can't survive in this place." Hari complained about the building.

"That's the point." Bhuvan told without realizing what it would mean to Hari.

"What the fuck did you mean? You, son of a bitch... How dare you say I'm not human?" Hari grunted as he held the boy savagely by his collar.

"I didn't mean that. I actually meant that this would be the least sought place and hence most secure place for that reason." he reasoned immediately.

"No wonder Victor prescribed inhuman treatment to him. He is not worthy to be treated humane." he convinced himself.

"This would be your shelter for a day or two. We move to a better place in Portshore, once the police noise comes down." he explained, though he didn't know if it would be better or worse.

"I better get away from him as soon as possible... filthy animal he is." Bhuvan thought to himself.

"Let's get inside before someone sees you." Bhuvan advised him.

"What the fuck? Do you command me, you half grown bum?" Hari growled.

Bhuvan was no more shocked by his rudeness, but hated him more.

"How could he have ever co-existed with anyone?" he wondered.

He convinced himself that he was only carrying out the order of Victor, and would get rid of him the very next instant he got further instruction.

"What the fuck are you staring at? Move your ass now." he shouted at Bhuvan, who led him to the entrance.

Hari was shocked just as he entered the serpentine entrance. He suddenly turned blind. He could only hear continuous chirping of the crickets. As he walked a few steps, he tripped onto a charred concrete block and fell on his face with a crackling sound that resounded throughout the building in a fearsome echo.

"I'll kill you… son of a bitch…" he screamed referring to Victor.

"I'll kill you… son of a bitch…I'll kill you… son of a bitch …" It was the echo, which repeated the same to him, horrifying him. He felt as if it was spoken by some hidden enemy. He felt something scary about the building, as he recalled the van driver's words about the building. As he got up and walked a few steps, he again stumbled upon a few more blocks.

"Stay calm and get up slowly." instructed Bhuvan.

Hari listened to Bhuvan this time. He slowly got up and switched on his mobile phone torch which lit their path. He noticed Bhuvan walk towards the stairs. Hari followed him, grudgingly.

"The stairs are in pretty bad condition… So be careful as you walk on them." Bhuvan warned him.

"Yes master." Hari ridiculed him so despicably.

Bhuvan didn't expect anything better from him. He ignored his attitude and walked ahead casually. When he reached the open floor without any parapet wall, he looked back at Hari, who was far behind. As Hari walked up the stairs, the whole building shook with an eerie rattling sound which scared him so much that he tripped again on the stairs. He couldn't help but recall the words of the driver, again.

Hari was lucky that he was still holding his phone. He got up and steadied himself. Swallowing the lump in his throat, he put up a brave face to preserve his pride in front of the boy who didn't even budge. He walked in the light of his mobile torch and joined Bhuvan. It took him a couple of minutes to climb the stairs which was done in few seconds by the boy, who then led him into a room which used to be the operator's room during its days. Hari looked pale in fear coupled with discomfort.

"Make yourself comfortable." Bhuvan said and immediately realized his mistake.

"Comfortable??? Are you kidding me? Get me a fucking drink and a pack of cigarettes." Hari shouted.

"Drink…! At this hour of the day?" This only further proved his despicable nature.

"Fucking rotten day…" Bhuvan walked out, cursing his day.

He got him a couple of bottles of brandy and a pack of cigarettes from the stock they maintained.

"Do you drink?" he asked the boy, who replied in negative as he didn't want to have any cordial affair with him, although he loved to have a drink.

Hari poured himself a drink and gulped it down his throat. He hated hiding in burrows, escaping from the cops. He lit a cigarette and took a deep drag of smoke and blew it out, filling the room with smoke. The boy was never entertained by his savage behavior. He had been looking for a chance to escape his company since they met.

"I'll get you something to eat." Bhuvan said, desperate to find a reason to escape from him.

Hari stared at him with contempt for a few seconds and then replied "You think it's time to eat?"

"Neither is it time to drink." Bhuvan thought, though he knew that it was a bad excuse. He sat in silent suffocation for half an hour, helplessly watching him empty the bottle and intoxication take control over him.

5:00 AM

"Son of a bitch… Wish I could impale your ass on a skewer." Hari spoke to himself. It was evident that it was about Victor.

Hari immediately retrieved his phone to make a call to him and then realized that his phone had gotten switched off as the battery got drained.

"Damn it…" he shouted in frustration. Bhuvan understood the situation and decided to seize the opportunity.

"I can get your phone charged." he offered.

Hari stared at him for a few seconds.

"Take it…" he said, fetching relief for Bhuvan.

"I'll have your phone for the meantime."

Bhuvan didn't like giving his phone to him, but he couldn't get a better opportunity. Hence he immediately removed his sim card and gave his phone to him. Once they exchanged the sim cards on their phones, Bhuvan was eager to leave the place.

Just as Hari switched on the phone, he heard the phone ringing, scaring him with the unexpected sound tearing the silence of the night.

"Wait." Hari said, not willing to lose his company, as he sensed an inexplicable fear of impending doom.

"Pour me a drink." he ordered, snatching away Bhuvan's momentary pleasure.

"Yes...?" He replied in a gruff voice as he picked the call.

5:00 AM

They finally reached their destination through a rough ride. Sunny spotted an old house at a distance in the direction of Saloni's sight.

"Is he here?" he asked suspiciously.

"No"

"Then, where the hell is he? Are you playing games with me?" he shouted impatiently.

Saloni stared at him angrily for a few seconds.

"Give me your phone." she demanded him.

He threw his phone on the dashboard before her which she picked up and thought for a few seconds. She took a deep breath, indicating that she'd made a decision to carry out her plan.

She then changed the setting in the phone, deactivating the Caller Line Identification which restricts receiver, the display of the calling number. The receiver would only get 'no number' on his display.

He was silently observing all her activities and was stunned by her knowledge and rapid action capability. She tuned the radio on the car's music system to a blaring wrong frequency and set the volume to maximum. When she was satisfied with the irritating cacophony on the radio, she called Hari.

"The number you are calling is currently switched off." The IVR voice spoke.

"Damn it… He can't switch off his phone now." she shouted out of frustration.

Saloni tried calling again.

"What's the use of calling a phone that is switched off? Isn't it foolish?" he ridiculed her.

She didn't mind his words. She called again and again cursing her fate. She almost lost hope.

"I believe there is no good news yet." Sunny asked sarcastically.

She didn't respond to him this time either. She thought for a long time and decided to make one last try before thinking of another plan. She called the number with least hope, but to her relief, she heard the ringing tone. She prayed for the call to be answered.

"Yes…?" she heard a gruff voice after a short ringing. Hari received the call just as he switched on the phone which he had borrowed from Bhuvan. She kept the phone on speaker mode at the roaring radio and stared at Sunny for a few seconds as if asking him who was foolish. Sunny bowed his head down in shame.

"Who the fuck is this? Speak out, son of a bitch." Hari screamed. She listened to the call without any expression on her face and disconnected it after some screaming from Hari.

Hari wouldn't be able to call back as the number wouldn't be displayed on his phone. She sat there with her eyes shut, thinking about the best way to execute her plan. She believed that Hari would be in a place where there would be better network coverage, waiting for the call again to confirm who the caller was. Her mind was working in a flash. Sunny was wondering what she was up to. He was often hailed in his office as the sharpest computer programmer with impeccable logic, but what Saloni was doing, seemed to be beyond his intellectual level to comprehend.

She called Victor's number and followed the same procedure. She had to act fast before any one of them got busy on another call by any rotten chance. She didn't want to be waiting on another call, which could spoil her chance. It was common that sometimes the network blocks the caller line identification due to network issues. She decided to thrive on that point, but still didn't want to take chances. She then shut the radio and called Hari. This time he picked the call immediately. She did not waste time in calling Victor, putting Hari on hold. She feared he might disconnect the call if Victor delayed picking the call. To her delight, she instantly heard the click on the phone which indicated the call being connected. She immediately put the call on conference and muted the phone. At the same time she put the call on speaker. She knew that it was not a fool proof plan, but this time she had to dwell on her luck too. It was the best chance she had at that point. Sunny was only blankly observing what Saloni was doing. He wondered if all that was a joke.

"Yes... Hello..." Hari shouted on the call.

"Hello... why don't you speak up...?" Hari growled, but his voice was interfered by a thundering voice.

"Mother fucking mongrel... How many times should I call to reach you?" Saloni could make out Victor's voice on the other end. Victor was probably trying to reach him when Hari was out of network.

"I could get nothing better than that, in the cave you have put me in." he replied back.

"Can't find a better place for a troglodyte..." Victor ridiculed. He was the one who had deliberately devised the torturous treatment to him.

"How long do you expect me to rot here?" Hari replied.

"Well... It's your funeral." Victor shot back.

"It might as well be your funeral, if you don't have me well placed." Hari dared warning Victor, which was an utter mistake, only a fool like him would do.

"You filthy son of a mongrel... Stop fucking warning me and stay on your ground, or else I can very well have you placed beneath it." Victor said as he grunted through a deep breath, trying hard to suppress his fury.

Saloni shuddered as she visualized the menacing expression of Victor.

"I wan..." Hari started to say something.

"And get this into your shit head... Keep your voice down until the shit you have scattered here is cleaned up." Victor interrupted without hiding his irritation.

"Remember... I will talk only with that kid hereafter." he announced.

Hari stared at the boy who was mixing his drink, wondering how he was not bothered by the ominous atmosphere.

"This place is like shit. I wan..."

"Just shut the fuck up and stay where you are. And remember you, stinking asshole...Don't make any calls from your number anymore. Switch off your fucking phone." Victor warned him.

Then there was sound of a click. Saloni understood that Victor had disconnected the call.

"Fuck you… son of a bitch." Hari grumbled at the disconnected call, not having the guts to speak it up to him.

"I believe he didn't stop making trouble. Did he?" Victor's consigliere, David guessed as he ended the call.

They had an early morning meeting in Victor's apartment.

"Well… What can we expect from a mother fucker like him?" Victor screamed.

The loud scream of Victor woke up Pooja, who was sleeping nude on his bed.

"Having a fool as an accomplice is more dangerous than having hundred clever enemies. Didn't I warn you?" he reminded Victor.

"Now, I suggest you get him killed immediately?" he advised.

"Oh dear… Do you think that I need persuasion to get rid of him?"

"I would be fucking delighted." He mimicked a caricature of delightful expression.

"Let the uniforms calm down and then I'll chop him down to pieces and feed him to the Portshore fish." *Uniform* was one of the slang words they used for cops.

"Today is my lucky day." Saloni thought with a sigh of relief.

"Did you find where the bastard is hiding?" Sunny asked with unbearable curiosity.

Saloni just nodded in negative. He was visibly frustrated, but Saloni was not heartbroken. Though she had not gotten what she had wanted from the call, it wasn't a futile attempt. She knew that Victor was hiding him. She had to plan the next step to find out his location. She shut her eyes, drafting the next step. Sunny was reading Saloni's expressions, as if he was reading Greek. By now, he was convinced that she was an intelligent girl, but he didn't trust her for her materialistic desperation, so much that she was ready to dump her associate for money.

He drove according to Saloni's directions, eagerly expecting her next move.

"We stay there for a few hours." Saloni pointed to a house he had already seen.

"I hope I don't meet any more of their filthy companions." he prayed.

"Maybe another business centre for them." he bitterly thought.

"Switch off the headlights and drive to that house." She prompted him to the empty space behind the house. As he was driving towards the house, she removed the scarf which she had tied around her wrist with money. She then picked out 5,000 rupees from the bundle.

"Can you keep this with you till we leave the house?" she asked him handing him the remaining money. He thought for a few seconds and took it suspiciously from her hand, still staring at her.

"Wait here." she said as she neatly arranged her scarf over her shoulders covering her cleavage, rather fashionably. She then got out of the car and walked towards the entrance.

Hari slowly sipped his drink, hesitant to start a conversation, but was reluctant to lose his company. Bhuvan was desperate to get out of the place, but couldn't muster enough courage to declare it. They sat in silence, listening to the chirping of the crickets and the occasional rustling sounds created by the pests and reptiles which inhabited the ruined building.

5:15 AM

"Please make yourself comfortable." Saloni said rather politely, showing him a bed and walked out of the room. He sensed something fishy. He waited until she left and then dropped onto the bed as quietly as possible. He wondered where she had led him and where she went leaving him there. He switched off the light to let the darkness swallow the room. He kept thinking of the events of the day and the suspicious behavior of the girl, but his tired mind was getting defeated by his sleep.

As his eyelids gradually draped his eyes, he sensed footsteps approach him. He gathered the focus of all his senses to his ears and listened very cautiously. The sound of the footsteps seemed to approach him. He gently opened his eyes and looked around to found nothing but darkness. He concentrated hard. He silently searched for the light switch with subtle movement of his hands, careful not to attract the attention of the intruder, but was not successful enough to hit the switch. He saw a silhouette of a person slowly approach him across the window and stop there. He kept a cautious watch on the movement of the silhouette which seemed to have frozen at the same position for quite a long time. Unable to comprehend the purpose of the man standing idle, he wondered whether he was just scaring him with the anticipation of what harm he might inflict on him. The situation was even more threatening than the one where he fought against people armed with knives and rods. His body temperature began to rise. He thought of making the first strike, but he was not sure if there was only one person.

"If there were more than one person, why would they waste so much time standing still? They could have attacked me with brute force." he thought.

"They are probably careful not to attract the neighbors." he clarified himself.

After sometime, he sensed a slight movement of the silhouette. When he sat up to be prepared for the attack from the man, he suddenly felt his neck strangled from behind. As he struggled to free himself throwing his hands and legs, his hand accidentally flicked the light switch and he saw Saloni's face with a cunning smile.

"I should've known." He cursed himself.

She held a wire wound around his neck tightly, suffocating him. As he was gasping for breath, he shifted his sight towards the silhouette and got an unrecoverable shock. It was Hari with a devilish grin. He immediately got hold of Sunny's legs.

Sunny's thinking sense was deteriorating, but he still attempted to understand what was happening. He tried to set the pieces in place.

"So... It was their plan. She, along with Hari had been planning to kill me using my own phone for their planning purpose. It was a trap all along." he bitterly thought.

His vision was veiled with a film of blood. As he was drifting away from life, the face of Imran appeared before him which instilled a new wave of energy in him. He freed his legs with a violent yank and kicked Hari with both his feet and pulled the wire off his neck and rolled off the bed.

9:05 AM

As he fell off the bed, he got up in panic. He looked around in confusion as he found no one and the room was not dark anymore. The clock denoted that he had slept for nearly 4 hours. He was sweating like hell. Much to his relief, he realized it was a dream. He however suspected it could be a premonition. He was not able to move his arms and legs for a few minutes, as he lay paralyzed on the floor for some time. He gradually regained his mobility. As he returned to normalcy, he debated whether he should walk out for fresh air or stay in the room till he knew he was safe out. He was not prepared to face any more surprises, but he felt suffocated in the room that he wanted to break free. He decided to take a walk out whatsoever. He stood up, dusted his trousers and walked cautiously out of the room. What he saw surely surprised him. He expected this to be a den of some of her associates, but what he saw was unexpected. An old woman was staring at him with a twisted mouth, probably from a paralysis attack. He was not able to make out whether she was pleased or annoyed by his presence. He scanned the room and found another person lying on the bed, probably in deep sleep. There was a wheelchair beside the bed. Saloni was missing. Then he shifted his sight back to the paralyzed lady. He noticed that the old lady was still staring at him, frantically swinging her deformed hand outwards, supporting her good hand to lift her up. She was shouting something in a muffled voice, as she was trying to get off the bed. He understood that she was asking him to get out. It was his misunderstanding. She was only calling Saloni, who came in running towards her and feigned a smile at him. He noticed a mobile phone in her hand, which seemed to have a call, still intact. "Call you later, baby." she said as she disconnected the call.

She then turned to him and said "Good morning sir." as she set the old lady comfortably on bed, which puzzled him.

He observed that she had taken her chiffon coat off, exposing her arms. A green patch on her left arm attracted him. It was the tattoo of a sun.

It took him back to the school days when he used to find his books filled with the sketch of sun adjacent to his name.

"What's this Sandy candy?"

"Well… It's your logo."

"Logo!!!"

He could still feel the excitement he had then. He recalled his sweet memory, still staring at her.

Saloni still kept the smile on, as she pleaded him with her eyes to cooperate.

"Good morning." he replied, still sounding rather rude.

"Boss is in bad mood as the business trip was troubled by headlight failure." she explained them.

"I told them about our trip to expand our business boundary, sir." she told him, gesturing him with her eyes, signaling him to comply with her story.

"Aah… huh… ya." he replied half-heartedly, hating to play along with her.

He suddenly witnessed the man lying on the bed creep upwards with difficulty with the support of his elbows until he was able to lean his back on the headboard of the old battered bed. Saloni rushed to his help, before which the sheet covering his limbs got discarded. It exposed his amputated legs. He brought his hand close to his chest and bowed down gently to him, with his eyes tear filled. Sunny understood that he was thanking him, but didn't know why. He bowed slightly in return.

He involuntarily walked towards the man who seemed to bear all the world's sorrow in his eyes. The man seemed to be struggling to pull some words out of his mouth. As Sunny approached him, he held his hands and began to cry.

"I… I…" He tried to get the words out of his choked throat.

"I can't thank you enough for all the support you have given to my little child." He managed to speak out vaguely.

"You need to calm down papa." Saloni soothed him down.

He was totally dazed with all the senseless events and weird people.

Saloni fed them and gave them medicine as she relieved the maid for the morning. They denied the breakfast offer on Sunny's insistence as they were chasing time.

"Papa… Take care of mama. I'll visit you some other day." she told, as she kissed them on their forehead. She walked out of the house, curious to resume their mission.

Sunny drifted back to his usual state of confusion, trying to differentiate hallucinations from reality.

9:20 AM

Victor wanted the boy to stay with Hari all the time. The boy, although didn't have the guts to defy Victor's orders, he felt suffocated in his presence. It was more difficult than he expected.

"Want something to eat?" Bhuvan asked searching for an opportunity to get rid of him.

"No." Hari replied without even looking at him.

Bhuvan thought for some time. "Shall I get your phone charged?" he sought a different excuse.

Hari stared at him for a few seconds and then said, "Fuck off." to his relief.

He didn't waste a second, as he scurried off the place.

Hari was never a social being, but the circumstance was different. Though he would deny, he was definitely terrified of the ominous atmosphere. He suddenly felt so lonely that he was dying to have company for the first time in his life. He retrieved his phone and checked for the recently called numbers to find the boy's number. It was then he realized that the call history got cleared when he switched the phones.

"Fuck it…" he screamed as his words echoed back to him from all over the place in a ghostly tone. He never wanted anyone's company so bad ever before.

"Come soon, son of a bitch." Hari screamed, within himself this time.

Though he was gripped with fear, his inebriated state helped him fall asleep.

MUTUAL HATRED

9:30 AM

"Now…Where do we find him?" Sunny asked her as he got into the car at the driving wheel beside her.

"Drive to Portshore." she said, leaning back on her seat, drifting into deep thoughts.

Portshore was a picturesque coastal town which ran along the breathtakingly beautiful beaches of the east coast, which was five hours drive from their current location. The name struck nostalgia in him. The beautiful town offered him a few beautiful childhood memories, but he wasn't sure if he had heard it right.

"Are you sure?" he asked doubtful about her confidence, as he didn't have a clue about how she knew it.

She just nodded in approval, trusting the information she received on her call that morning with Pooja.

"Are you…"

"You must trust me. Why would I fool you when you are paying me sufficiently?" Saloni interrupted his probe.

"Give me my money back?" she demanded him.

He gave her an obnoxious stare and dropped the money on the dashboard in front of her.

"Now drive." she said, as she tied the money in the scarf around her wrist as she did earlier.

They silently drove along the highway. He was really getting suffocated being in the same car with her. She pushed herself up from the sloping seat and switched on the music. He felt like slapping her. She kept changing the channels until she found some melodious music.

He took a deep breath trying to control his anger. He pressed the accelerator hard.

"I can't take it anymore." he thought as he pulled the car by a shop.

He opened the door and walked to the shop to get cigarettes.

"Give me a pack of cigarettes." he asked the shopkeeper as he gave him a hundred rupee note, but the shopkeeper was looking beyond him, which puzzled him.

"Where is he looking at?" he thought as he followed his sight which led to Saloni. She was wearing a provocative dress, which embarrassed him.

"Give me a pack of cigarettes." he shouted which shook the shopkeeper off his trance and also drew Saloni's attention.

She looked at the encounter and just shrugged casually and turned back closing her eyes, enjoying the music.

The shopkeeper hurried to get him his pack of cigarettes which he snatched from him, stuffing the hundred rupees note in his hand and didn't mind to get the change.

He resumed his drive for a few kilometers and stopped sideways at an empty spot and got out of the car. There was no reaction from her. He went to a huge tree on the sideway and sat beneath it. He leaned back and closed his eyes, trying to heal himself from the excruciating mental injury, but it did otherwise.

He feared closing his eyes because the gory images kept flashing in his mind. Then again he did so as to add fuel to his vengeance as he didn't wish to forget nor forgive the brutal killer. After a couple of minutes, he opened his eyes as he was unable to bear the heat of the thoughts and looked inside the car. She was still enjoying the music. He frowned at her indifference to such a brutal slaughter.

"These women do not mind earning money over dead bodies." he thought bitterly.

He took out a cigarette and lit it. He drew the smoke deep inside, closing his eyes and released it slowly. He never earlier thought he could yell at someone, but he was longing to kill a person with all his heart. As he was lost in deep thoughts, she got out of the car and walked towards him.

"Maybe she is coming to me for cigarettes." he thought as he offered her a cigarette, before she said anything, as he hated to hear her talk. She gave a puzzled look, without picking one. He didn't want to talk to her too. So he just took it back.

"Give me your phone. I need to make a call." she asked in a tone which was rather authoritative.

He threw the phone to her which she deftly caught and walked away from him. She called the number which she had already dialed on the phone. Strolling along the road, she waited for response.

"Hey Pooja, it's me again."

The rumbling of the thunder warned him to get moving. It looked as if the sky was ready to pour through the ominously dark clouds. He saw her walking towards him with the phone in her hand.

He wondered whom she might have called.

"Should be one of her customers." he thought.

"I do not like any filthy business to happening on my phone." he thought scornfully.

"It's only a personal call." she explained as she looked into his eyes, handing over his phone back. She had deep mesmerizing eyes.

"Did she hear my mind?" He was stunned at her intelligence and mindreading ability. He hated appreciating her, but it was a fact.

He snatched the phone from her and dropped it in his pocket.

Cold wind started to blow as if it could freeze them where they stood. He had his jacket on, so he didn't know feel it that much. Saloni wrapped her hands across her chest and started rubbing her palms against her exposed arms. He ignored her inconvenience as he walked past her and opened the door loudly, prompting her to get in. She ran to the car as the wind was growing wilder. She opened the door and jumped into the car to escape the brutal assault of the freezing wind. She sank in the front seat which did not help her as the AC was on. He switched off the AC, not for her convenience, but for his. It still didn't help her. She rubbed her palms to generate heat, not sufficient though.

He didn't mind her. Even he was feeling slightly cold with his leather jacket still on.

"Am I brutal to her who is out to help me?

Nonsense... She is only after money, not to help me...

Whatever, she is a girl in trouble...

She does not deserve sympathy with her arrogant attitude and cunning motives."

He argued within himself, careful that his positive inner voice would not succeed. He feared it would. He abruptly stopped thinking about it. The reason for his hostility was that he didn't want to establish friendship with her by showing soft corner.

Neither did she expect any help from him, nor complained for the lack of help.

"She is a proud girl for a prostitute." he thought.

She seemed like an odd fit in her profession with her pride and dignity that he sometimes couldn't stop appreciating her. He shook himself from his thoughts.

"I hate her... I hate her... I hate her." he reminded himself.

"Is that because I am in a vengeful mood that it has filled my entire mind?"

"No... I hated her arrogance, her attitude and her profession primarily. What a cheap person without morals should she have been to sell her body for money?" he thought.

She sat sideways away from him wrapping her hands tightly not only for heat, but also to hide her shivering. He consciously kept his attention away from her as he thought it was just a matter of time when he would get rid of her, forever. When he was driving steadily towards his destination with deep thoughts, the sound of pattering rain attracted him. The magical melody carried him back to his blissful past.

It was a winter evening. The school had rung the closing bell. All the students started to leave with their umbrellas spread open or raincoats to shelter them from the rain. The pattering sound of the persistent rain on the thatched roof of the classroom was enticing. As Sandy looked admiringly through the wooden grilled windows at the beautiful rain inviting her, she noticed that Sunny was looking at her with amazement. Her joy was so contagious to him.

"It's such a joy to watch the rain wash the whole town clean and bright. The leaves of the trees are as fresh as newly bloomed. The droplet of rain water dripping down the leaves is such a beautiful sight. Isn't it?" she spoke with curiosity.

"Rain is what I like the most." Sandy said, though she knew that he knew it.

"I love to get drenched in the rain. I love the thunders and the lightning. I love the delightful chirping of the birds. I love to run in the water pools. I love to shed the deposited water droplets from the leaves of the trees." Sandy spoke breathlessly.

"How about catching cold and fever and sneezing the whole day?" He ridiculed her.

"Oh yes… I forgot to mention. I love that. Wrapping myself in a thick blanket with heat in my body and cold outside is such a beautiful feeling." She spoke with childish charm.

He laughed aloud at her crazy admiration. He initially didn't like the rain, but started to love it as much as she did. He always saw the world through her eyes.

"What do you like about the rain?" she asked.

"I like it because it makes you happy. I like anything that makes you happy." He winked.

She stopped appreciating the rain and looked into his eyes. That sent lighting into his heart.

She gave the most beautiful curve with that fascinating smile. He loved watching it as much as she loved the rain.

"I would love to walk in the rain holding your hand." she said with her eyes sparkling like a dazzling diamond.

"Shall we have a walk in the rain" she pleaded

He didn't need an invitation.

"No umbrellas." She ordered, just as he was about to spread the umbrella.

He was always happy to oblige. He folded the umbrella and stuffed it in his bag. He took the bag which had books carefully wrapped in a polythene cover to save them from the rain, on his shoulder and outstretched his hand to her. She held it happily.

"Do you really like rain or just doing it to please me?" she asked.

"I love it." he said sincerely.

She stared into his eyes for a couple of seconds and then smiled. She led him outside into the persistent drizzle. As soon as the first raindrop hit her face, she turned electric with delight.

That was the greatest gift anyone could give him. Her happy face glimmered like the silvery moon. As she walked out raising her face upwards facing the drizzles directly, he also walked along with her, gleefully holding her hand.

"Truly amazing feeling." Sunny thought as he felt a thin rain drop on his face. There was a loud thunder rumbling

in the sky. At that instant she held his hand tight. He responded by holder her hand tighter. She removed her sandals and held it in her free hand. He did the same and they started walking through the scattered water puddles. As they walked along the moist road, she suddenly jumped into a small puddle gathered at the roadside, spilling water all over him.

She giggled with her usual childish gleam, as he responded with a surprised expression.

He loved it so much that he wanted to do it all day. He chased her playfully, as she dodged him, running ahead of him and halted breathlessly beneath a tree. He ran behind her and joined her. She surprised him by pulling a branch of the tree spilling down the raindrops deposited on the leaves. It gave a sizzling feeling which he liked very much.

She kept laughing as he brushed the water droplets off his hair.

He pulled a branch this time to let more raindrops shower upon them. She was delighted.

"Do you like it?" she asked.

"I love it." he replied.

"Take it then." she said, pulling another branch, giggling like a baby.

"Wow... she is so cute." he thought, as he captured her blissful image in his heart forever.

"We better start moving, else mom will kill me." She remembered.

"Ok... Let's move." he said as he led her to the road where there was a water puddle accumulated and jumped into it, splashing water onto her. She was taken by surprise and she loved it. There was constant rumbling of the thunder.

They started moving. His home was on the way to her home. So he would usually break off in between. She would walk a little more distance to her home.

"I'll never break off in the journey of life." he promised himself.

A rumbling thunder dragged him back to the present. Saloni, who too was lost in thoughts, was also disturbed by the thunder. He saw a satisfied expression on her face which was a little less than a smile.

"What could have made her so happy?" He wondered, as he had not seen her smile till then.

He didn't want an answer to that. It started to rain heavily. He turned on the windscreen wipers to clear his view.

12:30 PM.

"Stop at a restaurant. I am feeling hungry." she said.

He didn't reply as he kept driving. When he noticed a restaurant, he drove towards it. There was quite some crowd at the restaurant. He then remembered how embarrassed he felt walking with her. He stopped the car near the restaurant, but held the steering for a while.

"I hate walking with her in the public. What do I do?" He thought looking around for the least crowded restaurant.

"You don't have to degrade yourself by walking with me. You stay. I'll get something to eat." she said with disgust, about to get out of the car.

"Wait." he said.

"She's literally reading my mind, like she is reading a magazine." he thought awestruck.

"I'll bring you something to eat." he said and got out of the car, still hating her.

He hurried to the least crowded restaurant as he wanted to get back to the car soon.

His mind also feared that she wouldn't be found in the car when he returned.

"Get me a parcel of anything that can be quick." he asked the restaurant boy who gave him a suspicious look.

HeHeHe then tried to be calm and ordered for chicken fried rice. As he waited for the parcel, he gobbled up couple of doughnuts and a glass of fresh orange juice. He snatched the food parcel from the boy who was puzzled by his hasty rush. He was out of the restaurant in a jiffy and ran to the car. To his shock, she was not inside the car. His fear had turned real.

"Did she escape with the money? Did she just pretend to help me only for money? Then why didn't she wait till she got all the money? Maybe she wanted to keep out of trouble and escape at the safest time." He debated in his mind.

He ran around like a mad man in search of her as she was his only chance to avenge his friend's murder. He splashed water as he ran through the water puddles. Finally, he found her beneath a tree along the sideways of the road, fully drenched. The flimsy dress she was wearing dangerously revealed her skin. He glared at her with burning rage, tempted to slap her, but controlled himself as he didn't want any more complications with her.

"What the hell are you doing here? Go to the car." he spoke with suppressed rage, straining to keep his voice low. She stared at him for a couple of seconds and obeyed him.

He didn't want to have any conversation with her, but his mind was turning heavy with questions. Unable suppress his rage, he stopped the car.

"What the hell were you doing there? Looking for some customers? Am I not paying you enough? I don't know what to say. You greedy prostitutes always look for some activity. Can't you hold your urge for some more time?" he shouted

"Shut up…" He heard her words like a whip lash.

She breathed hard.

"Don't you know who made us…? There are always sex-hungry beasts hounding for hapless victims. They derive pleasure by treating us like a pile of meat. You are no better than them. You think we are disgraceful, because you are one of them. You filthy men think we are piece of flesh not fit to be humanly treated. You can never see the human side of us. We have family, we have self-respect, we know pain, we know shame. We are human… You try to be human." She screamed at the pitch of her voice and wept with her face covered in her palms.

Her words stung him like the fangs of a cobra.

He was stunned as he saw her wipe her tears and regain composure in a few seconds.

He started driving as they sat in absolute silence except for the pattering sound of the rain drops on the windshield.

"When did I turn so cruel?"

DEVIL OR ANGEL?

"*Never hesitate to apologize for your mistakes.*" Sandy always said.

There could never be a better situation to follow her words than this. He didn't know how to draw her attention. She was indignantly looking outside when he stopped at the sideway near one of the gulmohar trees spread across the length of the highway and looked at her. She gave him a quick glance.

"Forget about it. I am here with you only for money. You give me the money and I show him to you... end of business." She said and turned away, lost in her thoughts again.

Unknowingly he started to appreciate her for her pride and intelligence.

"*I forgot about the food.*" he thought as he was still hesitant to interact with her.

He held out the food packet to her and gestured her to eat. She snatched it from his hand and kept it on her lap.

He took a short walk and sat beneath a tree, lighting his cigarette. Drawing in a long breath of smoke, he blew it out facing upwards, thinking about all the incidents that had happened in a shot span of time. He spotted water droplets on the leaves and flowers of the gulmohar tree. Nostalgia struck him, as he threw the cigarette away and walked up to the reachable branch of the tree and pulled it hard to let all the accumulated raindrops spill on him.

"Wow… What a relief that was." he thought, closing his eyes and faced upwards.

Rain always fetched abundance of joy to him.

He rubbed the raindrops all over his face with both his hands. He shivered in the excitement of reliving his favorite memory of Sandy. Every time he did it, the result was the same. Incidentally, he turned towards the car and saw Saloni watching him in amusement. When she met his eyes, she hastily turned away from him.

He took out another cigarette and lit it, giving her time to complete her lunch. He walked along the rows of trees, imagining how Sandy would have gone crazy with the atmosphere.

When he thought that she had enough time to finish her lunch, he walked back towards the car. When he saw that she did not have the food packet with her, he understood that she had finished her lunch. The journey resumed.

01:15 PM

After half an hour's drive, he saw that there was a traffic jam. He couldn't clearly see what was happening ahead as it was raining heavily and the road was not visible beyond a short distance. The vehicles were returning the way they came from.

"Why are the vehicles returning?" he asked a returning traveler.

"There's a bridge broken few hundred meters away. The vehicles cannot pass." was the reply.

Sunny knew that he needed to drive back a long distance for a different route.

"Thank you." he said as he raised the window.

He turned around and drove back for the alternate route which was not a regular one for him. On the peak of desperation, he sped through the slippery road. He bumped onto a speed breaker as the visibility was also poor, lifting both of them from their seats almost hitting the roof. He stopped the car abruptly on the sideway. He looked at her, expecting annoyed reaction, but was surprised to see her worried expression. He stopped for a while to catch the view of the road through the wind screen, cleared by the wiper. He started the engine again. She did not react in any way. He wondered what was going through her, as he started to drive the car again.

"Stop the car!" she shouted.

He screeched the car to a stop. He didn't even have a wild guess of what could have made her scream at the pitch of her voice. He stared at her, inquiring why she asked him to stop the car, but she was not looking at him. She was looking through the window. She opened the door and ran outside, confusing him. He looked in her direction and saw that a bike had skidded on the wet road. There was a man sprawled on the road and a little girl with bruises all over their bodies. She ran senselessly towards them without minding the rain and also forgetting that she was running on the highway. She ran straight to them as a car was just about to knock her down, probably missing by an inch as it sped away. He feared she might have been crashed to death, but she didn't seem to have cared. She first attended the little girl. As she was unable to stand, she supported her arm over her shoulder and took her to sit on a culvert below the protection of a tree. The girl didn't seem be not more than 13 years old. She now saw the man feebly wincing in pain as he was badly bruised and was in a semi-conscious state. She ran fast to him. The man was too heavy for her, but still she wrapped both her arms around the man and tried to lift him. As the man could not be of much help, she was not able to lift him all by herself. He saw her turn to him for help as he was dumbfounded with her sense of responsibility.

"Help." she shouted, waking him from his trance.

He got out of the car door and ran towards them, cautious about the traffic.

"We need to take them to a nearby hospital." She shouted.

He was amazed by her helping tendency. Everybody who had crossed the road had just ignored the people in pain, but she had done otherwise.

"I remember seeing a hospital few miles from here." he said.

"Good. Now, let us drive them to the hospital. Quick." She said as she carried the girl to the car.

"I have misunderstood the girl by her profession. She has heart of gold."

He carried the man to the car. He was quite heavy for him to handle alone, but he did it himself.

Saloni had accommodated the child on the front seat and she sat next to her, nursing her. Sunny came to the car and laid the man down on the rear seat.

"Do you have a first aid kit in your car?" she asked cuddling the little girl, who was wincing in pain.

Sunny returned in a flash with the kit. She immediately applied the antiseptic to clean the wounds. Saloni started the engine and drove towards the hospital as Sunny sat along with the man in the rear seat. With the rain obstructing the road view, she drove at a safe speed.

She parked the car in front of the hospital and helped the kid out of the car, while he helped the man out, who was staring at us with expression of gratitude. They were immediately shifted onto stretchers and then moved to causality. The child had lost lot of blood.

"We need AB Negative blood immediately. We don't have it in the bank. Go and check with the other banks." The doctor commanded the junior.

"Do you know anybody with AB Negative blood? We need it immediately." the doctor asked Sunny.

"Mine is." Saloni announced.

"My blood group is AB negative. You know Sunny bunny, it's the rarest of all blood groups." Sunny recalled Sandy entering the class room, holding the blood test report. He drifted back to his school memories, as he took a seat in the row of chairs in the waiting longue.

"What a coincidence?" He wondered, as he saw Saloni pressing cotton against the needle piercing, walking towards where he sat.

She sat on a chair as she was feeling weak. She was shivering due to coldness as she was already drenched in rain. Sunny removed his jacket and held it in front of her. She pretended not to have noticed. He dropped the jacket on her nearby chair.

Her self-respect again impressed him.

Just then, he got a call. He looked into the display and walked away picking the call.

When he walked back to the waiting longue, he found her wearing the jacket properly and feeling better.

He was eager to know that the duo were fine. At the same time, he was desperate to leave, as he had some unfinished business. He peeked in to the patient ward to found the girl's father unconscious after a dose of sedative and the girl with heavy monitor systems. He was looking for the doctor to inform him that he should leave. Sunny was relieved when he saw the doctor walk out of the treatment room towards him.

"If everything we could do is done, we are compelled to take leave as we are in a hurry." he told the doctor.

The doctor then announced "The kid's survival depends on an operation which should be started immediately. It costs 20,000 rupees. It might sound rude, but due to hospital procedures, we cannot proceed until the amount is paid. If you could pay the amount, we can start the operation immediately." he said apologetically.

Sunny thought that the money Saloni had could help the child. As he turned towards her for help, she got up and walked away towards the exit. Her character was so mysterious and inexplicably inconsistent. She was the reason he engaged in the noble act, but she disengaged herself at the very mention of money.

"The operation should happen immediately." the doctor reminded.

"Is there an ATM nearby?" he asked

"No" he replied.

"Well... Actually I don't have cash with me." Sunny said.

"Don't worry. We accept card payment." the doctor replied.

That was a pleasant surprise for him. He didn't think about that.

After paying the bill at the counter and completing other formalities in quick time, he informed the doctor that he had to leave.

"May I know how you are related to them?" the doctor asked Sunny.

"Just found them bleeding on the road. Thought they need our help..." he replied.

The doctor couldn't believe it was true.

"You must have a heart of gold to have shown so much kindness to strangers." the doctor was amazed.

He looked towards Saloni, who was an enigma to him.

"The credit goes to her." he thought, indignant of stealing her credit.

The doctor asked Sunny for his contact details so that he could help the victim in any gesture of gratitude.

"Please never mind about that, Doctor." he said.

"May god fulfill all your wishes." he blessed Sunny.

He simply smiled back and walked towards the car, where Saloni was standing by. He unlocked the door with the remote key, letting her sit in the car.

As he turned on the engine, he looked at her for a few seconds and then concentrated on the road. He didn't want to know the reason why she hadn't helped the victims when the money was needed.

01:55 PM

The car was whizzing through the monsoon winds. Sunny was so engrossed in his own thoughts that he was semi consciously driving through the sparse traffic of the state highway. When he was steering into a turn, he almost crashed onto a container truck. He suddenly came back to his senses and tried to control the car. In an attempt to escape the fatal accident, he turned the car away from the truck and hit the brakes, so quick that it stopped just a few inches away from crashing onto a tree on the sideway. He was totally out of breath with perspiration flowing down his temples like a stream, despite the cold weather. It took him about a couple of minutes to regain his breath. He was worried that he might have scared Saloni by the close shave with death. He froze in terror when he saw her motionless.

"Hey... Can you hear me? Hello... you... err..." He mumbled in fear.

"Hey... Hello." he increased his volume, but she didn't respond.

"*She's dead!!!*" He panicked.

"*It can't happen to me. I'm already in lot of trouble.*" he thought.

"*Loser... Loser...*" The voice of Hari started ringing in his ears and his image appeared again mocking him.

As he was fighting the images of Hari, there was a knock at the car door.

"Get out of the car. You are under arrest!" He turned around and was shocked to find a cop with cuffs in his hand. The sight of the cop froze his spine. He was terrified not with the fear of getting caught, but with the thought of failing in his mission.

The scene instantly dissolved into a puff of smoke.

Tonight's going to be life changing night for you. He recalled his friend's words and wondered what they meant.

He shook all his thoughts off and made up his mind to check her pulse. There was a very huge challenge for him. He needed to touch her to check the pulse. He swore not to touch her. So did he, not to see her again. He generally hated the company of girls. She was the topmost on the list.

"Fate is playing ruthless games with me." he thought and took a deep breath, praying that everything should be fine.

He slowly moved his trembling hand towards her wrist and hesitated for a few seconds. It seemed to be the most difficult task for him. Though he had developed some respect for her since some time, he was not prepared to touch her, or for that matter, any girl.

"I don't have time to waste. I'm running out of time." he thought and held her wrist clumsily in haste. He didn't realize that his hands were shivering in fear. He was not able to make out the pulse with his shivering hands. He could not remember touching any girl consciously for nearly two decades. Then he felt a strange sensation that he quickly withdrew his hand and cursed his fate. He was not lucky enough to check her breathing with the heaving of her chest

as she had covered herself with his thick jacket. He felt absurd to think about it.

When he looked at her face, he got an idea. He carefully took his trembling hand closer to her nose and concentrated for any flow of air through her nostrils. He was not able to make out immediately as his fingers were trembling like wind chimes on a windy day. Hence he stayed there for a couple of minutes to make sure.

He abruptly withdrew his hand and leaned backwards on his seat and shut his face with his palms. Wiping the sweat off his face, he thanked his stars for the mercy.

He looked for the water bottle and found it beneath the rear seat. He was also surprised to find the unopened food packet on the rear seat.

"She had been starving for almost a day and has also donated blood which must have added to her weakness." he guessed.

He opened the bottle and sprinkled some water on her face. She didn't respond. He then took more water and splashed the water harder on her face. She slightly showed sign of life by gradually squinting her eyelids. It was a great relief for Sunny. She opened her eyes slowly and turned towards him, wondering what had happened. She looked so weak.

"Didn't you have your food?" he asked, surprisingly sounding concerned, which he hated.

"You are a lot of trouble." This time he tried to correct himself, but sounded rather rude. He was unable to manage his own emotions. Some mysterious forces were fighting each other within him.

"Eat it." he said rather commandingly, picking the food packet from the rear seat.

She obediently opened the packet and started to eat without repelling. He was surprised at her sudden compliance. He stared at her for a brief moment and returned his sight towards the road. He turned on the engine and started the car as he didn't want to waste anymore time. As soon as she swallowed her first bite, she got hiccups. She kept the food packet back on her lap and picked the water bottle. She immediately started pouring the water into her mouth spilling it all over her and coughing at the gush of the water into her throat that she got tears in hers eyes. He stopped the car immediately. She composed herself, slowly subsiding the hiccups and kept the water bottle at her foot. He saw her eyes turn red. Once he felt that she was back to normal, he shifted the gear and set the drive back on the highway. She ate slowly fearing that she might get hiccups again. She finished the food and threw the empty pack outside.

02:10 PM

It stopped raining and the road was empty. They drove in absolute silence.

His mind drifted back to the nightmare as he couldn't get Hari out of his thoughts. Every silent moment brought his image back to his mind, reminding him of his unfinished job.

"What if he is still in Manchore?" he asked her without any preamble.

"He is in Portshore." She answered without turning towards him, staring out into the peaceful silence outside the window.

"How do you know that? Look, I don't have any time to waste." he said.

"Neither do I" she flatly replied.

Though he wasn't sure whether to believe her or not, he didn't have choice. As he was thinking about it, his phone started ringing. He took the phone out of his pocket and looked at the number which was not from his contact list. He was not in the mood to talk to anybody unimportant. Hence he silenced the phone and kept driving. The phone started to ring again. It was the same number again. Ignoring the call, he kept driving, but it did not stop ringing. He picked the call out of irritation, but was unable to hear the voice clearly as the signal was weak. The call got disconnected. He let it go, but the phone started ringing again. He slowed down the car and stopped beside a tree and picked up the call.

"Hello… Who's this?" he answered.

"Give the phone to Saloni." was all he heard.

He disconnected the call, the next instant. He wondered what more humiliation was waiting for him. Saloni stared at him with a hint of anger.

"Did she know who the caller was?" he wondered.

"How can she read the name of the caller from my expressions?" he thought sarcastically.

"Was it Pooja?" Saloni wondered.

His mobile started screaming again as he turned on the engine. He silenced the call as he started the car, but it didn't stop ringing.

"What have I got myself into?" He cursed himself as he handed over the phone to Saloni without even picking the call.

She gave him an obnoxious look as she took the mobile from him. She received the call, but the voice was not clear.

"Hey Pooja. I can't get your words." she said with the hope that whatever she heard was only a misinterpretation.

He slowed down the car involuntarily. She jumped out of the car even before it came to a complete stop. She frantically ran all around like a mad girl to find the place with best network reception. Finally she found a steady signal at culvert and sat on it.

He wondered at her desperation about the call as he casually stepped out of the car observing her seriously talking over the phone.

"Never mind" He forced the thought out of his mind and lit a cigarette, breathing in the smoke slowly.

"What are you saying? When is it supposed to happen?" she questioned Pooja.

"The doctor says her condition is critical. If we don't act fast, we may risk losing her." she responded.

"I have arranged for the money. I can get it in a day. Can it hold on till then?" she asked.

"Not wise to delay even a minute was all that doctor advised." Pooja said.

"All long I have struggled to earn money to take care of her. Now when I almost have it, you scare me like this." she spoke in trembling voice.

"I'm not scaring you. I'm scared. Her condition is too bad. Try to make it as fast as possible." Pooja said.

"I would do it at the cost of my life." she said.

She tried to hold her tears, but her emotions were irresistible that her tears formed a thin membrane over her eyes. She found it difficult to speak out.

"Take care of…" Her voice trailed as she realized that the call was already disconnected.

Her mother had suffered a second impact of traumatic brain injury, which required craniotomy surgery to deal with the intracranial hypertension, but Saloni had been short of financial resources. When she got the opportunity to earn the required money, she was elated by the lucky chance, but fate was again playing a rude tantalizing game.

Clenching the phone in her fist, she sat there motionless, trying hard to fight her tears. She couldn't afford to lose her only hope for life.

"I have to save her at any cost." she resolved.

"Be composed." she told herself as she drew a deep breath trying to compose her.

Just then she felt the phone vibrate. She picked the phone on an impulse. It was a message, not a call. She regretted opening it. She was about to close the message when suddenly something struck her. She read the message again.

Happy birthday buddy

She was trying to block her mind from thinking about it, but a part of her was tempting to probe.

"What a coincidence!" she thought, afraid to find out something she didn't want to. She closed the message and marked it as unread as she didn't want to let him know that she had just intruded into his privacy. She was mentally searching for something, but at the same time she was terribly scared about something.

Then she realized that it was very critical that she gather the money for her mother's treatment that she shut her mind from everything else. She got up with rejuvenated vigor and walked towards the car. Sunny dropped the cigarette and stubbed it as she approached the car. She suddenly became hesitant as she handed him the phone. She was about to say something, but thought otherwise. She was experiencing a lot of uncertainty.

She walked around and sat in the car beside him. As they resumed their journey, she took a long breath, closing her eyes, contemplating about something within her. Gathering all her will power, she made a decision.

"I want the full payment now?" The words came out so bluntly from her mouth that it shocked him.

"What?" he blurted out.

"I want my money immediately." she said vigorously.

"My money...?" He couldn't control a frown.

"Look, I am not going to cheat you, because I need your favor anyway. I will pay you as soon as possible." he said

"I want it now. Otherwise I'll drop off from here." she said stubbornly turning away, avoiding any further argument.

He was really unable to judge her. She would seem to be an angel at an instant and turn devil in another.

"You will have your money soon. I'm driving to a bank now." he said, pressing the accelerator hard. He didn't want to make any judgment about her as he would no longer be associated with her once her job for him was done.

As he was fighting hard to align the conflicting thoughts, he still kept driving as fast as he could.

"There's a bank ten kilometers from here." he announced which attracted her curiosity.

02:25 PM

As he drove in the direction of the bank, his phone started ringing again. The number on the display troubled him again as he hated these people even knowing his number. He threw the phone towards her which she caught promptly and returned an embarrassed look.

"Why does she have to call again so soon?" she thought as her prescient mind feared devastation.

"Hello…" she spoke in a trembling voice.

Her expressions instantly changed, which puzzled him. She actually couldn't clearly hear what her friend was saying, as the network was bad, but her tone conveyed the message.

"Hello… Can you hear me? Your voice is not clear." She choked. She was straining to understand what her friend was telling her, hoping her fear was wrong.

Sunny involuntarily stopped the car on the sideways of the road.

"Hold on… I'm getting to a better place." she said in a shivering tone, almost weeping as she jumped out of the car.

Something about her troubled him. She had been such a tough girl so far, which made him think that she didn't have emotions, but what he was witnessing then was something surreal for him. Her thoughts were straining his mind so much that he decided to put her off his mind and take a short walk along the sideway.

He turned back to see what she was doing, as it had been a while since she took the phone with her. What he saw stunned him. She was leaning against a tree and weeping uncontrollably. He couldn't guess what could have broken her down. He didn't want to disturb her, so he sat in the car, silently waiting for her to come in, but she didn't make a move for a long time as she seemed to have frozen where she stood.

"I don't have time to waste." he bitterly thought.

"No more time to waste. Let's move." He looked into her grieving eyes as he spoke the words. That was the first time he felt ashamed of himself as he saw the hatred in her sorrowful eyes, which had carried arrogance so far. He turned away and didn't speak another word.

"Was I rude?" he questioned himself.

She didn't move an inch as she leaned against the tree, hiding her face in her palms and wept for some time. Sunny waited in the car as he didn't dare approach her again. His heart melted unknowingly when he saw her weeping, but he again tried to ignore her. After what seemed like an eternity, he heard the click of the door as he saw her seated beside him. She handed him the phone, looking away from him. He took it and turned on the engine as she stared outside with stoic expression. Though he felt guilty, he had a stern expression masked on his face. He noticed her swollen eyes which bore some unknown vengeance.

2:30 PM

It had been a long time since Bhuvan had left Hari in the ghostly building. The kid knew that he couldn't take too much advantage of the chances to keep away from Hari. Reluctantly, he took the fully charged phone, along with the lunch for him and walked towards the building. When Bhuvan reached the place, he was delighted to find him lying on the ground motionless.

"How glad would I be, if he was dead?" he prayed, as Hari suddenly started to blabber profanities about Victor and abruptly stopped. Bhuvan understood that he was talking in his sleep. He sat beside him, unsure about what to do. He was yearning for some entertainment.

"Let me play some games on my mobile." Bhuvan thought as he picked the phone from his pocket. He then remembered that his phone was exchanged with Hari's. He thought of switching back his sim card into his phone, but didn't have the guts to do it without his approval. Hence he dropped down Hari's phone and picked his which still contained Hari's number. He then got lost in his phone games as usual.

2:35 PM

As he kept driving, focused on the road, he suddenly noticed that the fuel was so low on the indicator.

"Damn..." He cursed himself as he did not know how far the next gas station was. He also didn't know whether he had fuel to drive till there. If the fuel tank dried somewhere before he found the gas station, he would be in trouble. He didn't have anyone to guide as the roads were empty. As he was about to lose hope, he luckily located a fuel station on the highway and he immediately zoomed in.

"Fill the tank." he said

"Do you accept credit card?" he hastily added

"No sir. Only cash." the guy at the gas station said.

"Damn my luck" he thought as he looked into his wallet, which had a few hundred rupee notes which could not afford him enough fuel.

"Fill the tank." He heard Saloni speak.

He turned towards her in surprise.

He wondered why she was suddenly willing to spend when she had been cutthroat about the money till then. She again drifted back into her world with her fiery eyes staring at an invisible enemy. He took the key out after switching off the engine and opened the fuel tank. As he looked back at her, he found that something about her was intriguing him. He didn't understand whether she was attractive or repulsive, but whatever it was, was very strong, as she thoroughly dominated his thoughts.

"Here's your bill, sir."

He took the bill and walked towards her, wondering whether she really intended to pay for the fuel. As he stopped by her side, she sensed his presence and offered the wad of money to him. He hesitantly retrieved two 1000 rupee notes and handed it over to the boy. She blankly stared at the remaining money wondering what she would do with the useless bunch of papers rolled in her palm.

Sunny immediately drove out of the fuel station.

"Drive right." she said in an expressionless tone.

He wondered where it would lead, but still followed her instructions. He then saw the board which read:

Infant Jesus Orphanage

"What does she have to do with an orphanage? How does she relate to it? Maybe she was brought up here." he explained himself.

"I don't have time for all this." he thought of saying, but refrained himself from saying so, as he didn't want to displease her. She had a very important favor to do for him.

He drove silently as directed by her. They finally reached the orphanage. He drove in and stopped at the parking. She got out of the car and walked straight to the donation box. He thought she might be willing to donate a small portion of the money she earned, to cleanse her from her sins.

"How can your sins be washed away by sharing the benefits you have reaped from the same?" he wondered.

He was utterly shocked by what followed next. He saw her pull out the bundle of money he had given her as advance and dropped it in the donation box. He was gobsmacked by the visual as that was truly unexpected.

A person, who was only concerned about money and was willing to do anything for money, just dumped the money in a box she didn't own. More importantly it served unprivileged kids.

He saw her walk back to the car. He was still in shock when she opened the door and sat beside him.

"You have donated a huge amount. Why didn't you let them know? Aren't you losing the credit?" he curiously asked still not sure why she did that.

She closed her eyes and leant her head back on the seat facing the roof of the car.

"Credit is not the purpose." she replied in an expressionless tone.

He felt loss of words as he couldn't explain how he felt. He didn't realize for a while that it was the first time he had spoken cordially to her.

"The guy at the fuel station said that there is a bank nearby. I'll drive there." he said.

"Money...? What do I do with it now?" she wondered. With no one to love, vengeance turned into her ultimate goal.

"Forget about the money. We have some unfinished work." she spoke in a steel voice with ominous determination, which scared him.

"We...?" he wondered. This was the peak of an intellectual challenge for him.

"She was prepared to dump a person who had been her associate, for money. I thought she was such a mean girl. Then she proved to be such an intelligent girl, which I felt was a dangerous combination. She looked out of place though. Then she was so sympathetic to people in distress and bold enough to take the responsibility. Then again she denied helping them financially. When I thought that she would help people with physical effort but not money, and that she values money more than people, she does such a big charity and does not wait for credit. With her last words, it proves that she no more needs money. Despite the lack of need for money anymore, she is willing to help me kill one of her associates. The most confusing part is that she seems to be personally involved now."

The whole analysis was spinning his head.

"I am an absolute failure." He brooded, as he was constantly taunted by her mystery.

SALONI'S FLASHBACK

2:50 PM

Sunny was so completely lost in his thoughts that he ran the car on a rough patch of the road, which caused bumps and the car shifted towards left as though being sucked in by a depression. He knew that he got another obstacle in the form of a flat tyre. He slammed the steering wheel and cursed his fate.

"It is not my day, definitely not my day." he thought.

He was unable to control his frustration as he was turning mentally volatile. He felt like he was breathing fire. He banged the door open and dashed back to the boot of the car for the spare tyre. He then dug into the tool box and pulled out the jackscrew. Saloni sat expressionless, as if she was unaware of what was happening around. When she saw him rolling the tyre, with the jackscrew in his armpit, she calmly walked out of the car and stood in a corner.

He didn't expect her to help him. He didn't fail this time, as she just stood there indifferently. He unknowingly smiled at his rare success in judging her. He squatted down and set the jackscrew beneath the car at the front wheel which got punctured. He removed the cuff buttons and rolled his sleeves up to his elbows. When he raised his hand above his head to pull up the sleeves, Saloni flashed a look at his right wrist from where a golden bracelet rolled down and settled on his forearm. Her heart skipped a beat when she saw that. She immediately floated to a faint world like a cloud of smoke in a strong wind, where she was hit by a lightning bolt from invisible striking point. Her mind was whipsawed between curiosity and fright. Her heart started beating so fast and hard that she could feel hammers crash her rib cage. She began to feel weak on her legs. She shook her eyes and her mind to oust the mounting curiosity, but again she wanted to explore it. She was caught in a frenzy wind of emotional fluctuations as she was ambivalent about what she might discover. She was both excited and terrified. A part of her was blocking her mind from the truth and the other part was forcing her to open it. She finally decided she wanted the truth. She was prepared for the flight of which she dreamt of everyday, yet she was hesitant. Transforming into Sandy, her innocent childhood form, she travelled back to the blissful past of her school days.

Sandy was so excited that she was counting down seconds to meet Sunny that morning. She kept staring at the rectangular box in her palms in excitement.

She slept forcibly as she feared she would wake up late in the morning. It had been a long struggle that she didn't know when she fell asleep. When she suddenly woke up from her sleep, she saw that it was already 7 AM. She was late.

"Mom, why didn't you wake me up? I'm late because of you." she complained.

"Oh really…? Didn't I wake you up? I was actually fed up of waking you up, my darling. Now don't delay anymore." she warned her.

"Thanks for reminding." she said hastily getting up from her bed, kissing her mother as she walked past her. Her mother was amused by her curiosity, but resisted herself from asking her.

Sandy worked in a flash as she got ready in a record time. Her mother set her breakfast ready by the time she was dressed in school uniform.

"Bye Mom. See you in the evening." She said as she walked across her mom carrying the hefty bag on her delicate shoulders.

"Stop there my dear… Have your breakfast and then leave." her mother ordered.

"Sorry mom, I'm getting late." she pleaded.

"This is one contest, you will lose, darling. Don't waste your time arguing."

Sandy agreed and hurried to dining table. She gobbled up her breakfast ending up in hiccups.

"Easy baby" her mother said as she handed her a glass of water.

She gulped the water along with the food and returned the empty glass almost dropping it down as she was in such a hurry that she didn't notice whether her mother had held it or not. Her mother noticed Sandy's bare hand without the diamond ring which she had gifted her for her last birthday.

She didn't wish to ask her about it, as she was happy that her daughter was happy.

Sandy floated like the wind to the school, unable to wait any longer.

"You are late today." Sunny, who was already expecting her, said as she stepped into the classroom.

"Hmm… I'm at the receiving end today. Would you please pardon me for my delay?" she said mockingly as she approached him.

"Apology accepted…"

"See how noble I am. I easily forgive, unlike you." He invited her into a playful quarrel.

"I agree, O noble prince." She mocked obeisance. She didn't argue as she was in no mood to procrastinate the experience of the joy she had been dreaming all night.

"Would you please do me a favor?" she asked

"Command…" he said

"Close your eyes and stretch your hand." she said unable to hold the excitement.

He didn't know why she was asking him to stretch his hand, but looking at her joy, he himself was already in boundless joy. He hated closing his eyes, as he felt like watching her enthusiastic smile all day.

"Here you are." he said closing his eyes and stretching his right hand. He didn't know what to expect, but he didn't care about that. She was happy. That was all he wanted. He felt something cold around his wrist.

"Now you may slowly open your eyes." she said with joy transparent in her eyes.

Sunny looked into her eyes before he looked anywhere else, amused by her excitement.

"Happy birthday, Sunny." She reminded him that it was his birthday.

Sunny stared at her with pride and joy.

"Do you like it?" she asked even before he had a look at it.

He stared at the beauty wound around his wrist. It was a golden bracelet with solid alphabets interlinked to each other to form her name - 'SANDY'. It was a custom design.

"Beautiful bracelet." he exclaimed as he wiggled the golden beauty around his wrist.

"It's not a bracelet. It's the Thread of Love." she announced.

Sunny knew that he should be expecting another fairy tale from Sandy.

"Enlighten me Sandy Candy." He encouraged her to proceed.

"Here you go." she said as she continued.

"Eons ago, god created the world. It was nothing but a huge ball of rock: stark and dull. He was not happy with his creation. He wanted to make the world, colorful. Hence he created the oceans, the mountains and the trees with beautiful flowers. It was beautiful, but He was still not satisfied. He wanted to make it eventful and interesting. Hence He created the animals, fishes, insects and birds, which made his creation interesting, but there was no order in the world. The world was just wild and uncivilized, which demanded his governance every time. He wanted someone to rule the world, so that he could relax and just watch. Hence he created the humans, cloning himself.

"Hah… My job is now complete." The God prided.

The humans ruled the world well, but they seemed to be listless and detached from each other. He kept wondering what he had missed. There was no bond between the humans, there was no love. The world was a mean place, only with materialistic purpose. He wanted to infuse love in the humans. It was the biggest challenge for him. He could easily create a zillion creatures in a jiffy, but to infuse love in them was a herculean task. It was a task bigger than creating life itself. He finally thought of an idea. He planned to tie the beloved hearts with a special bond which could make the human life on earth very special. Now he needed a special material to bind the hearts together. He summoned the divine goldsmith and ordered him to make special threads of gold. He imbued the threads with his divine soul. He called it 'The Thread of Love'. He then created the Kingdom of Love. The spirits of people who have selfless love for somebody earn a place in His glorious kingdom and they can physically communicate with the person they love, through the thread of love. Deeper the love, stronger the thread."

"It's beyond your consciousness that your soul lingers with the person you love, and hence your mood will affect the one you love. This is the reason why you sometimes sense your mood changing mysteriously with no reason."

"Nice fairy tale, Sandy Candy... I'm enthralled actually." he ridiculed playfully.

"Thoughts are not physical, how can they physically affect the others?" he questioned.

"You can only feel, but not see air. Air is physical.
You can only see, but not feel light. Light is physical.

You can see and feel your thoughts. Then why can't thoughts be physical?" Sandy's logical observation was irrefutable.

"Perfectly logical…" He was amazed by her ability of logical reasoning even for a fictitious fairy tale.

"Tell me about it." Sandy asked with curiosity.

"It's priceless." he exclaimed staring at the exquisite beauty around his wrist.

As she was carried back from her joyful reverie to the painful reality, she wondered if it could be a coincidence that someone was wearing a bracelet engraved with her name on it, similar to the one she had gifted her best friend, long back.

"It is not real. It's just a brutal coincidence, tormenting me." she explained herself.

However, she couldn't conclude that and her mind was so desperate to find out.

"How do I find it?" she thought.

An idea struck her.

She took a deep breath as she felt she was running out of oxygen and walked hesitantly towards him.

"Hmm… huff huff…" She was unable to speak out.

"Can you please lend me your phone for a few seconds? I need to make an urgent call." she asked in a shaky voice.

Sunny was puzzled that he couldn't understand the sudden change in her approach. She was such a confident and proud girl, but suddenly turned hesitant and timid.

"She is an absolute enigma." he thought, carefully picking the phone from his pocket as his hands were smeared with dirt from the wheel.

She took it from him and walked a distance and stopped at a tree. She turned away from him and stared at the phone. Her hands were shivering.

She hated intruding into his personal space, but nothing could hold her curiosity. She fumbled while operating the phone as she hesitantly looked through the messages and found the birthday message sent by his friend.

She started to get a million voices in her, shouting different opinions. Some were objecting and some encouraging her to do it. She cleared all the voices and called the number. She heard ringing of the phone and kept waiting for the call to be received. Her heart skipped a beat as she suddenly felt a click of the phone. She felt like hanging up the phone.

"Hello…"

"Hey dude…"

"Are you there?" the voice kept calling.

She didn't get what she wanted. She was expecting something, but also expecting it not to happen. She had two personalities within her with opposite feelings fighting each other with equal power. Nobody would win. That was her problem.

She held her breath as she kept waiting without speaking and without disconnecting the call.

"Hey Sunny?" the voice called

There it was. The words came down on her like a bolt of lightning. The whole world seemed to be closing in on her. Her head started spinning. She disconnected the call still holding the mobile phone to her ears.

"*This is supposed to be the happiest moment of my life…, but here I am, praying that all this should be a dream. A sweet dream…*" She cried within herself.

"*This is too good to be real. What do I do now? I do not want to disclose my identity and embarrass the person whom I loved more than my life. Would he accept me in this state? I am sure that he hates me because of the way I have behaved with him. Who would like a person like me? Even if he accepts me, will I let him ruin his life by choosing a person like me? I can continue living in this hell, but I do not want to drag him into it. He always thought good for me, how could I think bad for him for my selfish reasons? If he is still wearing the gift I have presented him almost two decades ago, I can understand how much he loves me. I'm glad about that. Let him be in love with the sweet girl whom he knew during his school days. I hate to introduce the scum to him, saying 'hey, this is the same girl, you adored during your school days.' Let him marry a nice girl and lead a happy life.*" she thought, not realizing the tears flowing uncontrollably. She wiped her tears and tried to compose herself. She didn't want to give him any clues. She shivered at the unexpected turn of events. She tried her best, but she could no more act normal. She was still holding the phone to her ears, pretending to be still on the call. As she was lost in her thoughts, she was suddenly awakened by the rumbling of the thunder. She wished that the thunder would kill her, but to her horror, she found that it was the phone ringing. She was so occupied with thoughts that she forgot about it.

"*What do I do now?*" she thought. She planned to ignore the calls until the caller gave up. She silenced the phone and let the caller give up his attempts.

She turned towards him shyly and started recollecting all the events of the day. The bracelet on his wrist reminded that her love was not unreciprocated.

"This is enough for a lifetime." she thought happily.

She also wondered how they shared the same goal. It was the most pleasing fact for her. She felt that there was something supernatural binding them with a common goal. Perhaps – *The Thread of Love.*

"I'm kidding myself." she thought to herself. However she couldn't eliminate the supernatural elements out of the reasoning for all the happenings so far that day.

She didn't know whether her tragic life would have a happy ending, but she always believed in fairy tales.

"This dream is heavenly. I would relish it for as long as possible. No harm." she thought.

She felt the mobile ringing again. She ignored it again as planned. The phone stopped vibrating. When she was sure that the caller gave up, she cleared the missed call alert on the screen. She waited for some more time to confirm and then put the phone back on ringing mode. She began recollecting every minute of his company since last night, reliving it.

"It's done. We'll move." Sunny said which shook her off her thoughts with panic that she rushed towards the car rather hastily and tripped on a stone on the path. She suddenly noticed the locket gifted by Sunny which she was wearing had become visible as it popped out of her shirt as she fell forward on her knees resting her hands forward. Her tripping drew his attention towards her.

"Any problem?" he asked turning towards her.

"No problem." She said as she skillfully pulled out the locket and slipped it into the jacket pocket before she stood up straight, without letting him see it. She walked to the car and took her seat. As Sunny sat at the driver's seat, she handed him his phone, inconspicuously staring into his eyes for a few seconds.

"How did I miss the magnetic glint in his eyes?" She cursed herself.

FRIENDLY SALONI

3:05 PM

He drove silently for some time as both of them were hesitant to look at each other.

"I'll drive to the nearest bank." He broke the silence.

He remembered her telling him to forget about the money, but he didn't know if he should take it seriously. Moreover if he passed the bank then, he may not find another one for a long time and he would be in trouble if she demanded for money, later.

It was the most painful situation she had ever faced. She was experiencing the pinnacle of emotions - grief, vengeance and love, all at the same time.

She sat silently looking out of the window, without saying anything for some time.

She wanted to keep herself away from him, yet wanted to get close to him. She didn't want to talk to him, yet couldn't resist the urge. She didn't want to think about him, but it was a definite impossibility.

"I no more need the money. Sorry, I troubled you so much." she told sincerely, when he expected a rude answer from her.

"Then, why do you want to help me without any benefit?" he was tempted to ask, but didn't.

Saloni had been longing to talk something to him, but couldn't find a lead to the conversation. Silence prevailed for a few minutes as she kept thinking how to initiate the conversation.

"Why do you have to fight with a criminal like him and spoil your future? You report to police and I'll testify." she said spontaneously.

Her concern for him surprised him. He didn't answer for a few seconds, trying to figure out what she had just said. He felt that she was genuinely concerned about him, but didn't understand her sudden changes. He convinced himself that unpredictability was the definition of her character.

"That wouldn't do justice to the sacrifice of my friend." he responded in a low voice.

She too relished the thought of killing Hari and had been running it in her mind over and over again for many years until then. She desperately wanted to kill Hari, because he was the reason for all her suffering and even her split up with Sunny. Also Sunny had a reason to kill him, which made it her reason too, but she didn't want him to spoil his life. She was quickly thinking about how to save him from the trouble and fittingly punish Hari at the same time.

"I can't ask him to forgo his vengeance. How do I keep him out of this and settle the scores with Hari at the same time? Can I do it?" she was seriously arguing within herself.

"What will you do with him?" she asked, looking outside, although she knew that it was a foolish question.

"Kill him. What else can I possibly do with him?" he replied.

"What next? What about your future?" she asked with concern.

"You do not calculate consequences while dealing with emotions. I would be a traitor if I look for my comfort, when he sacrificed his life to save me. How do I repay for his sacrifice?" he shot back.

She was proud of his sincerity, but not pleased with his plan.

"Can you bring back your friend by killing the killer? Had he been watching you, would he be glad you are risking your future trying to avenge his murder?" she asked him.

Sunny didn't have answer.

"I believe he would be annoyed with you for what you chose to do." she said.

He knew that she was right, as always.

"My friend was killed. It's all about payback." he bluntly said.

"Killing someone would not settle scores. It will do more bad than good." she tried her best to stop him before he got into something he would regret for life.

"I don't care." he replied with finality, recalling the hellacious images of the brutal night.

She understood his tone and stopped questioning further, but she was worried about the consequences of his act, as Sunny's safety became her priority.

Saloni's words pleased Sunny, but her intent added to his confusion. He felt guilty for whatever he thought her to be, but still, he couldn't conclude anything about her. He wondered if there could be anything more mysterious than her. He was still confused why she had been trying to talk him out of his killing plan.

"Is she concerned about Hari? If she is, then why did she agree to help me find him? Is it for money? Not a chance. She, in fact denied the payment. Why would she help me without any benefit? And why is she worried about my future?" These questions were unanswerable.

He was also unable to comprehend her multiple transformations in a short journey. He was back to the same state of confusion, which he had been experiencing whenever he probed about her. This time, it was a notch higher. He stared at her eyes for a couple of seconds and immediately looked away, as for some reason, it only aggravated his confusion. He avoided her eyes as he had been doing till then.

"Do we have anything to cheer about yet?" he asked Saloni to know whether her friend had offered any further information.

"I expect a call anytime." she hopefully said.

"I promised to help Sal, but why do I have to deal with Sam again?" Pooja whined.

She shuddered at the thought of dealing with him, as she recollected her clumsy breakup with him.

Pooja liked Sam as he was not an opportunist like others, but she also knew that she couldn't continue with the affair. She waited for a genuine reason to break up with him, which she knew she would never get. The more time she spent with him, the more she knew about him, the more she was impressed with him. Sam had a very positive approach of life. He never complained despite being orphaned twice. He was a religious yet mischievous guy, principled yet wayward, all within the threshold though. He believed that the only form of god is love. He was a rare blend of contrasting traits, which made him irresistible. Besides all this, he was very sincere in his love, which was the most annoying part for Pooja.

"This affair is freaking me out, baby." Pooja told Saloni hopelessly.

"Sam?" Saloni asked.

"Who else could that be?" Pooja shot back.

"What's wrong?" Saloni asked

"He's not in for a fun affair. He's…" Pooja hated to spell it.

"Serious?" Saloni completed.

"Yes…" Pooja answered.

"Are you?" Saloni asked her.

Pooja hesitated for a couple of seconds

"No…" she responded.

"And I have no intension of wasting any more time with him." Pooja declared.

"So… What's holding you back?" Saloni asked her.

"Well… You know…" Pooja fumbled.

"You want to have an amicable break up, isn't it?" Saloni guessed.

Pooja nodded in affirmative.

"As you keep waiting for the opportunity, you would only aggravate your position." Saloni said which Pooja rightly agreed with.

"Yes... I will do it immediately." She did not know when that would be. She still hoped she would get an opportunity, which she knew was not even a distant possibility.

Sam never demanded anything. He never treated her with disrespect. He always listened patiently. He never lost temper. He never thrust his opinions on her. He knew how to pamper his girlfriend. He was fun loving and fun filled. He was intelligent.

Pooja could never find a genuine reason to break up with him, but she had to find one.

"It's a beautiful morning." Sam told as he sat before Chris at a table in their regular coffee shop.

"Beautiful? Look at the scorching sun roasting my skin." Chris complained rather rudely.

Sam was unperturbed by her rudeness.

"Well... Everything seems beautiful when we are in beautiful company." She smiled mildly despite her strong intent to be rude with him.

"Now that you have made my day with your beautiful smile, it's my turn to recompense. Mind you... I can't gift you anything more beautiful than your smile. So please accept my modest gift." Sam said as he drew out a box which he had kept hidden from her sight all the while.

It was an exquisite gold necklace with flowery design studded with a few tiny diamonds within. It was an impressive design and unbeatable choice, but she had different thought about that.

"Are you trying to buy me out with your lavish gifts?" She burst out.

Sam thought she was joking and he laughed at her comment, which helped her maintain the seriousness.

"Stop laughing. I'm not for sale." she blurted out thoughtlessly and immediately regretted about that because her comments contradicted her life as it was. She felt ashamed at that very instant. There was nothing she could do about that. Words spoken cannot be taken back.

Sam was badly hurt. She knew that the reason was not good enough for a breakup, but she couldn't face him anymore. She was cornered by her own words.

"It's over." she said and stormed out of the Café without looking back.

Sam stood where he was, with his jaws dropped in disbelief and eyes wet.

3:15 PM

"Good morning. This is Sam. How may I help you?" Sam spoke into his headphone, when his mobile phone disturbed the whole floor with its loud ringtone. His manager, who was just walking past him, gave a scorching stare which he could easily read - *How many times should I tell you to switch off your mobile phone?*

Sam immediately silenced his phone and gave an apologetic look to his manager, who shook his head in disbelief and walked away towards the cafeteria. Sam, who was normally very polite and patient listener, was in a hurry to wrap up the call. As soon as the call was completed, he changed his status to inactive and threw the headset on his desk and rushed out into the corridor.

He dialed the last received number and waited with delightful curiosity. He leaned against a pillar and kept tapping his fingers to an arrhythmic tune on the corridor railing, waiting for the call to be answered.

"Hello…" Saloni spoke in a hesitant tone.

He sprang back to life on hearing the voice.

"Today is my lucky day?" he said.

She could not find words to begin her conversation.

"I need a favor from you." she bluntly told.

"Today is really my lucky day." he responded with an audible smile.

"After deserting you abruptly, I now call you for a favor. Won't you think I'm mean and selfish?" she questioned him with surprise.

"I'm proud that you turn up to me for help."

"Moreover I don't think that you deserted me. I firmly believe that there must be a strong reason for what you did. I don't expect an explanation. A person like you could do no harm to anyone. I love you, Chris. I love you, no matter what may come." he said, reflecting sister Teresa's upbringing.

She couldn't bear the burden of his trust that she regretted raising the topic.

She ignored her emotions and concentrated on her motive.

"I need a help." she told plainly.

"At your service, my angel…" Sam responded.

She kept silent for a few moments, not sure how to proceed. Sam waited.

"Well… There is some guy troubling me. I have his phone number. I want his calls list?" she spoke in a rush.

Sam was in a tight corner. It was the first time she had ever asked him for a favor. He could not disappoint her, nor could he risk his job to fulfill her wish. Telecom industries were very particular about customer data confidentiality.

It was his turn to maintain silence.

"You there…?" She disrupted his mental debate.

"Ya… Yes baby." He stuttered, still contemplating her request.

She knew that it was no ordinary task. She knew about the sensitivity of the matter, but still she had to persuade him.

"Well… If you are not willing to do it, then it's okay." She expressed disappointment, trying to cajole him and strangely felt uncomfortable manipulating him.

"Hey… Don't think so… Well… you know… It's risky." he paused

She knew that.

"I only care about my conscience, and my conscience says that you can't be wrong…" He paused for a few seconds.

"I don't want to know why you want the details, but I'll do it for you." he said.

"Thank you." She wanted to add something more to show her gratitude, but she could not.

"I want the calls list of a number since last evening." She said.

"Send me the phone number. I'll do it for you." he said as he ended the call.

She cursed Saloni for having her deal with Sam again, after she had broken up with him. Sam, who was determined not to disappoint her, kept thinking about all the meager possible options to get the job done. Since the company dealt with sensitive data, they were not provided with internet to refrain external data transfer. He could neither take a printout, as the facility was denied nor a soft copy as the USB ports were disabled. They had a rule to keep the mobile phone switched off, which he always broke, though.

"That's the only way." he thought.

He slipped the mobile into his pocket and quietly walked to his desk. Though he knew that he had only option to do it, he still kept thinking, not whether to do it or not, but about consequences. He was prepared for any consequence. He still kept himself in inactive status and unlocked his system. He retrieved the bill details of the given number. It was a prepaid number in the name of Hari. He turned on his mobile camera and scrolled the call details displayed in his system monitor. It was not a huge list, though. He was also cautious about his manager, who would always be on the prowl, but he was relaxed as he saw him walk into the cafeteria. He slowly scrolled down, making sure he didn't mess it on the video being recorded on his phone. He saved the video and quickly looked around to see if anyone had noticed his act. He gave a deep sigh of relief, when he found none. He then picked a number from the recently received calls and sent the video to Pooja through MMS.

Sam felt as though he accomplished a secret mission. He didn't notice his manager watching him suspiciously through the tinted glass of his cabin.

When Pooja saw her phone beep, she couldn't believe she did it.

BREEZY BREAK

3:25 PM

They seemed to have reached the benighted end of the road. Sunny knew he had to wait. Everything for him happened on extempore planning. He admitted that Saloni had done a brilliant job and he had no complaints about her purpose, though he had hated her in the beginning. He drove aimlessly, looking for an empty road as he felt uncomfortably naked on the busy roads. He was successful in finding an almost empty road along the east coast. He set the drive on the road that ran along the mesmerizing east coastline. Saloni was delighted with the sight of the deep blue horizon and the rippling waves glittering like streaks of diamonds in the late afternoon sun. Sunny noticed her enjoying the sight. As she constantly stared at the deep blue ocean with fascination, he drove the car straight to the beach and stopped it. He turned off the engine and stared at her for a few seconds.

He wanted to tell her to enjoy the beach, as he felt indebted to her. Though he had repealed his hatred for her, his pride was obstructing him from announcing it. Saloni was doing her best to avoid his embarrassment by her extraordinary ability to read his mind.

"Thanks." she said as she removed her sandals and got out of the car.

Sunny was glad that she was helping him in more ways than expected. He thanked her within himself.

She strolled gracefully towards the seashore with her beautiful dark hair fluttering like waves in the sea breeze, challenging the beauty of the deep blue sea waves. He couldn't help appreciating her elegance. She serenely walked towards the roting waves of the inviting sea.

"She is beautiful, intelligent and cultured. Then why the hell did she choose her way of living?" he wondered. He leaned on the bonnet of his car and admired her walking along the shore as the undulating waves caressed her delicate feet.

As she raised her face against the wind with closed eyes, letting the pleasant breeze wash her face, the inevitable ruthless reality dawned on her, which slowly eclipsed her joy. She deemed that of all the world she knew, only two people bore meaning for her life – Sunny and her mother. She missed one for most of her life till a day ago, living with her only reason to live – her mother. When she lost her, she miraculously found the one whom she thought she had lost forever. And much to her grief, her fate was so cruelly designed that she was certain to lose her only and newly found hope – the love of her life. As she was brutally dragged back to reality, the barricade of her tears arrested for quite a long time broke like a dam beyond the threshold.

She turned away from Sunny, not wanting him to notice her grieving. As she turned away from him towards the horizon, she noticed that the vast sea seemed to merge with the sky. She wondered how farther it could be from truth. It seemed to serve as a metaphor for her life. As she looked up at the sky with a sigh of despair, she witnessed the sun being hungrily gobbled up by the black clouds. Though it was not blindingly dark, it was so frightening for Saloni. She began to realize that the whole universe was bent upon incinerating her hope. Her hope for love, her hope for life…

She ignored the bitter facts all through her life, dreaming of the impossible, but fate was so persistent on getting her to realize it. It had become extremely difficult to extenuate her grief that she wanted to cry aloud and dilute her agony with her tears. Though she believed that her crying would be subjugated by the high decibels of the waves and the noisy strong breeze, she didn't want to take a chance. She walked as far as possible from him, pretending to enjoy the walk. She walked the shore which she had once walked along with Sunny, gaily holding his hand. She wondered why she was constantly being reminded of the blissful past, when fate had decided to take it back, soon, forever. She cried aloud to her heart's content in solitude.

Sunny took a cigarette and tried to light it, but the sea breeze was making it difficult for him. After many unsuccessful trials, he realized that the wind wouldn't let him light his cigarette. He then turned away from the direction of the wind and lit it successfully. As he let the sea breeze sooth him down, reminding him of his delightful childhood memories, he heard a feeble sound of the phone ringing. He immediately retrieved the phone from his pocket and before he picked the call, it got disconnected. He noticed that there were already missed calls from the same numbers. The roaring waves and the whistling wind had subdued the sound of the phone ringing. He couldn't make up his mind to call the number back and speak with the caller. He expected Saloni to take the call, but he didn't know how to attract her attention towards him. He dropped his cigarette and held the mobile in his hand, contemplating what to do. He hated wasting time, but couldn't snatch her momentary pleasure for his purpose. Unable to decide what to do, he gazed in her direction.

Saloni walked along the beach bemoaning the tragic events that had occurred to her in rapid quick succession. She took advantage of her loneliness and silently exhausted the unending stream of tears that ran down her cheek. When she felt that she had walked more than enough distance, she turned and started to walk back. As she turned around, she saw Sunny gazing towards her. She understood that he was in need of her. She turned towards the sea for one last time and subtly dried her tears with the sleeve of the jacket. She then turned casually and walked towards him.

As she walked towards him, an inexplicable melancholy in her eyes attracted him, which had been haunting him for quite some time. He was not able to understand her state of mind, but he felt something very familiar about her. Whenever he attempted to find out, his mind blurred out. He accepted his defeat and stopped thinking about it. He outstretched his hand with the mobile, prompting a phone call. She gaited faster, sensing the urgency. She reached out for the phone and checked the call history. She found three missed called from Pooja's number. She called the number and eagerly waited as the phone rang for a few seconds.

"Sal…" Pooja spoke out.

"Tell me…" she spoke in a groggy voice and waited for her to continue.

"Are you okay?" Pooja asked, troubled by the pain in her voice.

"Tell me." Saloni repeated.

Pooja stayed mute for a few seconds, sighed and then continued.

"I got the numbers called from Hari's phone after the incident. He made a very few calls." She paused.

"Ok…" Saloni waited for her to continue.

"He called only two numbers of which one is Victor's." Pooja said.

"I sent message with the call details."

"I also want the billing address of the other number which you gave me now." Saloni instructed her.

"I'll try my best darling." Pooja replied reluctantly.

"And hey…" She paused.

"I expect to receive mother's body by evening…" She again paused unable to continue as she understood Saloni's pain. "I'll take care of the rituals. You don't return until I advise you. Situation here is getting worse than expected." Pooja explained to her.

Saloni tried her best to conceal her emotions, but whimpered on a reflex when she heard about her mother, which Sunny promptly noticed. She immediately turned away from him and tried to compose herself with all her willpower.

"How can... How can it happen without me?" Saloni asked her in a shivering tone.

"I know you want to be here, but your safety is more important." Pooja argued.

Saloni didn't contend her opinion as she herself had some unfinished business. She disconnected the call still replaying what Pooja spoke.

Sunny stared at her sorrowful eyes, unable to comprehend their conversation and why Saloni had broken down during the conversation. Saloni took few deep breaths and then turned to Sunny.

"We have only one new number which Hari called after the incident, which means that it could be the number of someone on whom he depended in the crisis, who could have even sheltered him. I asked my friend to get his address which could help us locate him." Saloni elaborated to him in a shaky tone, evading his stare.

Though Sunny was thoroughly convinced with her plan, he wanted to know why she had broken down during the conversation. He unknowingly started worrying about her.

"We wait till Pooja calls back.'" she said.

He nodded gently as he walked a few steps forward and stretched his arms to relax as he had been driving continuously for a long time.

Saloni loved the delay in the proceedings which enabled her to spend more time with Sunny, as she knew that she had to part ways with him as soon as her job was done. They needed to wait until Pooja called again with necessary information. Until then she had time. Now that they had informally come to a truce, situation seemed to have become ironically more uneasy than before. They were finding it very difficult to act natural. Sunny admitted that Saloni was a perfectly adorable character, but he debated why he should make friendship with a girl, whom he knew, would be associated with for not more than a few hours. However, she had been disturbing his thoughts for quite some time and he had been constantly forcing her out of his mind. At least he was trying to. Whatsoever he couldn't be rude with her anymore, as he respected her and was grateful too. He lit a cigarette with the experience from his earlier trials, averting the powerful wind and walked towards the roaring waves. Saloni stood against the strong wind with her arms crossed against her breast and observed him walking towards the shoreline. She stayed behind just looking in his direction. Sunny glanced at her, leaning on the car, through the corner of his eye and instinctively checked his trousers pocket for the car keys. He instantly felt ashamed as he found that Saloni had caught him in the act. He didn't do it intentionally though. The fact was that his subconscious mind had firmly registered her as a wily and untrustworthy person. However she didn't seem to be bothered by his rude manners.

"Hope she understood that I regretted doing it?" he wished as he walked through the golden sand.

Saloni watched Sunny walk slowly away from her and wondered whether he would walk away from her forever. She wanted to stay close with him at least as long as they were together. She was scared to think about permanent separation when she was not even able to bear the momentary separation. The breezy wind turned brutal as she shut her eyelids hard in agony. Reality was harsher than hell for her. As she was feeling the pain, she had an uncanny sense of someone approaching her. She guessed who it could be, but didn't understand the reason. She shut her eyes harder praying for some miracle to happen.

She suddenly felt respite from the brutal wind pounding her face, by someone standing in front of her, who blocked the path of the wind. She shut her eyes even harder.

"Sandy…" She heard a faint voice.

She didn't respond.

"Sandy Candy…" This time it was louder.

She opened her eyes slowly and cautiously, and found Sunny smiling in front of her in ecstasy, to her ecstasy. Tears started rolling down her cheeks instantaneously. He immediately wrapped her in his arms tightly and wept like a child. He kissed her all across her face like mad. Though she prayed for it every day, she was afraid it could be a dream, as she had a few puzzling questions which were unanswered.

"When…" She was unable to speak the words out as her throat seemed to have chocked. She held his hand firmly, took a deep breath, cleared the lump in her throat and then continued.

"When did you…" She was short of breath after a few words. She again inhaled deep for another breath.

"When did you know?" She successfully completed her question.

He was also in equivalent ecstasy and was breathing hard, unable to gather words to speak his thoughts.

"When did you know?" She repeated the question as she tightened her grip on his hand, tears still rolling down her cheeks.

"I… I… I felt something so familiar with you from the second I met you, but my mind was somehow unable to recognize." He started to explain, as he paused to take a breath. He was short of breath, so much that he feared dying of it.

Saloni understood why.

"His subconscious mind probably was reluctant to relate the bubbly, innocent girl with what I am now." She thought.

She waited for him to continue as she didn't care what he talked, what he did. She wanted to hear him and watch him for as long as possible.

He took in a deep breath, expecting to talk for longer this time.

"I consciously tried to keep you away from my thoughts, but there was something more powerful than my willpower that brought your thoughts back to me. I wondered what that could be. As each minute passed, your thoughts started to grow stronger. I even used hatred to fight it, but it didn't work."

"When did you know?" She repeated her question again out of curiosity.

"I did not know exactly when, but it had been quite some time."

"Then what took you so long?" she complained.

"I was tempted to verify it every minute, but I was not sure if it was reality or only a figment of my imagination."

"I wasn't sure..." Sunny spoke slowly.

"How are you sure now?"

"Not sure even now..." He paused and then continued

"I thought it would be unbearably painful when I think that I came across you and let you vanish again as you often do in my dreams."

She rested her forehead against his chest and wept hard in joy. She held his shirt with both her hands and buried her face into his chest. Sunny held her by her chin and raised her head to align her eyes straight into his. He stared at her with pain stricken eyes. She stared at his eyes for a few seconds to notice tears forming in his eyes. When she shut her eyes in a silent prayer, she felt her lips moistened by a chill drop of water. She wondered how a drop of tear could be chill. She happened to taste it and found that it was sweet.

"I know that he's a sweet person. Does that make his tears sweet?" she wondered. She felt another drop on her cheek, another one on the forehead. More drops started drenching her face. She was baffled about how so many drops of tears could fall on different parts of her face at the same time. When she hesitantly opened her eyes, she saw the sky throwing more and more raindrops at her and mocking her with rumbling thunders. Then she saw Sunny running towards the car. Saloni let her tears flow freely as her fortitude was gradually getting demolished by the cruel game of the fate. She faced upwards to receive more rain drops on her face to camouflage her tears. As Sunny saw her getting drenched in rain, he opened the car door for her with his remote key. She heard the hooting of the car door, indicating unlock. Without hurry she opened the door and quietly slid onto her seat. She sat in the car and saw Sunny running faster now, as the rain started to slap the windscreen harder. She dried her tears off her face with the sleeve of the jacket and calmed herself, as he approached the car. He didn't waste any time jumping into his seat. He wiggled his head sideways scattering the rain droplets that soaked his hair all around, spilling some on Saloni.

As Sunny turned to apologize to her, he noticed a faint smile escape her lips, probably for the smallest unit of time. He thought hard for a few seconds, trying to figure out her expressions.

"Sorry…" he said, as he continued thinking.

"It's okay." she responded without revealing anything more.

She seemed to be the meanest girl he had ever seen at first sight, but later she turned out to be the most generous human he had ever seen. She seemed to be the most arrogant girl when she had a brawl with him in the hotel, but mysteriously turned calm as a saint. She seemed to bear all the pain of the world in her eyes, and suddenly seemed to have caught a smile amid the grief. His pain was that while she was able to read every word that ran in his mind, he was not able to reason her changes. He learnt to stop thinking about it. For him, there was one thing predictable about her – that she was unpredictable.

He wiped the rain drops off his hair, gently this time.

They began to feel uneasy again. Saloni was staring out at the sea through the windscreen, but the steady rain obscured the sight of it. She was trying to focus on the pattering of the rain drops on the windscreen and the roof of the car. On any given day, she would have gone crazy for it, but now, she couldn't set even a fraction of her attention towards the rain. Her eyes were greedy for his sight, her ears greedy for his voice and her lips greedy for his touch.

3:40 PM

Pooja felt so uncomfortable calling Sam once again for help in such a short time. She hated feeling indebted to him.

"Hi…" She greeted him.

"Hello" His voice missed his trademark zeal.

"Hope things are fine." she asked.

"Ya… fine." he replied.

Things were not fine. She was sure about that from his tone. She couldn't care as she had a task at hand.

"Tell me dear." Sam asked.

"I need another favor from you."

"Tell me, my princess."

"Well…" She hesitated.

"Would you do it?" she asked to confirm.

"Anything for you." Sam told sincerely.

Pooja hated his sincerity.

"Can you get me the address of a number which you gave me some time back?" Pooja directly asked, desperate to finish with him as soon as possible.

He was silent for some time.

"Is it so important? You see…" Sam was hesitant.

"It's important, very important." She was hasty.

"Oh baby… It's difficult now." He found it difficult to deny her request.

"Can I try some other time?" he asked her.

"You say you'll do anything for me, but not this small thing. Stop faking love. You people always make high promises. When the person you love is in need of help, you slip away with lame excuses. Don't ever say that you love me." She tried to extort him in utmost desperation.

"Don't say that, my love..." Sam still was in hesitation.

"Then why don't you do it for me?"

He was silent for a few seconds.

"I was fired from the job." He broke the pot.

"Yes... I was fired for breach of company's trust, as they caught me stealing customer data."

She was disturbed with the news.

"It was all because of me." She sobbed.

"I didn't want to reveal that, because I thought it might make you feel responsible for it, but you are not. I did it, knowing the risk." He tried to convince her.

She knew that she was responsible for it. She also knew how much Sam depended on the job.

Sam understood the silence.

"Hey baby... I'm not at all affected by this. I can get another job in no time." Sam tried to convince her.

Pooja felt as if she was stabbed by her conscience. She knew that it wouldn't be easy to get a job, when terminated for such reasons. Sam, though faced all the troubles because of her, still was convincing her that she was not responsible for it. Despite all his trouble, he was worried that Pooja might suffer guilty conscience.

"Why would someone be so nice to a miserable tramp like me?" she wondered.

She suddenly felt inferior that she could no longer continue the conversation with him. She abruptly disconnected the call and switched off her phone and wept like a child. She couldn't remember the last time she had cried like that. The angel, who was buried within her by her evil doppelganger, had been resurrected by the pure love of Sam.

3:45 PM

Both Sunny and Saloni sat in the car pretending to enjoy the rain, each lost in their own thoughts, occasionally stealing glances at each other. The pattering sound of the rain was interfered by a message alert. Sunny allowed Saloni to pick his phone. She picked the phone and opened the message. Her expression conveyed that it was not good news.

She retrieved the call history from the phone and called Pooja's number.

"What's wrong baby?" Saloni asked as soon as Pooja picked the call.

Her anxiety attracted his attention.

"Nothing" she replied.

Saloni knew that something was wrong.

"Tell me." She persisted.

"Sorry… I was not able to help you this time." she replied.

"I can see that. Now, I want to hear more." she asked.

"He got fired… He got fired from his job because of me." She wept. Saloni never saw Pooja cry like that.

"Come on, dear. Don't blame yourself. You are not responsible." Saloni tried to console her.

"Can you say that?" Pooja challenged her.

Saloni could not…

"Don't worry about me. You take care of yourself." Pooja said and disconnected the call.

Sunny gave her an inquiring look. She opened the message and handed over the phone to him which read:

Sorry… I couldn't help you further.

PURSUIT OF THE DEVIL

3:50 PM

They had reached so far on extempore planning at each level. It was like a puzzle, solving each level with the clues left out from the previous one. Every level seemed to be a dead end, yet they reached so far. They were back in the familiar situation, yet again.

"What next?" Sunny asked Saloni.

"There ought to be a way." She started thinking.

"It's remarkable that we tracked him down through the obscure path, with scarce clues."

"Thanks to you…" He mumbled in a voice just above the audible range, which was almost a whisper.

Saloni couldn't stop a smile, a small one though.

"We don't seem to have any hope this time." He was worried.

"We are sure that he's in Portshore." she said as she processed the bits of clues they had.

"The town may not be a big place, alright, but we can't knock every door or dig into every burrow in search of him." Sunny interrupted.

"We have the contact number of Hari's caretaker." Saloni replied.

"How is it going to help us? Agreed that the person is taking care of Hari, but how can we be sure that they stay together? How can we be sure whether the person is a boy or a girl? What kind of help could we expect from the person?" Sunny fired a volley of questions at Saloni.

"Let's find out." Saloni asked him to drive to a phone booth.

She dialed the number of Hari's caretaker from a pay phone and instantly heard an inebriated voice mumble on the phone.

"Hello…"

"Hello. Who's this?" she replied, unsure of what to talk.

"Tell me your name, bitch. You called." shouted a voice. Now Saloni indentified the voice of Hari, who had forgotten the fact that his sim card was in the boy's phone.

"The call is for me." Bhuvan shouted as he ended the game he was playing on his phone which still contained Hari's sim card. He was furious at him for the language he had used on his phone call.

Saloni immediately disconnected the call as she knew what she wanted to know.

"Luck is on our side." She beamed at the unexpected stroke of luck which confirmed that Hari was staying with his caretaker.

"Now we are sure that Hari is staying with his caretaker... who is a boy." Saloni told, not sure whether she had to mention that.

"That's good news. Can we get him to walk into our trap and force the information from him?" He sprang in rejuvenation.

Saloni was not excited with the suggestion.

"We don't know his strength. It wouldn't be wise to use brute force method, as we don't have sufficient strength." she said.

"It could be our last option though." She continued as she didn't like to shun his idea altogether.

"It would be better if we could track him down to his hide out, instead of pulling him out of it." she added.

"Pity that we don't have the magic crystal ball." he joked.

"We can extract something out from the guy on the phone." Saloni said, feeling uncomfortable with the thought of flirting with Hari's mate, who was a complete stranger to her, in front of Sunny. He understood her discomfort. Though he disparaged her in the beginning, he realized how unfairly he was prejudiced against her with his utterly wrong perception.

"People may not be strong enough to defeat fate, but it is the test of character to retain the purity of soul. Don't be hasty to judge people with their appearance, profession, association, or for that matter any incidents which convict them... For, first look can be deceiving." He enlightened himself.

When Bhuvan called back to check who it was, the call was unanswered as it was a public payphone.

4:00 PM

Hey darling.

Mom and dad are going out on a trip.
Come home tonight.
Let's have fun like we did last time ;-)

- Pooja

She messaged the text to the number of Hari's caretaker, assuming Pooja's name.

Sunny, who was seated beside her, didn't read the message, but just looked at her vaguely. He was curious to know what she was planning to do, but decided to mute his questions for some reason.

Saloni was not an expert in luring strangers, nor did she wish to learn the trick from Pooja. However her observation of Pooja's traits came to good use.

Saloni read Sunny's perplexed expression. She was not comfortable sharing her plan, but she felt that she was bound to.

"He might call in some time." she said briefly as she felt embarrassed to explain in detail.

He was good enough to grasp her embarrassment and didn't question any further.

"Been to Portshore before?" Sunny slightly stammered as he was not accustomed to casual talk with her.

"Huh?" Saloni was so happy about his casual talk, but still wanted to confirm it was real, as she had been having a lot of hallucinations since last night.

"Have you ever been to Portshore before?" He repeated.

"Well…"

The mobile started to ring, interrupting the conversation.

It was her first friendly conversation with Sunny since she met him last night and her fate couldn't bear the bliss of it.

"Damn the phone call." she cursed.

She put her finger across her lips and gestured him to stay silent. It was the same number she had messaged a few minutes ago. She shut her eyes and took a deep breath, still reluctant to exhibit herself as a vamp before Sunny.

"I got to do what I ought to do." She made up her mind.

"Hello darling… Ready for the fun tonight?" she attempted to speak in a husky tone, which rather sounded like whining. Thankfully it didn't make a difference to the boy.

"Hello… Who is this?" the boy on the other end asked. Saloni was happy about it, as Pooja used to say that young boys are always eager and hence easy to handle.

"Hey peter… What happened to your voice baby? Lot of drinks nowadays, huh?" she teased.

"Well…" There was some silence on the call. The boy seems to be an amateur with girls.

"That's an advantage." Pooja would say about amateurs.

"You can play them the way you want." she would explain.

Whatsoever, she was not experienced in enticing strangers through phone call.

"Peter, there…?" she stressed this time.

"Well…. Actually no." the boy said hesitantly, fearing that the conversation would end, as he loved the female voice.

"Oh. Must have used the wrong number..." she murmured.

"Sorry to have troubled you." She mocked an apology, closing the call with a chiming giggle rather obviously.

She felt so embarrassed to act like a coquette. She cursed her fate that she had never done that before and when she had to do it for the first time, it had to be before Sunny.

However the turn of events changed his opinion about Saloni, which enabled him to think positively about her. He wondered why she terminated the communication after they were lucky to get a call back from the person.

"Never let yourself seem like an easy target. It would give you the edge." Pooja would tell. Saloni, though was never interested in her lessons. She finally found good use of them.

Sunny was unaware of what was happening. He learnt to trust her on her judgments. Hence he dissolved all his questions. Silence prevailed for a few minutes. Saloni suddenly started to turn nervous with the thought of failing, which was a rare sight for Sunny.

"Have I made a mistake by ending the call?" She began to think of alternate plans.

She made a decision.

Sorry to have troubled you :-)

- Pooja

She messaged him and wished Pooja was there to help her.

"Amateurs are unpredictable. They are curious, yet might get disengaged out of fear or shyness. Nothing wrong in taking the lead..." Pooja would always say.

Saloni gripped the mobile with both the hands, close to her chest, in a silent prayer. Sunny could sense her determination in not letting him down. He confessed to himself that he was proud to have her as his partner. It was strange that he appreciated her without any ambiguity. He seemed to have got in terms with reality.

The mobile buzzed with a message alert in less than a minute.

No trouble at all. You have fun tonight ;-)

"Got him…" She was delighted. Now she had to be careful in hiding the desperation of getting him into the conversation, yet she had to keep him engaged.

Pooja: No fun tonight ☹

Hari's mate: Oh Sorry… Parent's trip cancelled? ;-)

Pooja: Parents' trip's confirmed, but my boyfriend is on a trip too ☹

Hari's mate: Oh… So sad. Can I help ;-)

He was hasty this time, but Saloni retained her composure.

Pooja: So kind of you… but, no thanks.

Hari's mate: Please don't be so rude to deny my help

Pooja: Sorry… I didn't mean to be rude. Just that I don't know you. See, I don't even know your name.

Hari's mate: Oh… If that's your problem, I'll solve it. My name is Bhuvan. Now, can I help you?

Pooja: Fine. What kind of help?

Bhuvan: Anything you miss tonight from your boyfriend

Pooja: That's a big help… I can't accept

Bhuvan: Why not?

Pooja: We are still strangers

Bhuvan: I have an idea for that too. Let's meet up and know each other. Then we won't be strangers

Bhuvan gained confidence from her responses.

Pooja: You seem to be full of ideas... Let me think about it.

Bhuvan: Sure... I hope you won't break my heart.

Pooja: Hey... Gotta go now. Catch you soon. Bye...

Bhuvan: Will be waiting. Bye

Saloni sighed with relief as she was satisfied with the outcome of the idea, despite her inexperience. She wanted to let Sunny know about the status, however, she wasn't comfortable sharing it with him. Yet she had to do it.

"We have him on track. We can use him in our plan."

"What is our plan?" he asked with controlled curiosity.

"We can use him to locate Hari." she informed.

"You can't ask him where he's hiding him." he queried politely.

"Yes, I can't ask him where he is hiding him, but I can ask him where he is." Saloni erased Sunny's doubts.

"Why didn't I think about that?" He felt embarrassed at his silly question.

"We can start with knowing the area he is in." Saloni said.

Sunny was tempted to ask her to call him immediately, but he let her do it at her own pace.

"Want a drive around?" he asked her, which even surprised himself by his cordiality with her.

"Thank you so much. I prefer sitting here." She gave him the broadest smile, which she couldn't hide. She hated saying no to him, but driving around, she insanely felt as if the time was flying. By sitting still, she felt as if she could slow down the time, and savor his company longer.

They sat there silently staring emptily at nothing, captured by myriad of thoughts, occasionally stealing glances of each other, but not for long. They were interrupted by the ringing of the phone. She hated it.

She checked the number on the phone display.

"So soon..." she thought.

Saloni nervously glanced at him through the corner of her eye.

"I'll be back." he said and walked outside into the humbled rain as he understood her embarrassment.

She thanked him within herself for understanding, and also wondered how there could be a time when she would be glad off his company. She hated the possibility.

"Hello." she answered the call, desperate to complete it as soon as possible, so that she could have Sunny's proximity back.

"Hello... Oh, it's you. I dialed your number by mistake." Bhuvan spoke in hasty explanation.

"It's a trademark excuse of an amateur."

"Got him!!!" Saloni thought.

"It's ok... Catch you later... Bye." Saloni said, wishing that he would be persistent, and he was.

"Now, that I have called, can we chat for a while?" he pleaded. He hadn't call to say bye.

"What do you want to talk about?" she teased him.

"You know... It is so pleasant talking to you. Can we...?" He hesitated

"Can we?" She encouraged him to continue.

"Can we meet?" He completed the sentence.

"Where do you live?" she asked careful not to raise suspicion.

"I live at the Saltfort industrial estate." Saloni was hit by nostalgia when she heard the name of the place.

"Where do you live?" he asked her.

Saloni wasn't prepared for the question.

"Dad's calling. They're about to leave. Call you later." she told in a suppressed tone and disconnected the call immediately.

As soon as she disconnected the call, Sunny dropped the cigarette and walked to the car, as he was eager to know what was happening.

"He lives at the Saltfort industrial estate." Saloni told him.

The mention of the place brought many thoughts to him, but he focused on the task.

"What next?" he asked his usual question.

"Since he lives in an industrial area, it would be nice if we could get lucky to catch any sound in the background, during the call, which could earn us a clue." Saloni said.

"Trouble is if we don't have any background sound, which is more probable…" She opined.

As she was drafting a plan, Sunny was struggling hard to bring something out of his mind. Saloni noticed him rubbing his nose as he was thinking. The amaranthine images from the album of her childhood flooded back to her, where Sandy used to mock Sunny for his nose rubbing habit.

"Amazing that few things live forever…" she thought, shaking her back to reality staring at him with amusement.

"How about creating one?" he shouted in enthusiasm.

"What?" Saloni asked in confusion.

"How about creating a background sound?" Sunny repeated.

She seemed to have mildly understood what he said, but she was not clear about it.

"We know the area he lives in. As we know, Saltfort is not a big place. We can have his companion in conversation with you and then run some sound throughout the area and see if it hits the spot. We can relate the background sound to his location." he clarified.

"That's an awesome idea." Saloni spoke in loud appreciation which made him blush.

Sunny was finally pleased that he could claim a bit of respect for himself with some intellectual contribution.

"Do you think we can create one?" she asked in contagious spirit.

"I... think... we can." he spoke thinking deeply.

It was a difficult task, but he knew whom to trust.

4:22 PM

"What the fuck have you gotten yourself into? You better not get your feet in here, if you wish to continue breathing." Steven warned him.

Sunny felt like a bolt of lightning hitting him right on his head. He was visibly shaken. Saloni observed his change of expression, but thought it was not wise to interfere at that time.

He took a deep breath and continued "Do me a favor?"

"I will do anything for you, but you do me a favor... Don't come here... at least forever." he responded.

Sunny was not ready to let the fear dictate him. He made up his mind.

"Shut the fuck up and tell me if you'll help me or not." he screamed.

Steven was not so pleased with his carelessness.

"Tell me." he replied when Sunny explained him the plan.

Steven was shocked at what he had just heard.

"Are you kidding? Don't fool yourself and get back to a safe place." he told.

"Yes or no?" Sunny was persistent.

"I can't let you get killed." He was concerned

"Cut the crap and tell me. Don't waste my time."

There was silence for a few moments.

"Bastard... Would you let me say no?" Steven shouted with a sigh of resignation.

Saloni, who was awed by his brilliant idea, was bothered by his sudden grief.

"Was that Sunny?" Krish asked Steven as he completed the call.

"Now... Here's your part." Sunny explained Saloni with a bit of hesitation.

"You... You keep in continuous conversation with the guy." He was careful in avoiding words which could dishonor her.

She understood his intensions and her joy knew no bounds.

"Sure... you got it." she said with a mild smile.

"All set?" she asked.

"Not yet…"

"We need another phone." he said thinking of a way to get one.

Saloni was anticipating a solution from him, as she found it as another opportunity to see him blush.

"Payphone" he said with finality, as he couldn't think of a better option.

"Couldn't find a better option…" Saloni nodded in approval.

The sky gradually cleared the clouds shrouding it. Sunny drove past numerous payphones, looking for the most isolated one. He called Steven, as he drove, hunting for a favorable payphone.

"I'll call you from a payphone in a minute… You better be on your toes now." he disconnected the call and drove towards the most convenient payphone. He picked the most isolated payphone from the rows of shops. He stopped the car at the phone booth.

"Can't get a better one than this."

For a brief moment, his eyes locked with hers as he handed the mobile phone to her.

"This is the most crucial part of the plan. We have to have all our focus and timing on this one." He emphasized.

Saloni nodded in assurance and Sunny had no reason to doubt her capability.

He had another trouble to sort out - He needed a load of coins to make sure that the call would not end due to the lack of it. He walked to the provision store nearby as it didn't have customers. His arrival delighted the shopkeeper at the prospect of a customer.

"I'm in a hurry…" Sunny said.

"Please pick your item sir. You would be off in a jiffy." The shop keeper encouraged him.

"Well I don't need any items." The shopkeeper frowned as he continued.

"You see… I need coins to use for the payphone." he said.

"Sorry sir… Can't help you on that." The shopkeeper told in frustration.

"I need them badly." He didn't hide his desperation.

"Well… You will be charged extra for that." The shopkeeper told as he wanted to make the most of his scarce opportunity.

"Two for one. How many coins do you need?" the shopkeeper said without asking for his approval, as he guessed he wouldn't deny.

"All you have." was his response which shocked the shopkeeper and also raised suspicion.

"All the coins…?" he repeated the question as he wasn't sure what he heard was right.

"All the coins." he confirmed.

"You see… My mother is in depression and she wants to talk to me. She talks a lot." he explained unnecessarily.

The shopkeeper gave a suspicious glance towards him and turned to the cash counter.

Sunny didn't like his glance.

The shopkeeper turned towards him with fistful of coins.

"Twenty." he said as he dropped the coins on the table.

"That will charge you forty rupees." he told him, still trying to gauge his desperation.

"Can you get more of it?" he asked the shopkeeper as he paid the amount.

"I'm sorry, but nobody would be interested to trade coins, sir." the shopkeeper responded.

"I'll pay you triple." Sunny tried to make a deal, but the shopkeeper was skeptical about it.

"I can't promise you anything, but I'll see what I can do." the shopkeeper answered.

Sunny swept the coins on the table into his pocket and walked steadily towards the phone booth and shut himself in it. He knew that his plan couldn't offer a chance of success unless they streamed in all their focus to their ears and he also thought that the number of coins couldn't offer him the expected length of call.

4:40 PM

All set.

He dialed Steven's number and waited for the call to get connected. He then signaled thumbs up to Saloni who also dialed the number of Hari's caretaker.

"Hello..." The voice at the other end spoke.

"Hi baby... It's Pooja here. Missing you already honey." Saloni faked desperation.

"Can't be more than I miss you baby." he responded.

"On track." Saloni thought responding with a thumbs up to Sunny.

She didn't even think about what all she would talk with him. She was just trying to impersonate Pooja, but she wasn't sure she possessed her skills.

"Hope he carries on from here." She prayed.

"Steve… You're on now." He instructed Steven to start.

"Ladies and gentlemen… This is a message in public interest." Steven started his announcement.

"Life is a precious gift." He continued as he couldn't deny Sunny's request, as that was his first request for help in all the years of their friendship.

"Please do not throw away the gift due to some petty problems in life." He paused for a couple of seconds as per the plan to let Sunny get signal from Saloni to proceed further. If the announcement was heard on Saloni's call, they had hit the spot. Sunny believed it could take a very long time or for that matter, the ploy was not a sure success fetcher.

"Go on." Sunny signaled Steven to proceed further.

"Depression is just a temporary state of mind. It will pass, if you let it. Do not take hasty decisions. When you have one reason to end your life, you have hundred reasons to continue living."

"Go on."

"The decision you take in the spurt of moment will hurt your loved ones lifelong. Your family needs you… Don't forsake them. Join the campaign and Live stronger." He kept reading the announcement which was actually an NGO initiative assigned to him a week ago, as a campaign to control suicides. He was just repeating the message he had personally announced a week ago.

"Damn it… Why did I choose this message?" Steven thought, feeling uneasy about the correlation of the message.

"Am I walking into a suicide?" he thought sarcastically.

"Go on." Sunny signaled him to move further.

"I'm getting bored being alone." Saloni told faking boredom.

"I got an idea to get rid of your boredom... Guess?" Bhuvan said, inviting her for a naughty talk.

"I give up." She played along.

"I'll meet you at your place, right away." Bhuvan spoke with the enthusiasm of a child.

"That's a mind blowing idea sweetie... but you have to wait for some more time." Saloni told

"This is killing me, darling." Bhuvan expressed his disappointment.

"It's doing the same to me baby... but good things take time, don't they...?" Saloni responded.

"Well then... Perhaps I need to make use of the phone for now." Bhuvan told mischievously.

"What are you wearing now?" Bhuvan started to flirt.

"Bastard" Saloni thought. She composed herself, as she knew that he was their only chance.

"Don't worry about what I'm wearing now... They won't trouble you when we meet up." She responded as flirtatiously as possible.

"Damn you Pooja. How did you do this?" She cursed as she continued the conversation.

Although Sunny knew that it was not a cakewalk with the plan, was still hopeful. He was keenly watching Saloni, waiting for a signal. Saloni looked in the direction of Sunny as she spoke on the phone, but occasionally looked away from him, which explained to him that she was going through some uncomfortable conversation. He felt bad for her, but she was the only chance for him.

The conversation seemed to go on and on without any success. Sunny knew that he was running out of coins.

"Wish I had a recorded tape, so that I could just play it." Steven thought, as he felt very uneasy acting normal with such a serious motive behind.

He prayed that he should find the location immediately, so that he could get out of the hook as soon as possible. At the same time, he also wished he would never find the location, so that it could save trouble for Sunny. Meanwhile Sunny kept dropping the coins into the slot as he counted the remaining coins every time, which surely discouraged him. He kept staring at the shopkeeper with the hope that he would fetch some coins. The coins counted down to single digit, still no positive sign from Saloni.

"Is this plan viable in the first place?" he wondered as his wait didn't seem to end.

"Go on"

"Go on"

"Go on"

It went on and on.

"How much area is left to be covered yet?" Sunny asked Steven.

"Not much left." Steven told him, switching off the mike.

"Are you running fast?" he asked him fearing they might have already missed the target on the run.

"I wouldn't cheat you, Sunny." Steven told him, evidently hurt.

"Keep going." Sunny said, not willing to waste any more time.

The hungry telephone prompted him to drop a coin and he dropped one more.

It kept going on without any success.

"Go on"

"Go on"

He kept repeating the phrase, but to his embarrassment, he realized that he was speaking to the dead phone.

"Damn it. It was one idea I proposed and it had to fail so miserably. I'm no good." He cursed himself, brooding over his utter failure.

It was just then he realized that he had stopped looking at Saloni for signals. When he looked in her direction, he was flabbergasted. He noticed that Saloni was trying to convey some positive news to him with her thumbs up.

Sunny understood that his plan was on the verge of success and he feared letting it slip away.

He searched all his pockets and wallet for coins, but to no avail. In the phone booth, he struggled like a caged wild animal.

"Don't fail me now…" he prayed, searching desperately for coins. Luck was playing a prank on him. Saloni looked at him in despair, as the background announcement kept fading away and stopped after sometime.

Sunny noticed that her thumbs up gradually moved downwards and finally formed thumbs down.

He punched the booth in dejection. Saloni noticed his actions and understood that he was short of coins. She pitied him, as she was also in no position to help him.

"I need more coins... I need more coins." When Sunny thought of approaching the shopkeeper again for a few more coins, Saloni remembered him throwing some change on the dashboard, which he collected at the toll gate. She scanned the dashboard and found a few coins to her delight.

"Something is better than nothing." she thought as she picked them and waved at him, still continuing with the call.

Sunny was delighted when he noticed the coins in Saloni's hand. He swiftly ran towards her and nearly snatched the coins from her hand.

He threw himself into the booth and dialed Steven's number.

"Go back in the direction you came." he told Steven without any preamble, as he knew that he had only three coins with him, which meant he had only three minutes to track down the spot.

"Okay..." Steven drove back in the direction he had just travelled.

Sunny looked in the direction of Saloni, dropping one more coin into the slot just as Steven continued with the announcement.

After some a short wait, she held her hand gradually raising her thumb, indicating that he was approaching the target. He was ecstatic and anxious at the same time. She raised her thumb upright and then moved her thumb gradually down as Steven moved past the location.

"Drive back" Sunny told him and waited for Saloni to give a full thumbs-up. Just as she raised her thumb upright, he asked Steven to stop as he dropped the last coin.

"Just switch on and off a few times." he said willing to confirm that Saloni got it right.

Saloni put her thumbs up and down synchronizing Stevens sound.

"Now... Tell me where you've stopped without wasting a moment." Sunny asked him fearing the call would get disconnected before he got the information.

Steven paused a few seconds.

"Are you there?" he shouted in desperation.

"Yes." Steven replied as he revealed the location.

Sunny turned to Saloni and raised his thumb up to her as he gotten the details from Steven.

It was a ruined building, occasionally used by some college guys to smoke weed.

"You did it Steve..." The call ended with a beep before he could complete the sentence and he had no more coins to continue the conversation. He needed none.

5:04 PM

"Can't do without a drink now..." Steven thought, driving straight to his regular bar.

"We'll have fun tonight, at my place." Saloni said and disconnected the call, as she saw Sunny rush to the car. Saloni, with some knowledge of the places, gave him some random address which she was not even sure, existed.

"Let's move." he told triumphantly as he jumped onto the seat.

5:24 PM

Sunny and Saloni stared at the charred building in the isolated place, which looked as if it was painted with gloom. He studied the building for a few seconds and then turned to Saloni.

"Well... Here is where we split. Thank you so much for all your help. I couldn't have done this without you." he said with evident gratitude.

"I can't leave you alone..." Saloni turned hysteric that she blurted the words out of her mouth without her consciousness.

"Pardon..." Sunny asked in confusion.

"Well... I mean... you... you might need help out there." For the first time in their journey together, he saw Saloni struggle for words.

"That's so very kind of you, but I can't let you do this. I had already been so mean to get you so far for my selfish reasons." he confessed.

"Well..." Her heart was beating hard. She was unable to find words, as she was struck by immense grief of splitting with him, for the second time. Though she knew that some time, this had to happen, she wasn't prepared enough.

"I couldn't have asked for a better companion. Hope we meet again in a better circumstance." Sunny said sincerely, stretching his hand towards her.

She felt the whole world spinning around her.

"Please take me a few hours back in time..." she prayed as she unwillingly stretched her hand towards his. She shook his hand hating to think about departure.

"This is the end of the road for me!" she thought with excruciating pain.

"Take care of your life." She managed to say as she released his hand immediately and swiftly walked away from him without turning back. She did not even let Sunny bid farewell to her.

He saw her disappear at the curve of the road, but still was surrounded by her mystical air. Her thoughts were hypnotic, pulling him into a never ending pool of unanswered questions. He shook her off his thoughts and turned back towards the charred structure.

He stood still for a minute preparing himself for a violent encounter and then walked fast towards his destination, without wasting any more time.

It was still a well-lit day, as the sun shone well above the horizon. When Sunny reached the entrance, he walked in cautiously, ready to face his enemy from any direction. As he walked through a curly path, he realized that though it was not dark outside, it was inside. It was a huge building and he didn't expect to find him as soon as he entered it. He tried his best to see things around him, but he saw nothing and heard nothing except for the chirping of the crickets, which gave a spooky background to the demonic building. As he kept moving randomly in the hope of a fluke to find the way, he spotted a faint glimmer of light at some height. He faintly noticed the stairs lead to the bright spot.

THE ATONEMENT

5:27 PM

Saloni was so disoriented that it became a herculean task for her to focus on where she was and where she was walking to. She actually didn't know where to go and what to do as her world had so suddenly turned dark. She felt as if she was pitifully watching herself stagger on the road. She knew that she couldn't go on like that. She mustered all her strength and tightly wrapped her arms around herself, as if not letting her slip away from herself. She wondered what made her deserve the pain.

As she was mentally lost with all the questions, she was abruptly woken up by the ringing of the phone in her jacket pocket. It was then she realized that she forgotten to handover few of Sunny's belongings back to him. *"I wish I could go back to him under the pretext of handing him back all his belongings…"* she thought.

"All his belongings…?" She wondered whether she belonged in that category. She was drawn out of her

thoughts with the continuous ringing of the phone. She immediately retrieved the phone and found Pooja's number on the display. She really needed to talk her heart out to someone and she knew that she was the only one.

"Pooja…" She spoke feebly.

"Baby… you don't sound good." Pooja was concerned.

"No problem, dear." Saloni answered though her tone said otherwise.

Pooja was silent for few seconds.

"Get back here at once." Pooja instructed Saloni as she thought something was wrong with her.

It was then that a part of her numerous questions got answered.

"I'm not getting back there, darling." Saloni answered with certainty, which surprised Pooja.

She firmly decided that she was not going back. Her life had changed overnight.

"Are you alright?" Pooja questioned.

"Alright" she meekly said.

Saloni wanted to tell her something, but she was not able to put them in words.

"I'll tell you something, baby." Saloni opened up.

"Yes" Pooja answered careful not to miss anything.

"You know Sunny?"

"Yes…" Pooja was unable to guess what to expect.

"He was the one with me since last evening." Saloni spoke with a glint of joy, despite her pain, as she spelled his name.

"What…?" It was unbelievable for Pooja.

"Was she dreaming?" she thought as she didn't mention about him all through the time.

"You heard right… And I'm perfectly sane" She clarified.

"If that's really true… that's awesome news baby…" Pooja was ecstatic.

"Did he identify you?" She was curious too.

"Not yet." She frowned.

"What the fuck? Why don't you tell him?" she urged her.

"How would I tell him? And what would he think of me?"

"Look baby… If he really loves you, he won't care about all that. Just tell him." she advised.

"How can you be sure?" Saloni asked her.

"You'll never know until you try." she answered.

"What if he doesn't want to accept me?" she asked.

"At least you would have done all you could." said Pooja.

"You are right." she said.

"Advise is always easier that action." she thought as she knew that she would never do that.

"Then do it… Now… now… just now." Pooja spoke like an enthusiastic child. Saloni felt so lucky to have such a friend, who would be glad for her despite loads of her own problems.

"Sure baby…" She assured, though not sure.

"Would you do something for me?" Saloni asked Pooja

"Anything" she replied.

"Would you stop giving in to fate and try something better?" Saloni asked her.

Pooja was silent for some time.

"What do you exactly suggest?" Pooja asked her, seriously.

"Quit the joint, baby. Get married and have a family. Get settled in life."

"Are you kidding me? How exactly do I do that?" she asked, even though she knew where she was leading to.

"Just listen to your heart, dear. Don't go by your so called practical ways." She ridiculed her concept of practical thinking.

Pooja frowned.

"Listen to me...Open up with Sam." Saloni advised.

"Would Victor allow that?" Pooja revealed her concern.

"Forget about that bastard. He has nothing to do with your life."

"Just follow your heart, dear. Everything will fall in place." she assured.

"How can you be sure?" Pooja questioned.

"You'll never know until you try." she repeated her answer.

"You have already decided to lose him. You can't lose anything more when you are already prepared for the worst." Saloni said.

Pooja suddenly developed a sense of self confidence after she knew what had happened with Saloni.

"I'll see honey." Pooja answered.

"Promise me darling." Saloni was adamant.

"Sure baby. I'll do it... at least for my sake." she promised.

"Next time, call me with good news sweetie." Pooja urged her.

"I'll try. You take care darling. You are worth much more than what you think you are." Saloni assured.

"I won't let you down, my angel. Take care. Call me soon." Pooja said.

"Bye." Saloni. said. She disconnected the call, feeling a bit relieved.

A short journey with Sunny had changed her life altogether. However fate had rendered Saloni to lead a solitary life thereafter.

5:30 PM

Pooja pondered over her conversation with Saloni.

You'll never know until you try.

She recalled her words over and over again.

Though she feared her inherent misfortune, she was lured by the greed for a miracle.

She finally made up her mind to go for it.

She immediately picked her phone and thought for a few seconds before she dialed Sam's number. However, she prayed that her call shouldn't be answered.

"Hey angel… It's such a pleasant surprise." Sam said as he picked her call.

"Look…"

"I can't look. I can only hear." Sam joked.

Pooja ignored his attempt to humor her.

"I called to make a confession." she bluntly said.

"Not again… Won't you stop making confessions? You could do nothing that calls for a confession, Chris." Sam said.

"My name is not Chris…" She hesitated for a few seconds and then continued, "Pooja is my name." It was proving to be more difficult than she had imagined.

Sam patiently waited for her to complete.

"My affair with you was only a bet, which I had won by betraying your trust." she told.

There was silence for a few seconds.

"That could be easily forgiven. I still love you." Sam replied cheerfully.

Pooja was surprised that Sam didn't feel bad to have been manipulated by her. She was however sure that he wouldn't be generous enough to forgive her when she was finished her confession.

"Don't be so sure. I haven't completed yet." she warned him.

Sam waited to hear more.

Pooja couldn't muster enough courage to speak what she intended to. She took a deep breath and then continued.

"I make my living by hiring my body for sexual pleasure." She tried to present it as decently as she could.

There was silence again - longer this time. Sam was really shocked by the last part of her confession. He remained stunned without response. She then realized that rhetorics couldn't negate her sins. Pooja lost hope.

"Yes… I'm a whore. A bloody whore ready to serve my body on a platter for money..." she screamed and sobbed.

No response from Sam. Pooja composed herself after a minute of sobbing.

"It's time to say goodbye." she said.

Still no response

She suspected if the call was disconnected.

"No… The call is not disconnected." Pooja assured herself as she could hear heavy breathing on the phone. With the silence, his answer was understood.

"You have already decided to lose him. You can't lose anything more when you are already prepared for the worst." She recalled the conversation.

"It's better not to try when failure is a certainty. At least I could have avoided a heart wrecking encounter." She thought, regretting that she was encouraged by Saloni's words.

She finally heard Sam's voice just as she was about to disconnect the call.

"I hate to say goodbye on phone. Can we meet up at the Café tomorrow? One last time…" Sam said as disappointment was evident from his voice.

Pooja thought for half a minute. She feared looking into his disdainful eyes when they would meet up.

"No." was her stiff answer, as she made up her mind to end the game.

STAGE SET

5:30 PM

Steven had the day of his life, but he was sure if it wasn't a good one. He drove back to his shop after a quick soothing drink.

"Jesus... I wish I wake up in the morning knowing all this was a dream." he prayed as he unloaded the speakers from the vehicle.

As he stepped into the shop, the sight of Irfan shocked him to death.

"Good evening brother. P... Pleasant surprise..." he stammered.

"What brought you here?" he asked.

Irfan swiftly walked towards him and swung a hard punch on his jaw.

"You brought me here Steve. You." he said.

Steven was dazed for a few seconds that the shop seemed to spin around him. He didn't know whether it was the effect of the drink or the punch, but the shop didn't stop spinning. As things gradually got back to its positions, he spotted Krish in one corner of the shop. His swollen face revealed that he was already done with. When he looked back at Irfan, he knew that he had never seen him so furious. Steven absolutely had no idea what to do, as he stared back at Krish for any hint, who nodded in defeat as he recalled his short encounter with Irfan.

"What's Steve up to?" Irfan asked Krish wrapping his hand around his shoulder.

Irfan suspected the timing and the purpose of the propaganda, as he knew that Steven currently didn't have any contracts.

"I don't know what you are talking about, brother." Krish told innocently.

"Look... My brother is in a box now. I have prepared one more for his company. I believe you won't want to be the one." Irfan threatened.

"I don't know what he..." Krish could speak nothing more for a couple of minutes as he experienced a thundering crash on his ribs. Krish was terrified watching Irfan with his clenched fist and furious eyes.

He retreated a few steps to regain his breath.

"I believe you'll take me seriously now..."

"Don't keep me waiting for long... I have run out of patience." Irfan bellowed.

Krish knew that it was wise to take him seriously. He was also terrified of the moment that could land him another murderous punch on his ribs. He knew he wouldn't survive another one.

Just as he was struggling to make a decision, he saw Irfan raise his fist.

"He got a call from Sunny..." Krish said in a hurry.

"Steven got a call from Sunny... I... I don't know what it was about." he hastily confessed.

"Take me to him..." Irfan commanded.

Steven stared at Krish with contempt of betrayal. Krish was actually a tough nut to crack, but not for Irfan. He could make the bravest person shiver with mere rage in his eyes.

"You were like a brother to me. But by ganging up with the son of a bitch who got my brother killed, you've proved to be on the wrong side." Irfan spoke between his clenched teeth.

"Listen... I swore to kill my brother's killer. I won't mind killing anyone who protects him." he warned.

"Sunny would never be a reason for any harm to Imran. Believe me, big brother." Steven assured, but received a hard blow down his ribs in response.

"Now... You've started pissing me off. Better be sure of what you are going to talk hereafter, because I'm going to take it very seriously." He spoke in a menacing voice.

Steven's mind turned blank, as he stood perplexed, not knowing what to say.

"I want to know everything." Irfan grunted.

"I have no intension of wasting any more time with you. You have less than a minute to make up your mind. Believe me. Less than a minute..." Irfan further emphasized, pressurizing him.

Steven knew that Irfan was not kidding. He had to make a decision in less than a minute now.

Just as he was contemplating what to say, he saw Irfan raise his fist. It was then he realized that he had elapsed his minute already. He had never been so terrified in his life.

"I'll tell." he screamed before Irfan landed a punch on his face.

"I'll tell. Everything..."

5:30 PM

Saloni recollected all the events since the previous night.

"God... Why can't I be with Sunny, when he is alone in trouble?" She cursed her luck.

Suddenly something struck in her mind.

"Sunny is alone, alright. How can I be sure Hari is also alone?" She panicked.

Saloni decided to confirm. She immediately retrieved the called numbers and called a number.

"Hello, sweetheart." Saloni spoke in a husky tone.

"Hello..." Bhuvan whispered.

"What happened darling? Are you in the middle of a sermon or what?" She laughed. All this she was doing with great difficulty.

"Alright... I'll tell you why I called you now. My parents expect me to catch up with them on their trip, due to some emergency. I'll have to leave tonight. So... let's meet now." she said.

Bhuvan was not in a position to leave.

"Can we meet sometime later?" He knew that Victor was so particular about having Hari in his sight for obvious reasons.

"Never mind. Good bye. And don't call me again." she spoke with evident displeasure persuading him to make a hasty decision.

"Don't say that dear. I'm dying to meet you." Bhuvan swore.

"If you want to meet me, now is the time." she warned him.

"Do I need to babysit this stinking piece of shit?" Bhuvan reasoned his decision to leave him alone.

"Just a second baby…" he told as he closed the mouth piece and spoke to Hari "I need to go out for a while."

"Fuck off." Hari shouted which Saloni couldn't hear.

"Coming or not?" Saloni asked with finality.

"Sure darling. Coming right away." he told.

She was sure that Bhuvan would be away for enough time. She was happy that she could help Sunny in some way and hoped there was no one else with Hari. With that hope, she then started to walk towards a new beginning of her life.

FINAL RETRIBUTION

5:30 PM

Sunny carefully walked up the ruined stairs. The stairs shivered under his weight that he wondered how much longer they would stay intact. He walked, careful not to break them with his medium weight as he progressed each step with absolute caution. He sighed with relief when he successfully reached the end of the ascending stairs. As he kept walking towards the source of light, he still heard nothing but the chirping of the crickets and mild rustling noise of his own footsteps. They seem to be all over the building. He slowly walked away from the light, through what seemed like corridor. He settled down on a slab in a narrow corner and concentrated on the sounds, expecting to hear some voices. He occasionally heard rustling noises amplified by the hollowness of the building. Suddenly the noise of a phone ringing resonated across the whole building, bringing him to his feet in an instant

"I blew it." He cursed himself for his lack of thought to keep his phone on silent mode. As he swiftly fished his pocket for his phone, he realized that he forgotten to retain the phone from Saloni.

"Hello…" He heard a whisper which still tore the silence to shreds.

"Can we meet sometime later?"

"Don't say that dear. I'm dying to meet you." the person spoke. He was desperate to please someone on the call. Each word reverberated throughout the building.

"Just a second baby." he said.

"I need to go out for a while." he seemed to talk off the phone.

"Fuck off." Sunny heard the other person scream.

He immediately identified him as he had the registered his voice in his mind so vividly; he could identify the sound of his breath. As soon as he recognized Hari's voice, he involuntarily clenched his fist, ready to kill him with a punch anytime he would face him. Waiting for the best time to attack him, he stayed still in his position. He was not worried about his own safety, but was careful not to miss his chance.

"Sure darling. Coming right away." Sunny heard the person speak on phone.

There was a graveyard silence as the conversation ended. He silently waited, thinking of a plan to make the best attack. He then realized how badly he missed Saloni. When he saw a boy emerge out of the door, he guessed that he was the one who had unknowingly helped him find the location.

As the boy walked out, he augmented Sunny's trouble by closing the door, blocking the scarce light, which let him grasp things.

"Damn it." He cursed as he concentrated on the movement of his enemy's companion. He understood that he was walking away when he heard the stairs squeak under the careless footsteps of a person in hurry. The sound hinted that he was moving quickly in the darkness, which implied that he was well accustomed to the design of the building. What would have taken a few minutes for him took just a few seconds for the boy. He was relieved as he heard the footsteps recede towards the exit. He sat silently in the dark for some time, thinking about his next step.

"Now is the time." Sunny thought, as he finally planned his attack and walked cautiously towards the door from where the young boy had emerged. He dragged his feet slowly towards the entrance. As he reached the entrance, he slightly pushed the door ajar. He carefully peeped in without exposing himself much in the light. He ran a quick scan across the dimly lit room to find nothing but empty space. Just as he retreated from the light, he felt an iron grip on his shoulder, which hiked his heartbeat. He stood still for a couple of seconds, before he yanked off the grip, which pushed him back into the light. As he stared into the darkness, he saw Hari emerge out of the darkness like a beast.

"Son of a bitch, can't you find better ways of ending your life?" he screamed as he ran towards him.

Sunny immediately shut the door, blocking the meager light flowing out of the room. Now, there was nothing but darkness. Hari still managed to crash himself onto him, tripping and rolling onto the weathered stairs. They held each other tightly. As they rolled down a few steps, the perishing slabs of cement stairs crumbled under their weight, dropping them down onto the dusty floor below. Even as they fell down, they didn't leave hold of each other as they feared losing the other in the darkness. Hari ran his hand to his scabbard strapped around his waist, eager to drive his *kukri* into Sunny's chest, but to his disappointment, his weapon fell down somewhere during the fall. He growled in frustration like a mad dog. Sunny, though didn't lose his sanity, was equally furious. They wrestled along for sometime, knocking each other down. Hari pinned Sunny to the ground and slightly lifted himself, careful not to lose his grip and swung his fist to land hard on his face, but he was not lucky enough, as his punch grazed his cheek, hurting him very slightly. Sunny returned a mighty punch in reflex. His luck delivered the punch right on his jaw, throwing him a few feet away from him. There was rustling sound as Hari fell to the ground. Sunny immediately rolled away and stood up on his feet. He wasn't sure whether to go for him or wait for him to come to him. Skeptical about his next move, he slowly and carefully moved couple of feet away from where he stood, waiting for any sound to hint the location of his target. He then made up his mind and moved around cautiously throwing his fist randomly in air with the hope of hitting him. Hari on the other side was also doing the same, as he got to his feet. After some blind punching, Sunny stood still and concentrated on sounds around him to see if he could grasp the sound of Hari's footsteps. He didn't move for some time. Absolute silence dominated the hellacious structure for a while when he suddenly sensed a movement to his left, probably a few yards away from him. As he got prepared to run him down, he heard another set of footsteps to his right.

"Hell no… *The filthy bastard got his companion back*." Sunny cursed his fate.

"*I don't care if it's two or twenty; the bastard is destined to die in my hands*." he swore.

Hari thought that it was Sunny and ran mindlessly towards the source of sound. Sunny also heard hasty footsteps loitering around. Only the hearing sense was active for both of them as there was nothing around but rustling sound. He ran towards the direction of the sound, swinging his fists with the hope of hitting one, not caring about the noise he created. Hearing the second set of footsteps, Hari guessed it was Bhuvan. He was happy that he got some help, as he started to feel the effect of excessive drinking.

"Come on bum. Make yourself fucking useful." Hari screamed out, filling the whole building with the echo. They shot punches aimlessly in the dark. Sunny started to feel impatient with the frustrating game. He thought it wouldn't be a bad idea to throw some stones around in the dark, hoping he might be lucky to hit the bull's eye. He cautiously bent down, to search for some hurting mass of stones. As he carefully bent down, running his hands across the floor in the darkness, he was startled by the approach of a pair of legs right in front of him. He would have been definitely hit, had he been on his feet, as Hari was madly throwing his fists around. As soon as he felt Hari's legs on his head, he threw a heavy punch around his groin area, which tumbled him down. He quickly stood on his feet and moved a few steps away in reflex. The building resonated with the whimpers of Hari for a few seconds and then the atmosphere regained its silence.

The game of hide and seek started yet again. The eerie silence of the humongous ghost house was torn apart by the ringing of a phone. When Sunny focused on locating the direction of the sound, his luck smiled on him. Hari picked the phone from his pocket to see who was calling, exposing himself in the backlight of the phone. It was only then he realized his foolishness, but it was too late, as he saw Sunny storm towards him and sweep him off his foot. The phone in Hari's hand dropped down, as Sunny carried him with the hope of crashing him onto some pillar. Unfortunately, he tripped on a concrete block and fell forward, throwing Hari's body onto the disintegrating wall a few feet away, shattering a part of the wall. A stream of light flowed in through the hole, superseding a strip of darkness, although it was unable to defeat the darkness overall. Hari regained his position and stood up dazed as he stared at Sunny, who was also badly hurt with the tripping. He noticed that Sunny wasn't quick enough to regain his position. Eager to make use of the advantage, he was ready to pounce on Sunny. Just then a hollow concrete block crashed on his head. Sunny's expression changed from confusion to joy, as the silhouette of person moved into the light.

It was Saloni. She couldn't muster enough will power to walk away from him in times of trouble.

When she heard the phone still ringing, she picked the phone from the pocket and ended the call. Sunny understood that it was Saloni's intelligence that saved him, but he didn't know that it was Saloni again who had lured Hari's companion away from him, rendering him alone.

She shifted her gaze towards Sunny, who was grateful for her help. For some time they ignored the existence of

Hari who seemed to have fallen unconscious with the strong blow from Saloni. Sunny casually got to his feet and walked a couple of steps.

"Why did you do this? You could get hur..." Sunny was unable to complete his sentence as he felt unbearable pain when he shifted his weight on his left leg. He realized that he had cramped his left calf with the fall.

"You alright?" Saloni asked ignoring his advice, as she hurried to his support.

"Alright..." he said in an attempt to hide his pain, but ended up groaning in pain.

Holding his arm, she gently made him sit and knelt down beside him, examining the part of his leg that was hurting him. She was not an expert, but she tried to put to use, all the learning she had obtained at the NSS camps during her college days. Sunny experienced a strange sensation with her touch that he spontaneously recoiled his leg, resulting in more pain. As he winced in pain, Saloni took his leg with more assertiveness this time.

"You'll suffer more if you don't get it treated." Saloni warned him as she rolled his trouser off his paining calf.

Sunny couldn't deny her genuine care. She rested her right leg on her feet, placing his leg on her lap. Sunny experienced a stirring in his heart. Saloni observed the cramp on the calf. She slowly moved his toe towards and away from him, relaxing his calf muscles, followed by a short massage. The pain subsided with her treatment.

"Feeling better?" she asked.

"Lot better..." he answered with a mild smile.

She gradually moved his leg off her lap and carefully placed his foot on the floor.

"Now… rest your foot slowly and carefully. Don't put your entire weight immediately. Go slow." she instructed him.

"How many more times, would I be indebted to her?" he wondered, as he felt the pain fade away gradually.

"Thank you…" he said wholeheartedly.

"You still shouldn't have come here. It's dangerous…" Sunny said, suddenly realizing what he had forgotten for a while, but he was too late as he received a heavy blow on his jaw, reeling him a few feet away from where he stood. They gave him sufficient time to recover.

Hari, then got hold of Saloni by her throat in a savage grip, almost choking her to death.

"Filthy bitch… How dare you gang up with that son of a bitch?" He spat on her face in disgust. He enjoyed Saloni strangling to death by his fierce grip as her eyeballs literally popped out of the sockets with his savage hold. Suddenly, he felt dazed for a few seconds as he experienced a heavy knock on his skull. As he felt the vibrations in his head, he loosened his grip on Saloni's throat. She coughed vigorously, sucking in all the air she could to sustain breathing. She fell to her knees still finding it hard to normalize her breathing. Meanwhile Sunny jumped on him and rendered another brutal knock with his elbow right on the back of his skull. Hari couldn't recover from the second blow for some time. He rushed to the aid of Saloni and helped her onto her foot. She gradually regained her breath as she wiped her face with her scarf. Sunny didn't want to repeat the mistake he did a few minutes before. Once he made sure Saloni was fine, he turned to Hari who was still staggering from his knock. Gathering all his fury in his clenched fist, he paced towards Hari slightly limping and discharged all his fury on his lower jaw. Hari couldn't stand the continuous assault. Moreover, his inebriation was not helping him retaliate. Sunny, who understood his state, madly rained punches all over his face, throat and neck. Regaining her normalcy, Saloni watched Sunny in astonishment as she never knew he could turn so violent. He punched Hari as long as his fists ached and his cramped calf hurt.

"The bastard should have been a monster to survive all the punches." Sunny wondered as he threw incessant punches.

The strip of light flowing through the wall started to get diluted by the darkness that was looming around.

"Damn… How I wish I had a weapon!" Sunny cursed.

Hari, who had been pretending to be submissive till then, cunningly kicked Sunny on his cramped leg, knocking him to the ground. Before Sunny could recover, Hari clamped him onto the ground and delivered a heavy punch on his face. Meantime, Saloni looked around for some weapon and luckily got hold of an empty liquor bottle. When she turned towards the duel, they had already rolled into the darkness, to her dismay. She couldn't differentiate the two in the darkness. As they wrestled, they filled the whole building with a rattling sound, which echoed into a horrific crackle of the devil. Saloni realized that Sunny was in a bad position, struggling to match Hari, who despite intoxication and the nasty pounding, had overpowered Sunny. She saw silhouettes of two people, but differentiating them was difficult despite the slight difference in their sizes. She expected them to roll into brighter space. Then she observed one man get on top of the other and knock his fists on the other. She didn't know who the one punching was. She intended to make sure before she got into the act.

She got an idea. She quickly retrieved the phone from her pocket, turned on the backlight and pointed it towards the duo. It didn't take more than a second for her to identify the beast crushing Sunny beneath his weight and trying to land punches onto his face. Saloni didn't waste a second more, as she crashed the bottle on Hari's forehead and immediately switched off the phone's backlight. As soon as Hari fell on the floor, Sunny flipped back and moved to a safe spot to regain his breath. Sunny knew that it was a heavy blow that Hari received from Saloni, but he wasn't sure how long he would need to recover. He didn't have the backlight for a long time, but he saw Hari's face drenched in blood, the instant he was hit. Saloni was glad that Sunny was off Hari's control now, but not sure if he was safe. Hari fell where the stairs crumbled during their fall. He ran his hand along the floor to find a stone for attacking him.

"God's on my side." Hari thought delightfully when he found his *kukri*.

He didn't want to expose his weapon, as he intended to use the element of surprise to his advantage. He still had to find Sunny in the darkness. As he was drafting his attack plan, he felt so dizzy that he was tempted to ignore his enemies and sleep for a while.

"Never mind… I will finish them both in a minute and rest after that." Hari promised to himself.

He constantly wiped the blood that flowed over his face and sometimes into his eyes. His inebriation helped him in one way: it reduced his pain. Sunny knew that hunting him in the dark would take the whole night. He slowly dragged his feet across the floor, careful not to make noise. As he kept dragging his feet along the floor, he hit upon a palm sized stone. An idea struck him. He picked the stone and threw it near the dimly lit place at the broken wall, with a reverberating thud, expecting Hari to walk into the trap. Footsteps approached towards the source of sound. He was elated with the success of his plan. To his shock, he saw Saloni walk into the light with her hands tucked behind. She deliberately walked into the light, setting herself as bait for Hari.

"Move away Saloni..." Sunny shouted her name, bringing a wide smile on her lips, despite the fearsome scenario.

At that instance, he heard footsteps approach towards her, which meant that she was in danger. He knew that he was Hari's target. So he rushed towards Saloni into the light in order to divert Hari's attention towards him. Saloni, assuming it to be Hari, raised her hand with the broken half of the bottle which was hidden from sight. When she saw Sunny emerge into the light, she dropped her hand. At that instant, Hari barged into the light towards Sunny like a beast. To their surprise, he had knife in his hand. Saloni was so shocked with the unexpected danger, that she knocked Sunny on his chest with all her force to move him away from the line of attack and also from the light. All this happened in a lightning pace that Hari, in his inebriated state was unable to respond with equal pace. Furious with her intervention and betrayal, he swung the knife at her with all his vengeance. She tried to dodge him, but not before his knife sliced her forearm, making a shallow cut, forcing her to drop the splinter on the floor. He then wound his arm around her neck, capturing her in his brutal grip.

"Bloody bitch… What made you go this far for that son of a bitch?" Hari asked, hugging her tight from behind while he gently ran the blade of his knife across her face.

"What did he offer you that you didn't care for your own life?" he shouted.

Sunny reflected the same question within himself, but couldn't find an answer. Saloni knew that Hari was a skilled knifeman, but equally impulsive. She wouldn't be surprised if he drove the knife into her throat without a warning. She still put on a bold face.

"What's so special about him that you switched your loyalty towards him, you dirty swine? Does he have four balls? I'll prove that I can do better than that, slut?" Hari said as he licked her all over her face, pressing the edge of his knife against her throat. She did not even budge.

Sunny was inexplicably furious as Hari abused Saloni, as he suddenly felt a sense of belonging with her. He unknowingly took it personally. Hari purposely stood in the light to attract Sunny, as he did not want to prolong the fight any more. Sunny waited to attack at the best time as he didn't want Saloni to get hurt.

Hari looked around with animated expression and shouted "Did you look at that, whore. He doesn't have balls. You have been chasing the wrong guy." He chuckled as he spoke.

Saloni swiftly turned around and thumped her knee into his groin with all her strength.

"I guess you have four balls now. Useless though." Saloni responded with horripilating audacity, knowing he still had the knife in his hand. Sunny was awed by Saloni's guts. Hari groaned like a swine in pain, letting her off in an instant, as he was powerfully hit. The blow put him out of breath for a few seconds. As he gradually regained his breath, he furiously raised his *kukri* to stab Saloni, who fearlessly stood in front of him. Sunny took the opportunity and pounced on him, tumbling him to the ground, rolling into the darkness. Saloni was worried for Sunny as Hari was still holding the knife. Sunny tightly held Hari's fist, which held the knife with both his hands, not letting him use it. By doing so, he let his other hand loose from which he received unobstructed punches. After a long struggle, Sunny finally overpowered him and pinned him down spread eagled, holding both his hands above his head. As Sunny knew that Hari was badly wounded on his forehead, he gathered all his power on his forehead and crashed it on his. The knock hurt even Sunny, making him fall on his chest. Hari dropped his weapon in the encounter. Both of them were dead tired as they had no energy left in them. With all the meager energy left in him, Hari lifted Sunny off his chest and kicked him on his abdomen, throwing him back into the light. Saloni immediately rushed to Sunny's support and took his arm around her shoulder, helping him onto his foot. He stood on his foot, and for a fleeting moment, he was lost in her deep mesmerizing eyes. When he realized that they were in a vulnerable spot, he gently moved Saloni aside and faced Hari's direction, daring him to fight him under the light. Accepting the challenge, Hari trampled towards Sunny, swinging his weapon at him. Sunny gripped both his hands and violently tucked them behind him, hugging him tightly, curtailing his movement. Seizing the opportunity, Saloni unfolded Hari's fist, making the knife fall off his grip. Infuriated by her indulgence, he gave a backwards kick which landed on her abdomen, throwing her down the ground. Sunny became furious at Hari that he knocked his fist on his forehead, letting his hands off his grip. Although Hari suffered immense pain, he didn't want to waste the freedom of his hands. He returned a heavy punch on his jaw. When he gained control over Sunny, he arched him backwards by wringing his neck through his arm. As Sunny struggled hard to get off the grip, Hari tried to reach out for the dropped weapon. Saloni saw Sunny in a near fatal position, but was unable to quickly get on her feet as she was badly hurt by Hari's kick. The weapon was just a couple of feet from Hari's reach. Saloni knew that she didn't have much time as Hari would reach the knife in a few seconds. As she lay down on the floor, she spotted the broken bottle splinter at her feet, which Sunny noticed through the corner of his eye. She kicked the splinter to Sunny's reach and she was precise with that, but it moved out of his sight as he stood arched backwards with his face upwards, staring at the dark ceiling. Though it was right within his reach, he did not know exactly where it was. He ran his palm blindly along the floor, searching for some luck. When Hari was just a few centimeters away from the knife, Sunny luckily got hold of the splinter and drove it into his thigh. Hari immediately let Sunny off his grip and fell down, letting him retrieve the splinter from his thigh and aim his throat this time. Just as Sunny raised his hand, he received a powerful kick on his chest that sent him reeling across the floor. He was dazed with the kick. Nobody had noticed the entry of the unannounced participant. Sunny rubbed his eyes to gain clarity.

IRFAN FINISHES THE GAME

"Oh God…" he murmured when he saw Irfan.

He was one person on the earth that Sunny didn't dare to face. Sunny got on his feet and looked at him. He didn't fear dying in his hands, but facing him.

"Kill me brother…" he said as he outstretched his arms wide open inviting his death.

Hari who was observing all this didn't want to waste any more time. He immediately kicked the knife towards Irfan.

"Kill the son of a bitch." Hari shouted.

"No…" Saloni screamed as she ran straight up to Sunny and hugged him from his front, blocking him from line of attack. Sunny was dumbfounded and confused. He stared into her magnetic eyes, as he moved her aside, still holding her arm. She shut her eyes in fear when she heard the sound of sudden footsteps and a knife pierce through flesh, followed by a muffled groan. She felt Sunny's grip tighten on her arm. Saloni anxiously opened her eyes and stared into his tear filled eyes staring ahead of her. As she followed his sight, she could only see the handle of the knife on Hari's chest. The 9 inch blade was wholly driven into his flesh, sending a silent stream of blood gushing down. She started to have an illusion of witnessing the whole scene in slow motion as she felt herself in a mystery land.

Sunny silently stared at the man who marched ominously towards him. Saloni was glad that he didn't have the knife in his hand, but was still scared. He slapped his palm on Sunny's chest and held his shirt.

"What the fuck do you think you're doing?" he screamed.

Sunny let go off Saloni's arm.

"Actually… I…" He couldn't find words to answer him.

"Shut up… You think it's fun playing with knives?" Irfan shouted, which resonated in the whole building.

"Fun is the most inappropriate word…"

"Shut up. Shut the fuck up." Irfan shouted.

"What do you think you'll get out of this? Get your friend back?" Irfan shook him violently by grabbing his shirt."You don't prove anything by all this. Anything at all…"

"I'm not trying to prove anything… I am not." Sunny shouted, yanking himself off his grip.

They seemed to have ignored the presence of Saloni who just stood as a mute spectator.

Sunny took a few seconds to compose himself.

"I'm not trying to prove anything…" He repeated again, as if speaking to himself.

"I'm… I'm just trying to…" He lingered, as he found it hard to explain his reason.

"You can't explain it kid. You don't have to settle accounts this way. You only get your hands stained with crime in the spurt of emotions. It's hard to remain righteous, but easy to fall into crime. Don't go the easy way. My hands are already stained. You have a life ahead." Irfan said, despite his bitterness of having lost his brother.

"I have nothing to live for." Sunny answered dejected. Saloni got a twitch in her heart when she heard that.

"You think you are returning your friend a favor?" Irfan said as he slapped Sunny on his chest with open palm.

"Well… Yes. Return him the favor. Get the hell out of here and live a life." he said as he held him by his collar.

"That's what he always wanted." Irfan said, pushing him away.

Sunny let his tears roll out of his eyes and wept like a child.

The sirens of an approaching police vehicle alerted them.

"Get the hell out of here. Now…" Irfan screamed, but Sunny firmly stood on his ground.

"You slip out of here. I can't thank you enough for all your help." Sunny told Saloni as he gestured her towards the broken wall which created a rear entrance.

"How can I leave you in danger and look for my safety. Life or death, it's with you." Saloni spoke within herself.

"Go…" Sunny prompted the broken wall again.

She stood there without any response. The sirens got louder and then went off, which meant that they were on foot.

"What the heck are you still doing here? Didn't you understand what I said? Just get out of here…" Irfan screamed, pushing him away.

"You girl… Take him out of here." he ordered Saloni.

She didn't need any more persuasion as she held Sunny by his arm and hurried through the broken wall just in time to have escaped the cops' sight.

"Freeze... police." Irfan was surrounded by the cops.

"Stay where you are and raise your hands up." One cop shouted at him.

Saloni silently led Sunny along the perimeter of the building to Sunny's car which was parked at a safe distance.

A WALK IN THE RAIN

"Well. Adios again..." Sunny said with a hint of displeasure.

Saloni felt her heart sinking when she heard those words again.

"Nice knowing you." he said, offering his hand for a final hand shake.

She grabbed his hand in an instant and shook it.

"Nice knowing you." She repeated his words as she still kept shaking his hand.

Sunny let her hold his hand as he felt some inexplicable solace with her touch. When she noticed Sunny gently stare at her, she became suddenly conscious of her extended handshake. Unwillingly, she released his hand. The moment she left his hand, he felt nostalgic. Some invisible force kept pulling them together.

"Thanks for the jacket." she said, handing it over to him.

"I can't thank you enough for all your help." he said putting it on.

"It's nice helping nice people." She winked, pretending to be normal.

"Be careful with your life." he said, hesitating to add something more.

"You are an intelligent girl. You can become whatever you wish to. Think about it." He expressed his opinion about her that he had been bearing for a long time.

"Sure... Thanks." She wanted to prolong the conversation, but she felt mentally numb.

"You take care of yourself." It was getting more difficult for her to act normal.

"Sure." Sunny said, staring at her for a couple of seconds when he remembered something. He fished out his wallet and pulled out whatever money was left in it.

"Sorry... This is all I have for now." he said, knowing well that she deserved lot more.

"Hey... thanks... but you don't need to pay me." She refused the money.

"Frankly, it's beyond my capacity to pay for all your help. This is for your expenses. I know you don't have any money." He insisted.

She accepted the money with a smile.

It was farewell time.

"Bye." he finally said, shattering her hopes of a miracle.

"Bye." She said with half smile, briefly waving her trembling hand and turned to walk away from him. It was just a matter of minutes, when her life would turn meaningless. As she walked away from Sunny, her only reason to live, she felt like getting stripped of her life. She staggered along the frontiers of emotional breakdown, as she had lost all her reasons to live, on the same day. She felt some strong force stopping her from walking away from him. She felt like she was walking against a storm. Sunny was no stranger to the feeling. As he started walking towards the car, he found something unusually annoying. He felt as if he was gradually dissolving into thin air as he walked away from her.

"This is strange. She is a nice girl alright, but what is so special about her which I didn't find in any other girl for almost two decades." He could find no answer.

Desperate to have a last look, Saloni turned back to see Sunny walk to the car, drinking the sight of him with all greed. As he reached the car, he turned to have a look at Saloni who turned back just on time. Habitually, he plunged his hand into his jacket pocket for his car keys. He felt something else in his pocket. For some unknown reason, he exercised utmost care as he retrieved it from the pocket. He gently held it in front of his eyes. He felt a violent stir in his heart.

The whole world dwindled into nothingness and then expanded into a whole new world; the world in which he lived every day - his dreams. His mind turned into a kaleidoscope of all heavenly memories and the evergreen images flashing at random. For a few moments, he was too stunned, unable to realize, that it was not dream. It was too good to be real.

He gazed at the chain with a sun locket suspended in his hand oscillating in the gentle breeze, his mind floating in the whirlwind of thoughts. He suddenly felt so light that he feared he might be blown away by the gentle winds. He travelled back a couple of decades in an instant, appreciating the golden chain hugging the most beautiful neck.

This will stay with me… till my end. He recalled Sandy's words.

His mind abruptly travelled forward, back to few hours ago, to the hospital.

Do you know anybody with AB Negative blood?

The next instant he saw Saloni pressing cotton against the needle piercing, walking out after donating blood.

He once again boarded the incredible time machine and travelled few hours back to the unknown place that morning to witness the sun tattoo on Saloni's arm.

What's this Sandy candy?

Well... It's your logo.

The tattoo flashed in his mind again and again.

What did he offer you that you didn't care for your own life?

The question gradually seemed to make some sense.

The next moment he remembered Saloni hugging him, protecting him from being attacked.

His head started spinning with all the inexplicable events, gradually unfolding its mystery. The images ran in his mind like high-speed photography. When the agitation settled down, all the pieces fell in place.

"I have had clues all the time. I had been a fool to not have identified them." he thought.

"Fate had been toying with me all the time." He cursed himself as he had been denying the wish of his life, which had been granted to him in an unexpected camouflage.

He was so stunned in ecstasy, that he was unable to move or talk. He turned back to see her walking hesitantly away from him.

He wanted to shout her name on the top of his voice, but his throat was choked with joy that made it difficult for him to speak out.

"Sandy…" he called out in a barely audible voice.

Her heart skipped a beat when she heard that. She was habituated to hallucinations for the past few hours that she believed it was just another one tormenting her. Ignoring her presumed fictional voice, she kept walking away.

"Sandy Candy." Now he called louder, which was unmistakable.

She couldn't fool herself this time. After a brief attempt to defy the eventuality, she finally gave in, deciding to embrace her everlasting dream, tantalizing her for some time, testing her endurance. She abruptly stopped, still hesitant to turn around to face him.

Sunny didn't have as much endurance. He wanted to hug her tightly and fill his empty life with her love. Turning blind to the atmosphere around, he ran crazily towards the love of his life, tripping on an obstacle, tumbling noisily. She turned around in a reflex and staggered towards him on her weak legs. Meanwhile Sunny got on his feet and outstretched his arms, which had been waiting for her since two decades. Her legs almost failed to carry her just when she reached him that she fell into his outstretched arms. Fearing that someone would wake her from yet another incredible dream, she shut her eyes tightly as she hugged him and buried her face against his shoulder. He hugged her tightly, facing skywards thanking the heavens for the precious gift, which he thought he had lost forever.

He gently raised her chin, as she slowly and cautiously opened her eyes. He stared into her eyes from which rolled down streams of tears.

"Is this yet another dream?"

"No dream was as real as this. This is not a dream."

"How did I miss the magic in her eyes?" Sunny thought, looking into her eyes.

The familiar eyes brimming with innocence, though illuded by the scar, hinted resemblance, but his preconceived hatred for her obstructed him from examining the truth.

"I had been such a fool." He cursed himself for not being able to identify his own soul.

She looked into his eyes with wonder, as though they were the only two humans in the world, who had met each other for the first time. She wanted to kiss him, but felt shy for the first time after many years.

As he read her eyes, he slowly brought his lips close to hers. Close enough that they breathed each other's breath. They began to breathe harder. His senses rekindled after so many years. He then moved his lips close enough to touch hers. As she could no longer resist the urge for his touch, she gently pressed her lips against his. They then kissed as if their survival depended on it. Torrent of emotions flowed through the kiss. As they broke the kiss, they hugged each other tightly, feeling the warmth of each other. They suddenly felt alive with the kiss. He hugged her passionately scooping her off the ground. She reciprocated by tightly wrapping her arms around him, arching her legs backwards, swinging in the air, burying her face on his shoulder.

He gently landed her on the ground and unwrapped his hands. When she wondered what he was up to, he held the chain dangling in front of her. Sandy understood his gesture. She blushed as she shyly bowed her head down, brimming with joy. Sunny tied it around her neck in a frenzy of excitement. The pain they had borne for all the years got washed away in their blissful reunion. When he lifted her face up by her chin, she felt a pleasant drop of rain on her cheek. As she looked up at the dark sky with heavy clouds waiting to pour down, more drops came down as if approving their relationship and blessing them.

It was beautiful.

Sunny stared at her, cherishing the joy in her eyes. Unable to hold his ecstasy, he offered his hand and asked her, "Shall we have a walk in the rain…?"

EPILOGUE

Irfan was arrested for murder on the spot of crime. He not only confessed the murder of Hari, but also his participation in the havoc created at the brothel, which didn't take long to land him in jail. He was glad that Sunny was no more involved. He wished that Sunny would lead a happy life as his brother Imran always wished.

The brutal murder at the brothel had caused immense pressure on the law enforcement department as the butchery had sucked the whole media's interest into it. The police department formed a special commission commanding a team of skilled encounter specialists, who listed down the people and places of target. Then they simultaneously attacked all the targets, depriving Victor's gang of breathing space. The success of the operation gave relief to the whole region and freedom to the prostitutes who were confined in the brothel.

Pooja took care of the funeral and last rites of Sandy's mother as promised. Once things got settled, Pooja invited her to visit her mom.

"Bring Sunny with you. She'll be happy." Pooja told her.

"Sure darling. What would I do without you?" Sandy responded with a grateful smile.

"What about Sam?" She asked Pooja.

Pooja narrated her last conversation with Sam.

"Take my word, baby. Meet him up." Sandy advised.

"I need some time, dear." Pooja replied to which Sandy agreed.

Sandy visited her mom, along with Sunny.

Upon Sandy's advice, Pooja met up with Sam. It was the most uncomfortable evening for both of them. They took a corner table and sat face to face, yet not facing each other. Silence prevailed for nearly half an hour as both were lost in their own thoughts, pretending to enjoy their coffee. Pooja couldn't bear it any longer and wondered why she had to go through all this again.

"Goodbye." she said as she prepared to rise.

"I didn't come here to say good bye." Sam spoke out of the blue, which froze Pooja in her half standing position for a few seconds. She couldn't guess what he had in mind.

"Yes... I need to talk to you. Sit down." he said.

Pooja followed his instruction dutifully and waited for him to continue.

"Before I speak, I wanted you to know that my love for you was true, whatsoever." he said.

"Was true" Pooja anxiously waited to hear what he wanted to speak, wondering if the words had some bearing to his message.

Sam did not know how to start. He thought for a while before he started to speak.

"I have two questions for you." Sam spoke.

"One – Are you going to carry on with your... profession? Two – Do you love me?"

Sam waited for Pooja's answers.

Pooja almost choked with anxiety that she could not bring the words out of her mouth.

"One – No. And two..."

"Yes." She replied after a little hesitation.

Sam studied her answers for some time.

"I always believe that circumstances sometimes could force you to do what you hate the most."

"Life is not always fair." He recalled the words of Sister Teresa.

"I do not want to know how and why you chose to be what you were. I don't care about your past no matter how bad it was, as long as it does not interfere with your present. Moreover, I could have never possibly known the truth if you had not revealed it to me. You still preferred the truth. I believe that only a person with a pure heart would have the guts to speak the truth so bitter. Well... Chastity is not an attribute of body, but soul. I believe that your soul is pure." Sam spoke with utmost sincerity.

"I love you." He finally declared as he held her hand.

Pooja was so dumbfounded that she sat frozen in disbelief.

"How can someone love a person like me?" she questioned herself.

She could not hold back her tears which rolled down like a stream running down a hill.

Sam gently squeezed her hand in assurance as Pooja wept in joy.

"I have one more question for you." He continued.

Pooja was already dazed enough with the unexpected turn of events that she was unable to guess what to expect. She waited for him to speak.

Sam got off his seat, knelt before her, opened his arms and proposed to her,

"Will you marry me?"